A List of Cages is a hero story you

—TAMARA IRELAND STONE,
RD

...rses through every sentence of this novel, whether it is love, **compassion**, or bone-chilling cruelty. A triumphant story about the power of friendship and of truly being seen."

—KIRKUS REVIEWS
(STARRED REVIEW)

★ "A page-turner with a lot of compassion."

—BOOKLIST
(STARRED REVIEW)

★ "Written with honesty and compassion, this book will resonate with a wide range of readers."

—PUBLISHERS WEEKLY
(STARRED REVIEW)

"This is Roe's first young adult novel, and it's *impressive*. While the crimes she portrays are truly vile . . . their evil can't stand up to the goodness in her protagonists, and the lesson that every kindness matters—and that we always have the choice to be kind."

—NEW YORK TIMES BOOK REVIEW

★ "Roe, a social worker, has written a stunning debut about loss, friendship, and the power of family. A potent and *moving* work. Do not pass over this book."

—SCHOOL LIBRARY JOURNAL
(STARRED REVIEW)

★ "Painful, devastating, beautiful and *brilliant*."

—SHELF AWARENESS
(STARRED REVIEW)

"A remarkably *gripping* and moving tale of a life saved—in more than one way—by the power of friendship."

—EMMA DONOGHUE,
best-selling author of *ROOM*

A LIST OF CAGES

A LIST OF CAGES

ROBIN ROE

HYPERION
Los Angeles   New York

Copyright © 2017 by Robin Roe

All rights reserved. Published by Hyperion, an imprint of Disney Book Group. No part of this book may be reproduced or transmitted in any form or by any means, electronic or mechanical, including photocopying, recording, or by any information storage and retrieval system, without written permission from the publisher. For information address Hyperion, 125 West End Avenue, New York, New York 10023.

First Hardcover Edition, January 2017
First Paperback Edition, December 2017

1 3 5 7 9 10 8 6 4 2

FAC-025438-17335
Printed in the United States of America

Library of Congress Cataloging-in-Publication control number: 2015045422

978-1-4847-7640-7

Reinforced binding

Visit www.hyperionteens.com

SUSTAINABLE
FORESTRY
INITIATIVE

Certified Chain of Custody
Promoting Sustainable Forestry

www.sfiprogram.org
SFI-01054

The SFI label applies to the text stock

For my mother, who taught me to give and love with all my heart

and

In memory of Jamie, the beautiful little boy who reminds me:
we are more than what we can see

A LIST OF CAGES

PART ONE

ONE

JULIAN

THERE IS A room in this school that no one knows about but me. If I could teleport, I'd be there now. Maybe if I just concentrate—

"Julian." Mr. Pearce says my name sharp enough to make me flinch. "You're less than a month into high school, and you've missed your English class *six* times."

I'm sure I've missed more than that, but I guess no one realized I was gone.

The principal leans forward, two fists wrapped around his tall, twisted cane. It has a little creature carved at the top, and I've heard other kids talk about it, wondering if it's a gnome or troll or a tiny replica of Mr. Pearce himself. This close, I can see the resemblance.

"Look at me!" he shouts.

I'm not sure why people want you to look at them when they're angry with you. That's when you want to look away the most. But when I do what he says, the windowless office seems to shrink, and I shrink along with it. A microscopic boy underneath Mr. Pearce's gaze.

"It'd be a lot easier for you to look someone in the eye if you got a haircut." He glares harder when I start pushing my hair out of my face. "Why haven't you been going to class?"

"I . . ." I clear my throat. "I don't like it."

"What was that?"

People are always telling me to repeat myself or speak up. The main reason I don't like English is because Miss Cross makes everyone read out loud, and when it's my turn, I stumble over my words, and she tells me I'm too quiet.

Knowing this, I pitch my voice a little louder. "I don't like it."

Mr. Pearce lifts two gray brows, looking completely stunned. "Do you really think not *liking* a class is reason not to go?"

"I . . ." For everyone else, talking just seems to come naturally. When someone says something, they automatically know what to say back. But for me it's as if the pathway between brain and mouth is damaged, like a rare form of paralysis. I can't speak, so instead I fiddle with the plastic tip of my shoelace.

"Answer my question! Is not liking a class a good reason not to go?"

I know what I think, but people don't want you to say what you think. They want you to say what *they* think. And knowing what that is isn't easy.

The principal rolls his eyes. "Look at me, young man."

I look up into his flushed face. He grimaces, and I wonder if his knee or back is hurting him the way they always seem to be. "I'm sorry," I tell him, and his whole face softens.

Then all of a sudden, his bushy brows come together, and he slaps open a file folder with my name on it. "I should call your parents."

My shoelace slips from my frozen fingers.

His lips curl into a smile. "You know what does my heart good?"

I manage to shake my head.

"Seeing that particular look of fear cross a student's face when I say I'm going to call home." He lifts the phone to his ear. He and his little wooden monster watch me as the seconds tick by. Then slowly, he pulls the phone away. "I suppose I don't have to call . . . if you promise that I'll never see you in here again."

"I promise."

"Then get to class."

Out in the hall, I try to breathe, but I'm still shaky the way you'd be if you were nearly clipped by a speeding car but you leaped out of the way at the very last second.

When I enter Child Development, all the girls lift their heads like a herd of deer sensing danger. Then, the second they see me, they look away as if I was never there at all.

Since I'm late, I have to stand in front while Miss Carlisle glares at my tardy slip. Even though no one is looking at me, I can't stop thinking that my hair is too long and my jeans are too short and my shirt is too small and everything I'm wearing is ugly and worn.

"I already marked you absent." Miss Carlisle sighs. She's probably even older than Mr. Pearce, with hair that might have once been blond and eyes that might have once been bright blue before she faded like a photograph. "I don't know what I'm supposed to do."

I know the new online attendance system is stressful for her, because she tells us almost every day. "I'm sorry," I say.

"It's fine." She slumps, her posture weary. "I'll take care of it."

As I'm heading to my seat in the back, the only other boy in class, Jared, waves to get my attention. "I'll see you on the bus today, right?" he says.

I don't answer.

Miss Carlisle announces that we have to complete the assignments in groups, so everyone shouts the names of the people they want, and they pull their desks into circles.

I'm probably the only person in the school who hates it when the teacher lets us choose our own groups. I lower my head to my desk and close my eyes. I used to think that if I concentrated, I could make myself disappear. I don't exactly believe that anymore, but sometimes I still have to try.

"Julian," Miss Carlisle says, "you are really pushing it today. Find a group." I glance around at the ones that have formed, a tight anxious knot in my stomach. "Just join the group closest to you."

Closest to me is Kristin, a girl who looks a little bit like a goldfish with her orange hair and bulging eyes. She sends me a bruising glare, and I feel like I'm wearing a defective invisibility cloak—a device that works perfectly until I do something stupid.

I met Kristin at the beginning of school this year. In first period, she tapped my shoulder and asked if I was reading an Elian Mariner book. I nodded, wary, because no one ever starts conversations with me. But when she asked what it was about, my words just spilled out. Yes, it was an Elian Mariner book, probably my favorite in the entire series. Kristin kept nodding and asking questions, and she said her sister loved those books. Then she added, "My sister's *seven*."

When everyone around us started laughing, I hid the book in my backpack. It wasn't until my next class that I noticed it was missing. Then in sixth period, I was returning from sharpening my pencil, and there it was, sitting on my chair.

I opened it to find that every illustration had been desecrated with black Sharpie. Drawings of penises were jutting up from Elian's pants, and floating penises were pointed at his mouth. Eyes stinging, I looked up to find the entire class watching me. I caught Kristin's fish eyes in the crowd, then she fell headfirst into her desk, shaking with laughter.

"Julian!" Miss Carlisle calls out now. "Move."

I quickly drag my desk to join the girls.

"So, *Violet, Jen*," Kristin says, "should we split things up?"

I pretend not to notice that she's excluding me and open my textbook.

"Okay," Violet answers. "Julian, did you want to—"

"I want a good grade on this," Kristin interrupts her. "Let's just divide it between us."

Violet doesn't answer, and I keep pretending I can't hear.

After the final bell, it looks like someone kicked over a beehive. Kids are swarming and flying in a thousand different directions. There's a sudden explosion of noise—talking and cell phones beeping. But I stand frozen at the top of the steps just outside the school.

My father is leaning against a tall tree across the street.

When I was little, my mother was usually the one who picked me up, but every now and then Dad would get off early and surprise me. Instead of joining the pickup line of cars, he'd meet me on foot. His hands were always blotted with ink, like a child's after finger painting, and he'd say, *It's too nice a day not to walk.* He'd say that even if it was raining.

But of course the man across the street isn't actually my father. It's just some trick of the sunlight filtering through the branches on a jogger who stopped to catch his breath.

I stand here, heavy now.

So heavy that the tall steps become a mountain to climb down.

So heavy that it takes a while to summon the energy to start the long walk home.

Ten blocks from school, I start to shiver. Autumn is here, but it seems too soon. Almost like I skipped over the last three months because there are certain things that are supposed to happen every summer.

I'm supposed to go to the beach with my parents. We're supposed to see fireworks and buy sparklers and find seashells. I'm supposed to stay up late and sit on the front porch eating popsicles while my mother plays the guitar and my father draws. Then as he's tucking me into bed, he's supposed to ask, *How many stars?*

On a great day I'm supposed to say nine or ten. But if it was amazing, the best day I ever had, I'm supposed to cheat and say something like ten *thousand* stars.

But we didn't get to see fireworks or eat popsicles or do any summer things, and I have this ache inside, like how you might feel if you slept through Christmas.

The same heaviness I felt after school reappears the minute I walk inside the empty house. Every inch of it is dark, glossy, and neat. Every piece of furniture is strategic. Every color is coordinated by someone trained to do it. It's exactly the sort of house I thought I wanted . . . until I got it.

I enter my room with its polished wood floors, desert-brown walls, and heavy furniture. My eyes are pulled to the only thing out of place—the big steel trunk at the foot of the bed. My parents got it for me to take to camp the summer I turned nine. They told me I was brave to go off on my own, but I got so homesick I couldn't even make it through the first night.

I drop my backpack to the floor and lift the trunk's heavy lid. My heart squeezes as I look down at all the things I love: photo albums and Elian Mariner books and my mother's green spiral notebook. I leave that untouched for today and fish around for my own notebook. I flip a few pages, then pick up where I left off.

It's hours later when I drop my pen at the sound of a car pulling into the garage. It's after eight o'clock, but sometimes my uncle gets home even later. And sometimes, if he has to go meet with clients in other cities, he doesn't come home at all.

I watch my bedroom door, the way the light from the hall shines around the perimeter like an entryway to another dimension. I listen for the sound of him climbing the stairs to his office, because even when he's home, he's usually working.

Instead, I see a shadow fall beneath my door.

I close my eyes, but I can't teleport, and I can't disappear.

My uncle Russell once told me he used to be so tall and willowy that when his high school theater put on *A Christmas Carol*, he was asked to play the grim reaper. I've tried to picture it, but it's hard to imagine he was ever frail.

Russell doesn't speak, just lifts the conch that sits on top of my dresser and turns it slowly in his hands. His fingers are long and thin like stretched putty.

"Getting homework done?" he finally asks.

"Yes," I answer, and immediately feel guilty. It's late and he's just getting home from work, still neatly dressed with a tie around his neck, while I haven't even opened my backpack yet.

He returns the conch to its place, then takes the notebook from my hands. He squints at it, turning it upside down, then sideways, then right side up again. He does this sometimes, a sort of joke about my terrible handwriting.

"What is this?" he asks.

"A book report."

He gives me a sharp look, and I'm afraid he can tell I'm lying. I peek up at the deep fault lines in his forehead and under his eyes, trying to read him. Some nights when he comes home, usually after he's been gone for a few days, he can seem drowsy, relaxed, almost like he just finished a big meal.

Other nights it's as if there's something moving just beneath his skin, something crawling and scratching to get out. On those nights it would be better to hear his office door shut. Lonely and locked out, but still better.

His mouth twists to the side in an almost smile. "You misspelled *sinister*." He drops my notebook to the floor. "Come into the kitchen."

I follow him to the other room, where he opens a take-out container. He stands at the black granite countertop, slicing his steak with a sharp knife and eating dripping red bites. The house is quiet except for the distant metal thumping of the water heater, like the sound the dryer makes if you leave coins in your pocket.

"Your principal called me today." Russell's voice is deep, calm, and steady, but his words prompt a heavy thumping in my chest. Mr. Pearce said he wouldn't call if I promised to go to class, and I'd promised.

For just a second the image of my father standing to meet me outside the school flickers behind my eyes.

"Are you listening to me?"

I nod hastily, ashamed. I don't work hard enough. Not like Russell, who works harder than anyone I know. He's had to ever since his dad died when he was seventeen. Again I try to picture a young, frail Russell, but I can't.

He slices the steak and takes another red bite. "How long have you lived here?"

My stomach goes cold, like I've swallowed winter. He's going to kick me out. I've pulled this one too many times, and he's done. "I'm sorry."

"That's not what I asked you."

"Four years."

"In all that time, what's the only thing I've asked of you? What's our only agreement?"

"That you can trust me."

"And?" He takes another bite.

"You can trust me to do the right thing."

"And?"

"You won't have to look into what I'm doing."

"I don't ask too much of you, do I?" All the feeling that's not in his voice starts jumping in the vein in his neck.

"No."

"I understand your . . . limitations. I don't expect A's from you. I don't even expect B's. But sitting in a classroom isn't too difficult, is it?"

"No."

"I don't like getting called by your school. I want to be able to trust you."

"I'm sorry." I really am.

He sets the knife next to the clean bone. "Go get it."

TWO

JULIAN

SOMETHING TERRIBLE IS going to happen.

I usually wake up with that feeling at the bottom of my chest. It's as if I'm blind and there's something right beside me, and I could get away from it if only I could see. It's a vague but gnawing idea that's followed me into fourth period. The more I try to shake it off, the more it consumes me.

I realize I've zoned out when I notice my Art teacher, Miss Hooper, standing above me with a yellow paper square that reads: TO DR. WHITLOCK'S OFFICE.

I sigh.

The best part about finally getting into high school was that those meetings with the school psychologist were over. Then I found out the lady from my old middle school is working here now.

"Take your things," Miss Hooper says, so I grab my backpack and step out into the hall.

"Julian?"

I spin around.

And the moment seems to slow.

It's as if I'm standing still and the world is whipping past like a car down a dark street. And for just a second, headlights shine right on me. That's what it's like—standing frozen in the dark, then seeing him. Adam Blake. Leaning against the brick wall, somehow managing to look relaxed while fidgeting.

For just a second I feel a burst of pure happiness. I've always wondered what I'd say if I saw him again. Then it occurs to me that there's nothing to say, except maybe *I'm sorry*, and my happiness falls away.

He breaks into a grin. I glance around to find who he's smiling at, but no one is there.

"It's me," he says. "Adam."

I don't know why he's telling me his name. Even if I didn't already know, I'd know. I've only been in this school for a little while, but I've heard his name a hundred times, mostly from girls who are in love with him. Their fascination with him is a little confusing. He isn't neat the way my mom told me a boy should look when she used to brush my hair in the morning. His brown hair is sloppy, as if he tried to comb it in one direction, got bored, and combed it in the other, then switched five more times.

He's taller than me, but not all that big—nothing like the huge blond boy he's always with—and I thought girls liked boys who were really tall and strong. He doesn't even act the way popular guys should act. The boys in my grade walk a certain way, almost stomping as if they're angry, but Adam speeds everywhere like he's running late. I've seen him trip over his own feet more than once, but he just smiles and keeps going.

That's another thing. Boys don't smile a lot. I'm not sure if they're unhappy or if they're just pretending to be unhappy. But Adam always looks . . . kind. And kind and clumsy isn't cool. But in this school, I guess it is.

As Adam watches me expectantly, the anxiety in my stomach grows. Not knowing what to say is nothing new for me, but not knowing what to say to *him* feels a million times worse.

"I can't believe it's you," he says.

Suddenly he lunges forward, and I leap back. He halts, looking confused, and now I'm really embarrassed. It's *Adam*, and if he's lunging forward with open arms, it's probably just to hug me. But even so, the embarrassment and pain are all too much.

I see a split second of surprise on his face as I spin around, then I race down the hall, in the opposite direction of Dr. Whitlock's office.

Once I'm out of Adam's sight, I slow down so I don't get stopped by a teacher. I take a deep breath, turning over the crumpled yellow note in my hand. Soon Dr. Whitlock will realize I'm not coming. If she tells Mr. Pearce, he'll call Russell again, then Russell will want to know what I've been doing to get sent to her in the first place.

But if I do go to her office, Dr. Whitlock will stare into my eyes and ask embarrassing questions I can't answer, and my stomach will hurt. Afterward, she might call Russell just to tell him I'm seeing her again.

I stop, sick with indecision.

There's no good choice.

And with every passing second, it's more likely she's telling Mr. Pearce.

I should turn back, but I can't seem to force my feet in that direction. At the moment, the certainty of seeing Dr. Whitlock is worse than the possibility of facing Russell. I know I won't feel that way if it comes to it. I'll tell myself how stupid I was to risk it. But I guess I am stupid, because I've already made up my mind.

I skip the English Hall, because those teachers always stand at their doors like a neighborhood watch, and I head down the Science Hall. The air is thick with a sickening chemical odor, the smell of something being dissected. At the end of the corridor, I turn the corner and freeze. Mr. Pearce is standing there, bent over his crooked cane. Whether he's angry or just in pain I don't know.

I duck into the alcove with the water fountains and wait. I count to sixty, then peek around the corner. He looks up, glaring right at me.

I duck back, and now I can hear the clacking of his cane. I press myself against the wall, trying not to wince out loud. Mr. Pearce and his goblin are getting closer. *Clack. Clack. CLACK.*

Then he limps past me, as if he has no peripheral vision at all.

I wait until he disappears from view before running past the gym into the wide-open lobby in front of the auditorium. I slip inside the theater and let the heavy door fall closed behind me.

It's dark.

This is the scariest part of the whole journey. If I get caught, I'll definitely be in trouble, because there's no logical reason for me to be here. That thought spurs me to run until my toes hit the stage.

I climb the stairs, then slip behind the curtain. Back here it's even darker, and it smells like dust and candle wax. For a moment the air seems to thicken, as if something is standing right behind me.

I hold my breath and stretch out my arms like I'm blind. I keep stumbling until my hands close over what I was looking for—the black iron ladder bolted to the wall. I climb until, finally, there's light streaming in through the dirty attic window.

The attic is massive, with countless trunks and cardboard boxes overflowing with hats and plastic swords. In one corner there's a giant papier-mâché dragon with a glittering red eye.

The first time I came up here, I was so afraid someone might discover me any minute that I spent the whole period pacing. But then I found the passageway.

Behind the old armoire I locate the two crooked boards dangling from their nails like fence posts. I push them to one side to see the room beyond this one. In the crawl space between the attic and my secret room, the floorboards are crisscrossed, and there are a couple of feet of dark void where there is no floor at all. I have to jump.

And now I'm standing in my room. The walls and floors are much darker and smell older here. It's empty and just big enough for me to lie down in one direction but not the other. There's one window, round like a porthole on Elian's ship, where I can look down at the courtyard where no one ever goes.

In my room that feeling, the one that sits at the bottom of my chest, practically disappears. I can see all four corners, and no one knows this place exists but me.

When the bell rings for lunch, I sit and pull the peanut butter and jelly sandwich and an Elian Mariner book from my backpack. This story is one of my favorites. Sometimes Elian just goes on adventures, but sometimes he saves people. In this one he saves an entire planet.

THREE

ADAM

WHEN I WAS a sophomore, Principal Pearce read some study on the inverse correlation between temperature and academic performance, and there was no turning back. He cranked the AC so high that even if it's scorching out, inside we have to dress for a Siberian winter. The cafeteria's the only room in the school that was spared his policy of Freezing Us Into Learning, so the second I walk in, I start tearing off clothes.

At the same time I twist my body sideways, winding through the dangerously crowded room. My friends and I have to cram into a table that shouldn't seat more than ten, which means finding a chair's like a game of Twister. When you combine the sudden heat, stripping, and intertwining limbs, lunch is basically soft-core-porn-time.

I manage to squeeze in next to Emerald, and our thighs press together. As usual, her reddish-blondish-brownish hair is up and twisted into a complicated style most girls would save for prom. Her eyes lock onto mine—so blue I'd figure she was wearing contacts if I hadn't known her since the fifth grade.

"Hi." I smile, kind of mesmerized by her, like always. She looks like a 1950s starlet with her perfectly painted red lips, pale skin, and the mole on her cheek—basically way too glamorous to be sitting here eating greasy french fries out of a Styrofoam container. There are about a million things I want to say to her right now, but I'm distracted.

Across from me, Camila's just whipped the scarf off her neck to reveal a shirt so low-cut that if she sneezes, her nipples are going to fall out. I try to pretend I'm not looking, mostly out of courtesy to her twin brother, Matt, who's sitting beside her. The pair of them stare at me for a second in that eerie twin way, reminding me how much they look alike—both small with dark hair and skin. When we were kids, they dressed alike too, till she started wearing tight skirts and four-inch heels.

I tear my eyes away from Camila when Charlie slams down his tray, looking even more menacing than usual, then with great difficulty folds himself into a seat. I used to envy his height till it got to ridiculous levels. When you're six foot five, you just don't fit anywhere. He's forever complaining about his cramped legs and sore knees. But then again, he's forever complaining, period.

Case in point: "Fucking freshmen. Do you know how long it takes to get through the line now?"

I do in fact know. He's been telling us every day this year. Allison (Charlie's on-and-off-again girlfriend since sophomore year) sits on his thigh, which is as long as a freakin bench, and gives him a sympathetic pat. Calming Charlie is a big part of her job description. The tall blonds look enough alike to be another pair of fraternal twins—the time I said that aloud to Charlie didn't go over so well, though.

"You should start bringing a lunch," I suggest, lifting my glass container.

"Tofu?" Camila asks suspiciously.

"I'm not going vegan or whatever you are," Charlie adds.

"It's lemon chicken. I eat meat—occasionally—as long as it hasn't been raised in a factory. Come on, try some."

Emerald spears a small piece with her fork and chews precisely, as if this is a formal dinner, then dabs her perfect mouth like her napkin's made of cloth. "This is amazing," she says. "Why don't you cook for me?" She takes another neat little bite, and this time she hums around it.

Charlie gives the two of us an annoyed look, so I wave a piece in his direction. "You sure you don't wanna try? This food's much better for you. It makes you stronger, gives you more energy—"

"Exactly what you need," he interrupts. "*More* energy." Everyone laughs, which seems to make him proud, because he doesn't get a lot of laughs. Then he takes a deliberately huge bite of his pizza. "I shouldn't have to bring a lunch. They shouldn't *be* here."

"LET IT GO, MAN." Jesse's voice is too loud, probably because an earbud is still stuck in one ear. He leans forward, his latest growth spurt making him look like a scarecrow, and he sets his drumsticks on the table. He carries them everywhere, but he gets away with it since drums are the one instrument you're allowed to play and not get called a band nerd. "It's been like a month."

"Come on, Charlie." I grin. "Don't you think they're just a little bit adorable?" I ask this knowing he hates kids even more than the word *adorable.* He looks like he's tempted to punch me, but then he always looks ready to commit an act of violence.

He was, in my opinion, irrationally livid when he found out we'd be sharing the cafeteria with the freshmen. Last year a group of concerned parents complained that their kids didn't have time to eat, so this year instead of four lunch periods—one for each grade—we have two. Longer lunches, yeah, but twice as crowded, and for people who actually eat school food, now half their time's spent in line.

We were told that putting the freshmen and seniors in the same lunch period was purely a numerical decision. We were the smallest class; the freshmen were the biggest. A few days into the semester I started to suspect a more deviously brilliant plan.

The cafeteria was chaos. Freshmen were running around like kindergartners. Worse maybe, because even kindergartners know to stay in their seats and not write on their tables in ketchup and pull each other's hair. It didn't take long for unrest to rise among the seniors. We all wanted sanctity restored, but the faculty just stood there looking traumatized.

Naturally it was Charlie who confronted them. He Terminator-marched to a table that was having some kind of green bean launching competition, and told them to sit down and shut the fuck up. As they looked up at him with fear and awe, they reminded me of a cage full of big-eyed, terrified mice, and I know exactly what that looks like.

My career as a pet store associate lasted less than a day. I got to work early, stoked and ready to play with dogs—I never got to have one, since my mom's allergic to every type of fur—but I soon found out my job was to clean up shit. The liquidy shit of anxious animals. I did my job, then removed a couple of the sadder puppies and rolled around on the floor with them to cheer them up.

I got yelled at by the manager—an old man who looked a lot like Santa Claus, only his beard smelled like cat pee. He ordered me to clean up more shit, this time from a pissed-off cockatiel that clawed and cursed me.

All in all, my day was going okay till a guy came in and asked me for a mouse—a nice plump one. I thought that was weird, then he added, "It's for my boa constrictor." I'd only been working there for, like, five hours at that point, but I already felt responsible for the collection of smelly, caged animals in my care, and these were the smallest of all. Santa told me they were in the glass case in the storeroom, and sent me off with the awful task of deciding which one was going to die.

When I opened the lid, a hundred mice with huge round eyes stared up at me. I stuck in my hand, grabbed a little white one. Cute and trusting with tiny ears. I held him for maybe a minute before I stuck him back in the case and watched him burrow under all the others.

What happened next was like a time warp where you'd swear you didn't do it—or at least you didn't *plan* to do it. But I guess sometimes, without thinking, you find yourself tilting over glass cases full of mice. One interesting fact: scared mice are *fast*.

When I heard the screeches, I bolted back out front to find the boa constrictor guy ducking a squawking cockatiel, freaked-out ladies hopping onto countertops, Santa soothing the ladies, little kids chasing the mice, and Santa's teenage helpers chasing the kids. Somewhere amidst all this chaos, I blurted out that I just couldn't give a living creature to that guy.

Later, as the manager was firing me, he laid a wrinkled hand on my shoulder and said, "Son, you don't have the stomach for the pet shop business." He was right. I did not have the stomach for mouse execution.

I didn't have the stomach for freshman intimidation either. I could see that it was a necessary evil, but I left that to Charlie. One harsh sentence from him that day and they sat down and shut the fuck up.

☆ ☆ ☆

Charlie's still looking pissed, worse even than his normal pissed, so I have to ask, "You all right?"

"My mom's having a baby," he answers.

"ANOTHER ONE?" Jesse says.

For some reason Charlie's mom waited seven years after he was born to have a second child, then produced a kid every twelve minutes after that. I remember our first-grade teacher telling the class during circle time that something *wonderful* had happened to Charlie that morning. He'd become a big brother. He responded by flinging himself into the center of the circle and screeching, *My life is ruined!*

"What's this one going to be called?" Camila asks with a little smirk.

"Shiv."

"Shiv?" I say. "Isn't that what they call knives in prison?" It's a good thing I'm sitting too far away to get punched.

"And," Charlie adds, "I failed my Chemistry test. I don't know why I let my counselor talk me into taking AP. I've gotta get her to switch me into Regular! Adam—"

"I'll talk to her." If I don't agree immediately, I'll have to hear him say that maybe his parents would have time if they didn't have nine million other kids—the bitter complaint he's been using since Brother Number One. I know I could refuse, tell him that he's totally capable of pleading his case himself, but knowing Charlie, he'd end up doing something crazy and get another in-school suspension.

By this point, Emerald's eaten the majority of my chicken. I'm debating whether to take my container back or to keep watching her chew.

"So are you guys coming or not?" Jesse's asking, and I realize I have no idea what everyone's talking about.

"Maybe," Matt says. "Could be cool—"

"No," Camila interrupts him as if that's the end of the discussion for both of them. It probably is. She's older by two minutes and has used this to rule over him ever since I can remember.

"It's too far," Charlie whines. "Like at least an hour drive."

"Yeah, it really is far." Of course Allison agrees with him. "We don't even know if they're good."

"They *are* good," Jesse insists. They must be talking about some obscure band he wants us to go see, because he has a prejudice against anything anyone might have actually heard of.

By now the entire table (Charlie, Allison, Camila, Joe, Natalie, Kate, Bianca, Michael, Josh, Maddie, Sean—basically everyone) is grumbling that they don't want to go. The concert's outdoors and not till the end of October. It'll be cold. It's too far. Jesse and Matt both look disappointed but seem to be settling into acceptance.

"I'm in," I tell them, already getting excited, because the mini road trip will be fun. "Yeah, it'll be awesome. Adventure! And we'll bring blankets."

Jesse grins and shoves one of his earbuds in my ear, painfully hard. "You will not be disappointed, man. Listen."

The screaming vocal and clashing guitar sound about like every other band he's shoved into my ear, but I smile and chew my last bite of chicken. I can only half-hear the table now as they decide how many cars we'll need to get all of us there.

FOUR

JULIAN

AFTER SCHOOL, I take a sharp right and cut through the park. It's not really much of one—no slides or jungle gyms or anything that might attract parents and their kids—but it's thickly wooded, with a few small ponds and some faint pathways. I like this route better than going through the neighborhoods not because it's faster, but because it's as if I'm doing this deliberately instead of avoiding Jared and the bus like a coward.

Sometimes, if I try hard enough, I can picture the Jared I met way back in kindergarten. I remember when Mom picked me up that first day, I told her there was a very mean boy in my class. Jared pinched kids when the teacher wasn't looking. He scribbled on everyone's watercolors with black crayon. He knocked down their towers in the block center.

Mom listened, nodding, then she said there was no such thing as a mean child, only an unhappy one.

"But you don't know," I told her. "You didn't see."

"I don't have to see. I know." She wouldn't tell me *how* she knew, but she swore that Jared deserved nothing but my sympathy.

The next day, when he kicked down my tower, I put a sympathetic hand on his shoulder. "It's okay," I said. "I know you're just unhappy." Then he punched me in the eye.

After school I told Mom she was wrong. Jared was evil—he'd *hit* me. I waited for her to be angry, to tell me she would call his mother. Instead she said no one is evil, only unhappy, and unhappiness festers inside like a sore.

Later, as I watched Jared on the playground, playing alone or hiding under the wooden beams of the jungle gym like a real-life kindergarten troll, I'd worry, imagining festering sores under his skin where no one could see.

But *I* could see. I can *still* see, and I can feel all the sympathy Mom told me I should feel.

But that never made me any less afraid of him.

As soon as I get home, I open my trunk, and today I take out the green spiral notebook. I found it on my mother's desk in our old house, and I grabbed it before everything we ever owned was catalogued, boxed, and stored away. Sometimes I can picture it: paintbrushes, tooth-brushes, shirts, quilts, books, and musical instruments, all in boxes in the dark.

For all I know, in one of those boxes there are a hundred more spirals like this one. But this is what I have, a single notebook, sheets filled front to back until the words stop right in the middle.

I flip at random, landing on a familiar page. The first time I read it, I thought it was a list of her favorite movies. I didn't recognize most of them, but I knew a couple were ones she really liked. But if they were her favorites, then where were all the Shirley Temple movies?

She loved those. And why were war movies on the list? She hated war movies.

So if it's not a list of favorites, and it's not a list of least favorites, then what is it? If she wrote them down, they must be important. Maybe something happened on the day she saw each of them. Or maybe . . . I don't know, but they have to mean *something*.

For the millionth time I wish she'd titled her lists, because the entire notebook is like this. A list of places. A list of colors. A list of songs. But no titles. No context. No way to understand what they mean.

FIVE

ADAM

I OPEN CHARLIE'S front door, and it's like stepping inside a bad Western. The life-size Sylvester the Cat doll he won at the fair last spring has been hanged and disemboweled. White fluffy guts explode from its stomach as it swings from the chandelier by its jump-rope noose.

One of Charlie's brothers flies by wearing nothing but a Superman cape. Three more kids, dressed in clothes that barely fit, are hot on his trail. One is carrying a jar of jelly, and the others are waving cap guns. I dive in between them.

Soon I'm surrounded by identical blond children. Two leap up, digging footholds into my ribs like I'm one of those climbing walls. The rest giggle and hug my legs, looking up at me with faces so dirty it's like they've been cleaning chimneys. This house is basically a Charles Dickens orphanage, except the kids are happy and the villain here is completely outnumbered.

Speaking of Charlie, he's just begun his menacing march down the stairs. The kids in my arms cling to me and bury their faces in my shoulders. The ones on the ground try to flee but don't make it before Charlie grabs the jelly from Tomás and orders Olivier to put on some pants.

"Gotta go," I tell the kids in my arms. They kiss my cheeks before hopping to the ground and following the other horde of children up the stairs. I don't know how they're growing up to be so sweet when they live under a constant reign of terror.

Charlie grabs his jacket from the dining room table, then glares at it in astonished fury. Something purple and sticky is dripping from the sleeve. I can't help but laugh.

"Tomás!" he bellows, and even I'm scared. Several more little blond heads scatter in all directions with frightened squeals. He takes an ominous step, and I grab his arm.

"We're gonna be late." There's actually no set timetable for playing laser tag and video games, but I'm trying to avoid bloodshed.

"I just bought this jacket." Charlie takes his possessions very seriously. Money's always tight—a side effect of having so many kids—so he works for a landscaping company, mowing and raking and hauling heavy things.

"I'm sure it'll wash out."

He King-Kong-roars. "I can't wait till I graduate!"

One pale head peeks over the banister. "Us too!" A few scattered giggles are heard from the shadows. Charlie hurls his jacket on the table and stomps toward the stairs. More frightened squeals.

"*Charlie.* Let's go."

"I'm gonna freeze," he says, which is ridiculous, since it's gotta be sixty degrees outside.

"Poor Charlie. You want to wear my jacket?" I make a show of taking it off, and he shoves me so hard I stumble, then trip, but luckily land in a pile of Sylvester guts. "Seriously, man, one of these days you're gonna really hurt me."

He smiles—the thought of that boosts his mood just a little. Anything I can do to help.

"Can you make this thing go any faster?" This time Charlie's complaining is purely perfunctory.

"Say whatever you want, but you know my car is awesome."

"It's a *station wagon*."

Technically, it's a 1968 Saab delivery van—one my grandfather gave my mom when she was a teenager. She's kept it all this time, strangely sentimental of her considering they haven't spoken in over ten years.

When my grandfather bought the Saab, it was olive, but decades have morphed it to an oxidized green. Outside it looks like an old-fashioned ambulance. Open the door, and you fast-forward a couple millennia. Most of the interior had to be replaced, so the dashboard and controls look like what 1950s television writers thought spaceships would look like one day. There's a lot of curvy silver and enormous red buttons, but the weirdest part's the centrally located heating vent that looks exactly like a robot's face.

Charlie turns on the heat—probably to make a point about his lack of jacket—and the round robot mouth glows red.

"Just be grateful I have a car," I say, "or I'd be carrying you on the front of my bike."

"My parents could afford to buy me a car if they didn't have nine million kids." I walked right into that one. "Anyway, pretty soon I'll be able to buy my own car."

"That's great, man."

"So," he says, "I hear you groped Emerald during English today."

"Who told you that?"

"Everyone."

"It wasn't groping. It was hugging. I needed the oxytocin." In third period our teacher went off on some tangent about the healing properties of oxytocin—the chemical produced when people touch. When I tried it on Emerald later, she consented like a princess allowing a peasant to kiss her hand, then attempted to break contact after about four seconds. I had to remind her that it takes twenty seconds for the chemical to activate, which was weird since she has the second-highest GPA in our class and should've remembered that.

Charlie rolls his eyes. "Right."

"It's true. Ms. Webb said that people who don't get enough physical contact can actually *die.*"

"I guess I don't have to worry about that. Me and Allison are making plenty of oxy-whatever."

"Good to hear."

"So you just happened to pick Emerald for this? At random?"

I know what he's getting at. Emerald and I went out for a *month*— in the *sixth* grade. But he's convinced there must still be burning suppressed feelings.

"You know she has a boyfriend," I remind him. Not just any boyfriend either, but a guy so badass he doesn't even sound like a real person. Brett's a college sophomore, on the rowing team, who's a pilot in his spare time. Like he flies actual planes.

"I know," Charlie agrees. "But if she didn't—"

"But she does."

Charlie heaves a defeated sigh. "Yeah, I guess. And if *that* guy's Emerald's type, there's no way you'd—"

"Let's talk about how much I'm gonna kick your ass tonight at laser tag."

"No! You said we'd be on the same team this time." He looks so upset, like a six-foot-five six-year-old, that I burst out laughing. Then consider pulling over to hug him.

"All right. All right." I'm still laughing. "No splitting up this time."

"Same side?"

"Same side."

SIX

JULIAN

AT TEN O'CLOCK I close the curtains on a flat wax-paper moon and get into bed. I'm tired, but my body won't relax. The house is empty. It looks like Russell won't be coming home tonight, and I'm always more afraid on nights when I'm alone.

Maybe it would be different if the house weren't so quiet. I wish I still had the little portable DVD player Mom and Dad bought me for long road trips. For years I could fall asleep listening to sitcoms or my favorite movie, *Swiss Family Robinson*. But one day the DVD player stopped working and nights became too quiet.

I can hear the rattling thud of the water heater. Below that, the hum of the refrigerator.

Above, the scrape of tree branches along the roof. None of these sounds is unfamiliar, but I still feel the vague dread that I can't stop or sort out.

I turn on my flashlight and roll over to gaze at my sand-colored walls. For just a second I see my old walls in my old room. Brilliant ocean blue. I close my eyes, and suddenly I'm teleporting—I'm there.

The yellow light beside me is not from my flashlight, but from my lamp, the one with the pedestal shaped liked a crescent moon. Beneath my window is the little bookcase with peeling red paint and shelves stuffed with movies and Elian Mariner books. And the blue of my walls is broken by bursts of color from all the posters I've hung.

The first time Russell ever punished me was for hanging a picture in this room. I should have checked with him first, I know that now, but I didn't think to do it at the time. In my old room I could hang pictures whenever I wanted. Russell's punishment wasn't all that severe, but that had never happened to me before, and it shocked me. After it was over, he asked if I would nail holes into a stranger's wall.

Crying, I shook my head.

Then why would I think I could do it here? he asked. These weren't my walls, just like this furniture wasn't my furniture. "Is this how you behaved with your foster family? Is that why they finally put you out?"

The day I moved in, he'd told me I'd caused so many problems and was so spoiled that my foster mother and brother were done with me. The way he'd said *spoiled* wasn't the way you'd talk about an overindulged child, but how you'd describe meat left out in the sun. Spoiled meant *ruined*. He'd warned me that if I pulled that in his house, he'd be done with me too.

"Yes," I answered, because I had hung pictures in my foster brother's room.

Russell nodded as if he wasn't surprised. Then he told me something he's told me a thousand times since: the problem with the world was that fathers weren't raising their sons anymore, so boys never truly became men. If these fatherless boys ever had sons of their own, inevitably they would fail. Boys could not bring up other boys.

Some words stay in your head long after they're spoken. Those words meant he thought little of my father, and that was because he thought so little of me.

Now my brain begins to fill with static until I can't see my old blue walls anymore.

The dread resurges, more intense now. I roll over, refocusing my attention on the ceiling, and tell myself, *Think good thoughts.*

Spider-Man pops into my head, but I quickly push him out. Those movies always scared me.

Think good thoughts.

If I can just think good thoughts, I can fall asleep. Again I try, and now I can see it. Elian Mariner. Only he is me, and I'm standing on the deck of a ship in his crayon-colored world, and my ship can go anywhere.

ADAM

I get home around ten and let myself in through the back door. The yellow kitchen's semiclean by normal people standards, which means it's immaculate by ours. Dishes done, garbage out, herbs in the windowsill all lined up. It also smells freakin amazing—freshly baked almond bread on the counter.

I don't bother getting a plate, just grab at it with my bare hands like a starving animal. It still shocks me that my mom knows how to make bread now. Till about five years ago, we ate practically nothing but fast food.

I push through the swinging yellow doors into the living room. Mom's still awake and sitting in the center of our yellow couch.

"She's a monster!" This is Mom's version of a greeting. I chuckle when I glance at the TV. *The Bachelor.*

"What'd she do this time?" I ask, dropping down beside her.

It turns out to be pretty much the exact same horrible thing she did last time—saying evil things to the other women but pretending to be a decent human being in front of the guy. I suffer through the Rose Ceremony, which would be a lot more entertaining if I were allowed to laugh, but I'm not.

When it's finally over, Mom says gravely, "I swear to you, Adam, if he doesn't send her home next week, I'm never watching this show again." We both know this is an empty threat.

She turns off the television, then pulls Connect Four from under the coffee table. While we play, she asks who I was hanging out with.

"Charlie."

"How's he doing?"

"Same."

She makes a mild noise of disapproval. She's known Charlie since he was six, so she can't outright dislike him—in her mind he'll always be a kid—but he's not her favorite person either. She thinks he's way too grumpy. I've tried to explain to her that's what makes him so entertaining.

"Emerald wasn't there?" Mom's tone is so casual that it doesn't sound casual at all.

"Nope." I drop a checker into the board with a grin. "Connect four."

"How did I miss that?"

"I don't know." I slide the tray, spilling the checkers onto the table.

After I win again, Mom suggests she may have early-onset Alzheimer's.

"You do not have Alzheimer's," I say. "You're only thirty-seven!"

"Don't remind me."

Which is my cue to tell her, "But you look way younger." Of

course, this is partly because she's extremely short—like only up to my shoulder. But there's no need to mention that out loud.

"Well, something's going on. I never used to lose!"

"Maybe I'm just getting better. You ever think of that? You could beat me when I was nine."

"All right, Punky Brewster," she says, which means she thinks I'm being a punk. It doesn't make sense. I found that '80s sitcom on YouTube, and despite the character's name, she was a nice little girl.

Same thing with the Rudy Ruettiger—what Mom calls me when she thinks I'm being rude. I've seen the movie about the plucky Catholic kid who finally got to play for Notre Dame. I've told her it would make more sense to call me Rudy the next time I persevere and overcome all obstacles, but she doesn't care about making sense.

"Besides," I say, "if you had dementia, how could you know where everything in this house is at, like, a photographic memory level?"

"That's a mom thing." She smiles. "We always know where our kids' missing shoes and schoolbooks are."

"Your memory's fine. I just happen to be better at Connect Four."

Now she frowns, but she's pretending to be more irritated than she is.

"Harvey and Marissa went at it again today," she tells me during our third game. At times like these I can tell she misses being a social worker. Her happiest days are when her office coworkers fight and she can sort it out. "I really think Harvey just needs some counseling."

Which makes me think of him.

"I saw Julian today."

Mom's face loses all animation, and her lips turn up in a creepy plastic smile, the way it does whenever she's upset but trying to pretend she isn't. "How did he look?"

"About the same." Still small for his age, still too much black hair falling into huge round eyes. Only he seemed different in ways that would just worry her—too quiet, and flinching away like a skittish kitten when I got too close. "I tried to say hi, but he took off." I don't add that he *literally* took off, as in turned and ran.

She places another checker in the board, but she obviously isn't paying attention anymore. "I still think about him every day," she says.

I drop another checker, but I'm not paying attention anymore either. "I know."

SEVEN

JULIAN

MISS WEST IS unhappy. I know this because she's mean the way Jared is mean, like the grown-up version of kicking over your tower. She teaches Physical Science, the class I have first period. It's a nerve-wracking way to start the day, but sometimes I think it's for the best. At least I'm getting it over with.

I find my seat in the back, and as soon as the bell rings, Miss West confiscates one girl's phone and screams at a boy for whispering. A moment later Dawn, the girl with cerebral palsy, is wheeled into the room. Miss West watches while the aide helps Dawn transfer from her wheelchair into a desk, a process that always has the girl wincing and sweating.

"Dawn," Miss West says once the aide is gone, "wouldn't it be easier to just stay in *your* chair?"

Dawn looks caught off guard, her eyes big and distorted behind her glasses. "I like sitting in a desk," she finally answers. Her voice is a little strange, like all the letters don't come out quite right, and every time she speaks it makes Miss West cringe.

"But none of us like having to delay class every day to wait for you," Miss West says. "If you're going to insist on doing this, then the least your aide can do is get you here early. All this coming in late and leaving early is very disruptive."

Slowly, Dawn nods, then Miss West says it's time to return our exams. The room was already tense, but now it's even worse.

"David," she says, handing a boy his paper, "seventy-six. Violet, eighty-five. Kristin, ninety-three. Julian . . ." She stops right in front of me. This close, she's much scarier. Her eyebrows are two black ink arcs, and her skin looks like wax. "Forty."

I never talk and I don't have a phone, so when I get yelled at, it's for failing.

"Can anyone tell me how someone could possibly make a *forty* on this test?" She looks around the room. "Alex, do you know?"

Alex and Kristin are the most popular kids in the class, and they're the only two Miss West seems to like. They can be tardy or take out their phones and she doesn't get mad.

Alex shrugs. "I don't know."

"Me neither," Miss West says. "I would have thought it was impossible unless you just randomly circled answers."

I wince and close my eyes. If I concentrate hard enough, maybe I really could teleport.

"Pitiful."

Or just disappear.

At lunchtime in my hidden room, my fingers itch to trace the words in my mom's notebook. I like the way it feels, but I'm afraid to bring the notebook to school. What if someone took it and drew ugly pictures in it? What if they destroyed it altogether? The thought makes me feel sick, like I'm in a speeding car instead of standing still.

No, it's better to leave the notebook safe in my trunk. I know most of the lists by heart anyway. There's one that if it had a title would be called A List of Fears. All of the words end in *phobia*, except for number sixteen: *kayak angst*.

I looked it up on a school computer and read that it's an anxiety disorder you can only find among the Inuit sailors of Greenland. The sailor feels fine as he's heading out in his one-man boat, but he panics once land disappears. Disoriented and alone, unable to see a shore in either direction, he's terrified.

It makes me think of Elian Mariner. He always sails alone, and he's never afraid. Maybe he isn't scared because he doesn't experience this aloneness for long. One moment his sailboat is airborne in the stratosphere with a beautiful view of a tiny earth and all the stars. Then, *flash*, like fireworks and a sonic boom, you turn the page and he's *there*. In another country or another world.

The travel looks instantaneous, but when I was little I wondered about it and asked my dad, *Where did he go?*

Dad pointed to the picture, his index finger a rainbow of ink. *He's right here.*

But in between? Where was he?

I don't know.

Dad turned the page and kept on reading as if the place where Elian disappeared didn't matter. Because when you're between two shores and no one can see you, you don't really exist at all.

EIGHT

JULIAN

A FEW MINUTES into fourth period, I've only taken one step in the direction of my hidden room, when I hear my name. Adam is behind me, exactly where he was the first time a week or so ago, and wearing an amused smile. "Going to Dr. Whitlock's?" he asks.

I just stand here squeezing the yellow hall pass.

"I'm her aide this year," he adds. He starts walking, then halts. "Coming?"

I hesitate before falling into step beside him. While we walk, I watch our feet. My sneakers used to be white but are now dirty yellow. His are new and bright white and moving like they always used to—fast, with a mixture of skipping and jogging.

The whole time, he's talking. "So you're in Art? Do you like it?"

I nod, but I don't like it. Maybe I would, if I could get the beautiful pictures in my head onto the paper. Miss Hooper says my drawings are good, but they aren't really.

"What teachers do you have?"

I steal a glance at him to see what looks like genuine interest.

"Uh . . ." My voice comes out rusty and strange. "For English I have Miss Cross."

"Oh, I had her! She was really nice."

She probably never had to ask Adam to speak up.

As we get closer to Dr. Whitlock's office, all the cells in my body start telling me to run. "I have to use the bathroom," I say, then rush through the door and duck into a stall. I stand here counting minutes until I'm sure Adam will be gone.

But when I come out, he's still there, pacing right outside the door. I must look pretty startled, because he says, "Sorry. Didn't mean to scare you." He reaches out, and even though I know he isn't going to do anything, it still catches me by surprise. He puts two hands up, backing away a little. "Sorry, now I *really* didn't mean to scare you."

He starts walking again, then stops when I don't follow.

"Um . . ." I don't know how to say this politely. "It's okay if you need to go somewhere else."

"Are you saying you don't want me to walk with you?"

I think he's joking, and I never know what to say when people are joking. I think most people tease back, but I can't come up with any jokes. But when you just stand there, you make people uncomfortable.

Finally he says, "Just kidding," which is what most people eventually say. "I heard you got lost on your way to her office the last ten times."

"I didn't get lost."

Adam grins. "I didn't think you really did."

"Oh."

"Well, now I'm your . . . What's a nice word for prison transport? Escort!" He bounces ahead, and too soon we're heading into what looks like a waiting room, one with a big desk and a moss-green couch.

Adam strides across the room and knocks on a frosted glass door to an interior office. I hear a voice, familiar and deep, say, "Come in."

Adam opens the door, bows a little to me, then drops onto the couch. With a sigh, I walk over the threshold.

ADAM

When I got to Dr. Whitlock's earlier, she explained that my assignment was to bring in Julian—a lot like a bounty hunter, only without the violence. Or the reward.

The first time someone assigned Julian to me, I was ten years old. I'd just started fifth grade when our teacher, Mrs. Nethercutt, announced that we were each being given a kindergarten reading buddy. Mrs. Nethercutt was one of those teachers who liked to remind you that you'd never have it as good as you have it right now. One day you'd be in the real world, instead of the fictitious world of elementary school. There'd be no friends or recess or lunchtime. Instead, you'd work hard and be still and never speak to anyone. All day. Every day. Until you retired, then, soon after, died.

Her classroom was designed to replicate the future silent-sedentary life we'd inevitably have, so when she said we'd get to leave the room twice a week to play reading games, I was stoked.

Our class hosted a party with sugar cookies and pink lemonade, and there was an elaborate ceremony to introduce us to the kids we'd be working with for the rest of the year. At the end, the kindergartners ordered their fifth grader to lift them up. Mrs. Nethercutt immediately ordered us to put them back down.

The boy assigned to me—Julian—looked like an anime character, with too much shiny black hair that fell just short of his enormous round eyes. As soon as I deposited him back on the ground, he grabbed my hand in that unself-conscious way little kids do, and told me to listen.

My attention had been wandering because the room was pure chaos. Kids were darting everywhere, someone had spilled the giant bowl of lemonade, and Charlie was wailing that his reading buddy had peed on him.

"I'm listening," I said.

Julian's little face got serious, and then he burst into song. His powerful voice grabbed the attention of the entire room, and even Charlie stopped crying for a minute. I can't remember what Julian sang, but he was good. Not just little-kid-good, but really good.

It took a few meetings with our reading buddies before I realized that kindergartners were a lot like manic-depressives, vacillating between euphoria and despair with terrifying speed. It was overwhelming to a lot of us, and one time Charlie got sent to the office for saying "This is hell."

But I got lucky. Julian never cried or threw fits or peed on me. He was just a naturally cheerful kid—always singing and wearing those crazy glasses you'd get at joke shops—so we spent our time in the library playing superpowers and having fun.

Well, that was until Mrs. Nethercutt demanded to know what I thought I was doing. I told her that Julian and I felt we'd been misled. We'd been promised reading *games*; instead, we just got reading.

She ignored my totally valid concerns and ordered me to make Julian read aloud from one of the kindergarten primers at the center of our table. I promised I would, and I had the best of intentions, but

Julian's pockets were full of distractions—coins, paper clips, a gooey hand on a long gooey string—all the kinds of things my mom made sure I didn't have in my possession before she'd let me out of the car in the morning.

Mrs. Nethercutt eventually got fed up and said if we didn't get to work, she'd assign me a new kindergartner, or even worse, Emerald would get two, and I'd have to sit alone and *still*. Emerald and her partner were seated right across from us, so when she overheard the threat she gave me a severe frown. Maybe she was still annoyed because I'd messed up her perfect hair with the gooey hand.

I didn't have much choice, so I got serious and told Julian no playing—just reading. The kid who was always singing and smiling dropped his dark head onto his outstretched arm, looking miserable, and kicked his little feet in the air.

I could totally sympathize. The books we had to choose from weren't exactly page-turners. Every line of every story was practically the same. Boy plus verb plus ball. Girl plus verb plus cat.

Completely out of self-preservation, I brought an old picture book from home. Julian took one look at it, sniffed with very adult disgust, and said no, he didn't want to read at all. I pleaded, telling him it was my favorite book when I was in kindergarten. He huffed that he wasn't in kindergarten. He was a *second grader*. He'd said this before, and I'd figured it was just little kid posturing. He was always trying to impress me—like telling me that when he was at home he could fly and move things with his mind.

"If you're a second grader, then why are you here?" I asked.

"I have dyslexia," he said. "I'm in Reading Improvement."

Hearing that, I felt like a jerk. I knew how much it sucked to be separated from your class for something you couldn't control.

I glanced over my shoulder to find Mrs. Nethercutt watching us with narrowed eyes, and I hastily promised Julian it was an awesome book—my favorite in second grade too.

This seemed to pique his curiosity, so he looked at the cover—a little boy with dark hair and round eyes standing on a giant sailboat—and tried to sound out the title. "E-e-el—"

"Elian Mariner."

"He has a ship? Like *Swiss Family Robinson?*"

I'd never heard of *Swiss Family Robinson*, but he was actually looking interested now, so I said, "Yeah, just like that. But Elian's ship is magic. It can go anywhere."

The next time I saw Julian, he sauntered into the library, beaming, his little arms weighed down with a stack of Elian Mariner books. He said his dad had gotten them for him because he was a good reader now. He went back to being cheerful-humming-Julian till the end of the year, when our buddies had to write an actual book report.

He glared at his blank page, refusing to write. After a while, I got impatient, took the glasses off his face—ones with eyeballs dangling from Slinkies—and pushed a pencil into his little fist. Sulking, he crossed his skinny arms over his chest.

I got bored and turned away, watching my friends help their buddies, till Julian tapped my cheek. "How do you spell *Elian?*"

"Elian? That's easy for you." I pressed my forefinger to cover up the *E* on the book's cover. "What do you get if you put *J-U* here?"

He frowned in concentration, then looked comically stunned. "That's my name!" He began to write, and he had the worst handwriting I'd ever seen. Staggered, backward letters—hieroglyphics, not English.

After a couple of sessions of working steadily, he read his paper aloud to me, since I couldn't make out any of it. Right away I was in, just like when my mom read me actual books. At some point he must have been pretending to read, because it was way longer than the single page he'd written, but I didn't care. His story was good—not just little-kid-good, but really good.

I said as much, and for some reason that moment—right after I told him—is frozen in my head like a photograph. His smile was enormous, and his eyes were shining like he was blowing out the candles on his birthday cake. But sometimes that smile is superimposed onto the face I saw the next time he was assigned to me. The day his parents died.

JULIAN

Dr. Whitlock smiles like she's truly glad to see me, but the intensity of her gray gaze is hard to hold. Her eyes are more curious than friendly, and she's dressed not like a teacher, but like a lawyer or a business-woman.

"How have you been?" she asks, folding her hands in her lap.

I nod, hoping she can understand that a nod means *okay*.

She asks me to take a seat, so I sit on the couch across from her orange cloth chair. It doesn't look like the kind of chair she'd choose. Actually, as I take another glance around, I realize none of the furniture looks like it belongs to her. The small coffee table is purple. Her desk is yellow. Nothing matches, and it reminds me of a living room from a show that I must have seen a long time ago on Nick at Nite.

"Julian . . ." That's the tone I remember: careful, as if she's about to give me terrible news. "Do you understand that this is a safe place, and everything you say here is confidential?"

She's being nice, but it just makes me more nervous, because she expects me to tell her things so personal that they need to be confidential. I don't know what to say, and it becomes awkward, like it always does. Not because she looks annoyed or uncomfortable like most people, but because she's not filling in the space either.

I start picking at the tip of my shoelace. The last bit of plastic comes off and falls onto the floor. Dr. Whitlock lifts the wastebasket toward me. I pick up the plastic and drop it in the can, then she tells me to choose a game from her shelf.

Board games were not something we ever did at home. When Mom and Dad and I played something, it was guitar or piano or pretend. But I know Dr. Whitlock likes games, so I choose Sorry, just like last year, because it's the only one I know how to play.

I learned it from Russell's nieces when we visited his sister Nora's house one Thanksgiving. They were obsessed with it, but it seemed like a mean and unnecessarily sarcastic game to me. If you draw the Sorry card, it reads something like SORRY! NOW I'M GOING TO TAKE MY PAWN FROM START AND KILL ANY OF YOURS I WANT.

I set the game onto the purple coffee table. Dr. Whitlock opens the box and asks what color I'd like.

"Any of them."

She frowns and already I feel like I've done something wrong. That's what playing feels like too: not fun, because she's watching as if she's evaluating me on how well I play. And the thing about Sorry is that you can't be good at it. It's all luck, so I don't know how I'm supposed to do well besides counting the spaces correctly and not landing on her when I have the option to do something else.

The only time I've ever taken out one of her pawns was when I got the Sorry card and had no choice. Even then I took out the player farthest from her HOME, so it wouldn't be as mean. But afterward I found her watching me, not the board, and she looked unhappy.

NINE

JULIAN

IT'S DARK OUTSIDE, cloudy and starless, when Russell calls me into the living room and aims one long finger down. The hardwood floor is stained, *spoiled,* like footprints left in wet cement.

Earlier this afternoon I cleaned my shoes using something I found under the kitchen sink. They were gleaming white by the time I set them on the living room floor, but I guess there was still some bleach on the soles.

"You have to learn to respect other people's things," Russell says, his voice calm and steady.

"I do."

"You do?"

"I'm sorry. It was stupid."

"Yes," he agrees. "It was." He pauses, and my stomach knots while I wait for him to decide.

Then he says, "Go get it."

I freeze for a moment, then walk to the massive cabinet against the dining room wall. Whenever we used to visit this house, my mother would always say how beautiful the cabinet was, the dark cherry wood with shelves of antiques and paper-thin dishes.

I open the long drawer at the bottom filled with lacy tablecloths and napkins. Underneath them is a thin willow switch. I watch my hand shake as I reach out for it, then return to the living room.

I put it in his outstretched hand.

There's a sudden leap in his throat and the slightest catch in his voice when he says, "Take off your shirt."

If I really had powers, I could turn off pain the way I can shut my eyes. But I can't. I feel it. Skin doesn't get thicker. Instead, it remembers. I know this is true, because the second the air touches my back, it starts to sting like the switch is already falling.

"Turn around," he says.

This part is hardest. A billion years of evolution tells your cells to run. But you can't run. You have to turn around and face the desert wall. You have to be still. He doesn't care if you cry, but you can't fight.

A sound fills the air, then pain so sharp, you feel sick. Slash after slash, cutting and deep, one on top of the other. They don't stop until you're screaming into your palms.

TEN

ADAM

"I TEXTED YOU." This is Charlie's pissed-off way of saying hello when he gets to Government. He hefts a chair and drops it next to my desk—he's too tall to fit his legs under one of his own. "Ms. Stone's being a bitch." Apparently Regular Chemistry's no better than AP Chemistry. I can see another visit to Charlie's guidance counselor in my future.

"I didn't get it," I tell him. "My cell phone broke."

"You broke another phone?"

"I don't even know how it happened. I guess it was in the pile of stuff I threw in the washing machine."

"Idiot."

Emerald and Camila breeze into class, whispering to each other in a way that looks more secretive than how I've ever talked to anyone in my life. Emerald's shoulders are back like she's a professional dancer. Below her flowing white dress, her legs are long and bare and strong like a Roman statue come to life. Her mixed-up-colored hair is in dozens of tiny braids that are somehow combined into a larger braid, and

54

then all of that is twirled on top of her head. Sometimes her hair alone makes me think she might be a genius.

She smiles when she sees me, and Charlie gives me a knowing look before he whines, "I'm starving."

"You're always starving."

We're still two periods away from lunch. After Government it's time to grab Julian and bring him to Dr. Whitlock's, then there's nearly an hour of just *sitting*.

"But I'm really starving." He looks pretty pitiful, actually.

"There might be some food in my backpack."

He dives for it, and looks disgusted when he comes up with nothing but a Ziploc of carrots. "Well, this sucks," he says, but he eats them anyway.

A minute later Mrs. Conner announces that we can work in groups. "We love you, Mrs. Conner!" I shout, then pull my desk next to Emerald's because if you're going to do an assignment with anyone, it should be her. I watch the totally engrossed way she works—for Emerald, every assignment's a major one. I have the urge to unravel her braids or maybe touch the mole beneath her eye. Instead I ask her how Brett is.

She looks surprised for a second, then her whole face lights up— beautiful except for *why* she's lighting up. "All right," she answers.

"Amazing!" Camila corrects, leaning over their desks so I have no choice but to look down her shirt. "He's taking her up in the plane this weekend." Emerald's blue eyes widen and she looks a little embarrassed, like maybe this whole sky date was supposed to be a secret.

"Seriously? That's awesome." Because seriously, it is. It's exactly the sort of badass date you'd love to plan for your girlfriend, but instead you end up taking her to the food court at the mall.

"I guess." Emerald lifts one shoulder in a graceful shrug.

"You guess?" There's obviously no way to impress her. "I mean, seriously, *I* want to be Brett's girlfriend." She, Camila, and Charlie start to laugh. "Do you think Brett would consider a sister-wife thing?" More laughs. "Be sure to tell us how it goes." Emerald shrugs again, looking more embarrassed than stoked.

For the rest of class I have this weird feeling. I'm trying to write, but for each word I'm picturing Emerald and the rower-pilot barreling through the clouds.

JULIAN

I take the note from Miss Hooper and step gingerly toward the hall. The pain has lessened, but I can still feel each cut stretching my skin when I move. When I open the door, Adam is there, only this time I'm expecting it, so I don't embarrass myself. He's smiling brightly, but I don't really know what he's thinking, because you can't always believe smiles.

"Hey," he says. "I wasn't sure you'd be here. Dr. Whitlock said you've been out the past couple of days. Were you sick?"

I nod.

The morning after the punishment I woke up to find a twenty-dollar bill beneath the conch on my dresser, which meant I was allowed to miss school and order pizza. Seeing the money, I had the usual conflicting feelings. Guilt that he'd be going to work while I stayed home. But relief too. If he was letting me miss school and order food, he couldn't be too angry anymore.

"Feeling better?" Adam asks.

I nod again.

"I hope you didn't take a bunch of pharmaceuticals. That stuff's poison."

"No . . ."

"Good. You ready?"

I nod and fall in step beside him, watching our feet. I'm wearing my bleached white sneakers. Today his shoes are red high-tops, like Superman's boots.

"So do you like to draw?"

I nod, even though I don't.

"Cool. You'll have to show me your work sometime."

This is what happens when I lie. Almost instantly I'm put in some situation where I have to tell more lies or I'll get caught. We walk in silence, but it's actually not that uncomfortable, because he doesn't seem to mind that I don't know what to say.

"I took Art my sophomore year," he says a couple minutes later, as if there was never any lull. "I sucked."

He smiles, and now I wish I had just told the truth, because then we could have had sucking at art in common. He launches into a story about how his friend Charlie was in his class and went insane during the third week of their hallway projects. The hallway project, Adam says, *sucks*.

"You have to draw these three-dimensional hallways using nothing but tiny squares." He explains that it requires a lot of patience and Charlie has none. "He tore up his paper and threw all his markers on the floor. He's kind of a giant first grader." Adam laughs, but I'm just staring in awe, because I'd be way too afraid to do something like that.

"I know, right?" he says, as if I said that aloud. "He got two days of ISS. Personally, I've never even gotten a detention. And . . ." He looks at me pointedly. "I've never ignored a faculty member's summons and hidden out in the school." He might be joking, but I'm not sure. "I really should stop hanging out with delinquents."

"Is . . . ?" Adam watches me, his expression patient, as if he doesn't mind waiting for me to finish my question. "Is Charlie your best friend?"

"You mean, do we wear matching friendship bracelets and have photos of each other in our lockers?" He smirks, so I guess I said something stupid. "I don't know. I mean, we've known each other since kindergarten. It's funny—he'd never gone to preschool or anything before, so that first day he was *flipping out*. He cried, like, all morning, till I gave him my cookies at lunch." Adam grins. "We've seen each other practically every day since then. Well, except for when we went to different middle schools. But I don't think I've ever labeled anyone as Best Friend. I just have a lot of friends."

He shrugs as if having a lot of friends is no big deal at all.

ELEVEN

ADAM

JULIAN PAUSES OUTSIDE Dr. Whitlock's office, one of his skinny arms dangling to his side while the other arm reaches across his chest to squeeze his bicep, like it's sore. He's not *that* small—about the size of any other freshman—but he seems smaller because he's always bent like he's ducking a low ceiling.

When he finally heads inside, I drop onto the couch, prepared for a good forty minutes of boredom. I'm not sure why Dr. Whitlock even has an aide. I deliver maybe one note per period. I can't even do any filing, because everything's confidential.

While I'm answering texts, I make out a voice on the other side of the door—just hers—which isn't surprising since he's so freakin quiet. But he wasn't always. Back in elementary school, he was anything but.

A memory pops into my head—Julian giving me this construction-paper card on the last day of fifth grade. All the kindergartners made ones for their buddies, and they were all really proud when they handed them to us. It was pretty adorable, actually. I think I still have mine somewhere. I didn't expect to see him again after that. Then two years later, I came home to find a little boy sitting in the center of our yellow couch, holding a stuffed dog under one arm. When he looked up, his enormous eyes were like glass, something reflective instead of animated.

"Julian?" I said.

Mom whispered, "You know him?"

"Yes." But it was like looking at a photo of a painting. Julian, twice removed. "We were reading buddies. Right, Julian?"

He didn't answer, just stared straight ahead like a sleepwalker.

"Julian is going to be staying with us for a while," Mom said.

Still, he said nothing.

"Julian." Mom spoke carefully. "Adam and I will be right back." She ushered me into the kitchen, and as soon as the doors swung shut behind us, she started to cry. My mom's a pretty emotional person, but when it came to the foster kids who stayed with us sometimes, she always kept it together—no matter how bad the story was.

Knowing this, I got a sick feeling in my stomach. "What happened?"

She shook her head and breathed in fast. "His parents were on their way to pick him up from school. They were all going out of town for the long weekend."

"What happened to them?" I repeated.

"They were in an accident."

"And . . ."

"They died."

"*Both* of them?" She nodded. "How?" I wasn't really asking for details—just questioning how one boy's life could be so instantly and completely obliterated.

She ignored the question. "He wouldn't leave the school. He wouldn't go with the social worker. He kept saying his parents were coming."

My eyes drifted back toward the living room. It scared me. If something happened to my mom, I'd be the one sitting in some stranger's living room.

"I need you to help me with him," Mom said suddenly. It was a weird request, since I was always nice to the kids who stayed with us. But I just nodded and said okay.

Julian didn't make a sound, not during dinner. Not when we watched TV. Not when Mom tucked him into the other twin bed in my room.

Then in the middle of the night, I was woken by a strangled whimper.

"Julian?" I climbed out of bed and stood over him. Tears were shining on his cheeks. "Want me to get my mom?"

He shook his head and began to cry, only I couldn't really call it that.

It was convulsing.

It was dying.

It was the most pained noise I've ever heard another human being make. No one should be capable of that sort of agony and still live.

I was scared to stay with him. I was scared to leave him.

I didn't know what to do, so I grabbed his stuffed dog and shoved it at him. He looked at it for a second, then convulsed even harder.

"I'll get my mom," I said.

"I want *my* mom."

I didn't know what to say—what could you say to something like that?

Still sobbing, he pulled a pillow over his face. Afraid he was going to suffocate, I pulled it away.

"I'm getting a headache. I need my dad. I need him right now!" He was hysterical. "I have a headache! I need him!"

"What does he do for it?"

"He *fixes* it."

"How?"

"Rubs my head."

I sat down beside him and rested my palm on his forehead like I was taking his temperature. "Like this?"

"No." He ran his fingertips across his forehead like he was playing the piano.

I tried to mimic it. "Better?"

He continued to cry.

I'm not sure how long we sat there like that before he asked in a soft, wiped-out voice, "Where are they?"

"Didn't . . . didn't anyone tell you?"

"They died. I know." He sounded so tired. "But where *are* they? Where did they go?"

At the time I didn't get that he wasn't asking where they were in a physical way. I didn't know what to tell him, so I rubbed his head with a little more pressure. "Go to sleep, okay?"

He looked up at the ceiling, eyes wide with despair. "They disappeared."

Julian had no relatives, no godparents, no anyone, so at the two-week mark, when most of the foster kids went home, he stayed. At first it seemed like he was never going to be anything resembling himself again, like he would always be sad. But then there were little things.

We'd go to the mall, and he'd want to wear those joke glasses you could buy at Spencer's—the kind with an attached nose and handlebar mustache.

Or Mom would be reading him a story before bed—he still loved Elian Mariner—and when she finished, he'd add this crazy-long epilogue.

Or he'd sing and talk about his mom—she could sing anything. And his dad—he could draw everything.

But sometimes, out of nowhere, he did this approximation of crying, where his face would scrunch up in pain and his shoulders would shake, only he wouldn't make a sound.

Months went by, and it started to feel like Julian had always been with us, like we were real brothers. After school we'd run around the neighborhood, and at night we'd run around the house till Mom told us to wind down. We'd watch TV—I'd suffer though all those Disney Channel and Nickelodeon shows he liked. He'd endure my superhero movies and endless questions about which superpower he'd want if he could only have only one.

That time we watched *Superman* still pops into my head every now and then. I wasn't really thinking when I stuck in the DVD. Then we reached the part where Lois Lane dies. . . .

It was like Julian stopped breathing—he looked that stricken—as a devastated Superman pulled her from the wrecked car and cradled her head. Julian covered his face and whispered, "Don't cry, Superman."

"It's okay," I said. "See?"

Julian peeked through his fingers. Superman was rising up through the air, into the clouds. Julian gasped as he spun the world backward and brought her back to life.

TWELVE

JULIAN

MISS HOOPER DOESN'T wait for Adam to knock on her door anymore every Tuesday and Friday. She just sends me on my way. Today, as soon as I step into the hall, he asks, "*What* is that?" He's laughing at me, but it doesn't feel mean the way it does when other people do it.

"It's for Child Development," I explain.

He takes the large plastic doll from my hands. "You have to carry this thing around all day?"

"All week."

"I'm so sorry." He shakes his head in sympathy.

"Miss Carlisle says we need to learn that having a baby is terrible."

Adam laughs. "I guess this would do it."

My parents never told me it was terrible. They always sounded so happy when they'd talk about bringing me home from the hospital, or the expression on my face the first time I tried baby-food spinach.

"Do your teachers get pissed when it goes off in class?" Adam asks.

"Sort of." Mostly Miss West. "But I think Miss Cross likes it." She says things like *You couldn't find a sitter?* Or *It must be tough to be a single dad.* I'm almost sure she's joking, but I can never think of a joke to say back, so I mostly wish she wouldn't say anything at all.

The baby suddenly bursts into loud mechanical sobs. "What do I do?" Adam panics, pushing it back at me. I type the correct code into its back to stop the crying. "All week," he repeats, shaking his head again. "Jesus."

When he starts walking, I fall into step beside him, and it's like trying to keep up with something that has too much energy for its container. It fills the hall and ricochets against everyone we pass. A teacher can be approaching, face stressed or sad, and body bent as if they're carrying something too heavy.

Then they see Adam.

They blink as if blinded, and their mouth spreads into a Christmas-morning smile. Sometimes they stop to tell him how much they've missed him, that Algebra or Geography isn't the same without him. Then they ask him what his schedule looks like next semester—does he have room to be their teacher's aide? Adam will ask about their family, mentioning each relative by name; then with a brilliant smile, he promises to visit their classroom very soon.

And now that smile is aimed at me. "Anything interesting happen today?" It's a question I get every Tuesday and Friday.

"Yes," I say. "Miss Cross is making us be in a play."

"'Shakespeare in the Spring.' The English department does it every year, and every year it's awful. Do you know which one you're doing?"

"The one . . . I can't remember his name . . . something weird."

"Not specific enough."

"The one where everyone dies."

"Still not specific enough." The nice thing about Adam is it's easy to tell when he's joking, because he's nearly always joking.

The doll starts to scream again. I have to punch in the code for Distress. "Miss Carlisle says the old egg method was better," I say. "Do you know what that means?"

"Yeah. Kids used to carry around an egg instead of a doll. You passed as long as you didn't break yours."

"Oh." That sounds a lot easier than this. "What play did you do?"

"When I was a freshman?"

I nod.

"*Macbeth*. Oh my god, it was such a freakin mess. So I guess you know, *every* freshman has to participate. They make the sets, the costumes, everything."

I nod again.

"Well, obviously there aren't nearly enough parts for everyone, so the English teachers just add them. Like when we did *Macbeth*, *eighteen* girls performed the parts of the three witches. It might've been okay, but we didn't have after-school rehearsals till a couple days before the show—we just practiced in class. And since the witches were all in different English classes, they learned their lines in different rhythms—the witches' lines rhyme, almost like a song.

"Anyway, the girls only got to have one read-through as a group, so when we did the actual show, no one was together, and you couldn't understand a thing they said—for the entire play. I'd say it was funny, but Emerald was Witch Number Eight, and she's, like, still traumatized."

"That's terrible."

"Do you know what's worse?"

"What?"

"When I was a freshman, they had two performances. The Saturday-night show for the parents, and another one on Friday afternoon, when the entire school was *forced* to come." I must look horrified, because he says, "I know, right? Consider yourself lucky. They just changed that last year."

"So the students don't come to the Saturday-night show?"

"Definitely not." He grins. "No one who doesn't have a kid performing would willingly put themselves through that." The doll starts to wail again. "Do you have to take that thing to lunch with you?"

"Yes."

"Where do you sit? I never see you."

"I don't go to the cafeteria."

"Then where do you eat?"

I can't answer that, so I don't.

"Oh, Julian." Adam sighs. "So secretive."

ADAM

I duck out of Dr. Whitlock's office a few minutes early—she never notices—and head to the cafeteria. Lately we've all become obsessed with The Game, which is basically Truth or Dare without the option to choose truth. As soon as you're given a dare, it's either comply or get ostracized. Then you get to dare someone else, so it's the game that never ends.

It's fun, but there's one unfair rule: guys can be dared to strip completely and make fools of themselves by ringing someone's doorbell or streaking down the street, but girls can't be asked to shed any undergarments.

Allison once cited safety issues, which is obviously a ridiculous excuse. It's not like a kidnapper-rapist is going to steal them while we're all pointing and laughing. Emerald, in her superior, yet reasonable way, said something about the female body being more beautiful and therefore more sacred—basically implying that seeing a guy's junk is equivalent to seeing a naked chimp at the zoo.

I'm one of the first to get a seat today, and soon all my friends squeeze into the table. I glance around for a suitable challenge, then spot Principal Pearce bent over his cane—the one that could be a prop from *Lord of the Rings*. All my friends are legitimately nervous as I look each one in the eye.

I freakin love it when it's my turn.

"Okay . . . Camila," I say. She watches me, her green eye shadow looking like a bruise that's starting to change colors. "I want you to go flirt with Mr. Pearce for at least three minutes."

"No problem," she says, way too smug. We all laugh as she sashays over and puts a seductive hand on his arm. I've got to give it to the old man. Camila's doing her best hair tossing and cleavage thrusting, but he doesn't look impressed. Suddenly she spins around and stomps back—high heels smacking the floor—and slaps a little piece of paper on our table. "I got a dress code detention."

We burst out laughing. When she storms off, we laugh even harder.

Just a few minutes later, Camila returns. "Adam," she says, leveling me with an icy smile.

Now, it's just understood that you *forward* the dare when it's your turn, instead of immediately striking back at whoever dared you. Otherwise, no one else would get to play. But apparently Camila's too pissed to play by the rules.

She reaches into her purse, then tosses a pair of tiny, Camila-size panties at me. "Put them on."

Everyone at the table starts laughing like crazy, but I have to ask, "Were you just wearing these?"

"No! You're disgusting! I got them from my locker."

"Why do you have spare underwear in your locker?"

"Just put them on," she orders, "and make sure everyone in your next class knows you're wearing them."

I give her a wide smile. If she wants to embarrass me, she's going to have to try harder than that.

Between lunch and fifth period—only moments after squeezing into Camila's miniature underwear—I trip and end up sprawled out in the center of the crowded hall. Charlie and Allison cackle like I did it on purpose for their amusement.

It takes me a little longer than usual to get up, and when I do—shit shit shit—my ankle *hurts*. I yell out in high-pitched agony. It really, seriously hurts.

Camila rolls her eyes and examines her long fingernails. "You're not getting out of this, Adam."

I moan, stagger-hopping to the wall, and lean against a row of lockers. The underwear's squeezing my balls, and I'm pretty sure my ankle is broken in ten places. Or at least sprained.

Allison stops laughing. "I think he needs to go to the nurse," she tells Charlie, sounding all motherly. I want to hug her right now, but that would mean letting go of the lockers. Then, to me, "Come on, Adam, let's go."

"I can't *walk*."

Camila stamps her tiny foot and pouts. "You have to finish the dare!"

Charlie squints like he's trying to figure out if this is some kind of trick. Then he apparently decides I'm really hurt, because he yells at me, "How can someone trip over literally *nothing*? Idiot!" I know this is his way of saying he cares.

Allison pats his back as if he's the one who needs comforting, then Camila snaps her fingers. "Charlie, Allison, help him." Sometimes she treats people like they're her brother, and it can be pretty intimidating. The two of them quickly obey and do this thing where they stretch out my arms and drape them over their tall shoulders. Allison's five foot ten—my height—but trying to sling an arm around Charlie makes things dangerously lopsided. We briefly consider switching him out for Camila, but that would just tilt us in the other direction.

The bell rings, and we're officially late to our next class.

"Oh Jesus, just climb on," Charlie grumbles, squatting low to the ground. Grinning, I hobble over and hop onto his back. He puts his arms under my knees, and we're on our way, piggyback-style.

"You boys look cute like that." Camila winks, snapping a picture with her phone. I smile back and nuzzle Charlie's neck.

"Dude . . ." His voice is low and threatening and hilarious. "If you don't quit it, I'm throwing you down, and you can crawl to the nurse's office." He drops my legs, and for a second they're dangling. I hitch them back up and latch on tighter with my arms.

"You make me land on this foot, and I'll kill you." But I quit it, because I believe him.

When the four of us file into the nurse's office, the middle-aged lady's face instantly sours. "All right, kids." She puts her fists on her wide hips. "Theatrics I don't need."

"Theatrics?" Camila puts her little fists on her own hips.

"He sprained his ankle," Allison explains as Charlie backs up into a chair and drops me. I really need to get this underwear off. It's like a weird version of choking.

"It doesn't take ten kids to bring in one kid," Grumpy Nurse says. "The rest of you can get to class."

Camila's clearly pissed, Allison looks afraid to leave me here, and Charlie is three seconds from imploding.

"It's fine, guys," I tell them. "I'll text you later." They leave grudgingly while the nurse grabs a thermometer and stuffs it into a thermometer condom. "The problem's my ank—" She shoves it under my tongue.

"No fever," she says when she extracts it a minute later.

"It's my ankle."

"Hmm." She lifts my jeans, then presses the bone with her cold fingers.

"Ow. Ow."

"I don't see any swelling."

"It really, really hurts."

"You've been awfully smiley for someone who's *really hurt*. Tell me the truth. Do you have a test this period you're worried about?"

"Ah . . . I do have a test, but I'm not worried about it."

She nods like she's figured me out. "Okay, you go take that test, then if you're still in pain, we'll call Mom."

"But my class is upstairs, on the other side of the school. I don't think I can make it." I look around the room. "What about that wheelchair?"

"What about it?"

"Can I borrow it?"

"That's for someone who is seriously ill. Not for kids looking for a good time."

"Looking for a . . . I'm not looking for a good time, I assure you. Just transportation."

"You go back to class, take your test, then we'll talk."

"But—"

"Right. Now."

She means it. She's seriously kicking me out. I get up, hobble-limp, then hop on my uninjured foot. So far so good. A few more hops— then I stumble, and every bit of my weight lands full force on my aching ankle. "Fuck!"

The nurse gasps, her hands flying to her chest like she's been shot. I hobble-limp back to the chair while she stomps in squeaky nurse shoes to her desk. "I'm writing you up," she announces, jerking out a pad of paper.

"I'm sorry. It was involuntary."

"And you're still not doing what I asked."

"I wish I could."

She starts writing furiously, reading aloud as she goes. "Refuses . . . to follow . . . instructions."

I'm starting to feel queasy. I landed too hard, and now my foot is freakin throbbing. Sweat beads on my upper lip. "I think I may actually have a fever now. Maybe you could take my temperature again."

Another shotgun-gasp and she writes even faster.

THIRTEEN

ADAM

I CRUTCH THROUGH the crowded cafeteria the next day, and everyone at our table makes room for me to prop up my foot. "What's that?" Camila asks, tapping her long red fingernail on the mason jar I pulled from my backpack.

"Water."

"Why does it look like that?"

"My mom added a few shots of herbal remedies for ligament healing," I explain.

Camila shudders. In all fairness, it does look like a urine sample.

Charlie's glowering his way through the crowd, then he spots me and his entire countenance becomes alarmingly cheerful.

"Oh god," I moan as he approaches, still beaming. "Who told you?"

"*Everyone* told me. I just didn't think it was possible."

"No one thought it was possible," Emerald adds, her blue eyes sparkly and amused.

Matt pulls up a chair and demands of Charlie, "Why are you so happy?" It's a reasonable question. I don't think any of us have ever seen his teeth before.

"You don't know?" Charlie sits up straighter, obviously excited about the prospect of telling someone who doesn't know.

"Know what?"

Charlie's mouth opens, but before he can speak, Camila says, "Adam got an ISS."

"Hey!" Charlie glares. "I was about to tell him."

"Adam?" Matt looks at me like I was just arrested for double homicide. "How?"

So I tell the entire table my story about the cruel nurse, maybe exaggerating things just a little to make it funnier, but also to gain their sympathy. Now everyone is equal parts amused and angry on my behalf.

Well, except for Charlie. He's just amused. "This is awesome."

I try to give him a mean look, but it can't be very convincing since I'm laughing. "It's not awesome. It's ridiculous."

Somewhere during my story Jesse actually removed both earbuds, and now he's giving me a knowing smile. "What'd your mom say?"

"What do you think?" My mom is sort of famous for making our fifth-grade teacher cry.

Charlie grins. "Can I watch her kick the nurse's ass?"

"I hate to disappoint, but she won't be coming. She wanted to, but—"

"You begged her not to?" Emerald accurately guesses.

"I just convinced her that it's not a big deal." Because it's really not. "She's more fight-the-system, and I'm more just-let-it-go."

"No kidding." Charlie stuffs four french fries into his mouth.

"Hey, I could fight the system," I protest.

Matt puts a supportive hand on my shoulder. "We know you could, buddy."

Everyone's looking at me like I'm something adorable and harmless.

"I *could*. It's not like I've never been in a fight before."

Now they're looking at me with perplexed suspicion. Emerald's eyes twinkle like she suspects I'm just trying to impress everyone.

"I *have*. Marcus . . . seventh grade?"

Jesse and Charlie look at each other for a second, then burst out laughing.

"Getting smacked in the face with a Harry Potter book does not qualify as a fight," Charlie says.

"First of all, it wasn't just any Harry Potter book. It was *Order of the Phoenix*."

Matt gasps. He knows that *Order of the Phoenix* is the longest and most potentially dangerous of all the Harry Potter books when used as a weapon.

"Still not a fight," Charlie insists. "Now maybe, if you'd hit him back . . ."

It honestly never occurred to me to hit him back. I remember standing there in stunned pain, then feeling even more shocked when Marcus collapsed and started crying and writhing around on the floor. "I couldn't. He was having a mental breakdown or something."

"Why'd he hit you, anyway?" Matt asks.

"I know," Charlie says eagerly. "I saw the whole thing. We were in the middle of Math class, and Marcus was trying to do his worksheet or something, and he just snapped because Adam wouldn't *stop talking*."

Now all the guys at our table are laughing hysterically, and the girls look like they want to join in but are trying to leave me some dignity.

"You don't know how much that sucked for me. My mom went insane."

This only makes them laugh harder.

It really did suck. When she picked me up from school that day, I still had an ice pack on my cheek, and she went ballistic. I tried to appeal to her social worker side, but it was like she'd had no professional training at all. She pulled me back into the school, then got even more irate when the principal wouldn't promise immediate retribution. When it comes to me, she can get embarrassingly mafia-esque.

"I'm serious," I say, pretending not to be as amused as they are. "She still has plans for that kid. She says she's just biding her time."

Jesse takes a breath from laughing. "Dude, your mom is awesome."

FOURTEEN

JULIAN

WHEN I GET to Child Development on Thursday, Jared is smashing his fists into the backpack beneath his desk like it's an arcade punching bag. I get the usual rush of fear/sympathy, but at the same time I feel a strange wave of contentment as I take in the room. It's a *nursery*. Babies are everywhere—lying on the floor, leaning against purses. Mine is safe under my arm as I find my seat in the back. I set him on the desktop, and look at his wide brown eyes and small smile.

The bells rings, and a moment later babies start waking up and wailing. A frazzled-looking teacher pokes her head into the room. "Mind if I shut the door?" she asks.

Miss Carlisle nods sadly.

And the door closes, trapping all the cries inside.

Stressed-out girls start typing codes into their babies' backs. The room falls silent, but only for a few seconds before a different group starts up.

"Do you understand now?" Miss Carlisle raises her voice so we can hear her over all the noise. "Do you see how this would ruin your lives?"

My baby has been with me every moment this week, and sometimes I think I can tell the difference between hungry-crying and sad-crying just like my parents said they could with me. Mostly I don't mind the noise, although I do worry when we're in my hidden room and his loud voice echoes to the rafters. But I worry even more in the middle of the night.

Russell has been away, but I've been afraid he'll come home after I fall asleep, afraid he'll hear and get mad, and I keep getting a cold pain in my stomach like I've swallowed a thousand winters.

But for the past three nights it's been only us—me and the baby— and I haven't noticed the strange noises the house usually makes, almost like they aren't there anymore. It's been nice and not terrible, but I don't know when Russell will be back.

Now the baby is looking at me with worried eyes. I smooth down his soft hair and run a hand over his round cheek.

"What the fuck?" Jared's voice finds me like a missile. "Are you *petting* your doll?"

Everyone is looking at me now. Kristin's rolling her fish eyes. Violet is staring, her eyes so inky dark, they look wet. A couple of other girls laugh.

I glance at Jared, and that's when I see what is sticking out of his backpack: a baby. Its rosy cheek is caved in. Jared launches to his feet, kicking over the bag. The baby's head thumps hard against the floor.

"Jared!" Miss Carlisle looks up from her computer. "These dolls are expensive!"

Jared scowls and grabs the baby by the hair to toss it onto his seat. Then he looks at me.

My eyes flit to Miss Carlisle, who's back to concentrating on her screen.

Jared starts toward me like a predator, like a wolf.

My heart begins to pound in my ears, and the next thing I know, I've pulled my baby into my lap and wrapped my arms around him. Jared stops in his tracks, almost as if he's startled.

Then he smiles with wolf teeth. "Someone *really* likes his dolly."

I hear a couple more laughs and feel my face getting hot. I should probably set him back on the table, because everyone is acting like it's weird to hold him, but if I do, Jared might grab him and do something to him.

"Jared," Miss Carlisle says wearily, "go back to your seat."

But he doesn't.

He stares me down, eyes full of angry black scribbles like the ones he used to make on my watercolors.

"Jared," Miss Carlisle repeats.

The scribbles start to swirl. They fill up his face—the whole room.

"Jared."

He growls, then begins walking backward, watching me all the way to his desk.

Then he shoves his baby to the floor and slams into his seat.

FIFTEEN

ADAM

I'VE NEVER BEEN inside the ISS room, but I can already tell it's going to suck. It's windowless, colorless, posterless—basically totally freakin bleak. There're five desks, all facing one gray wall so our backs are to the teacher. Floor-to-ceiling wooden partitions separate each desk like bathroom stalls. I guess they're to avoid distractions or the pleasure of looking at anyone, but it feels a lot like being stuck in the corner—a punishment I found unbearable when I was a kid. Within five minutes my skin's crawling. I need to move or see something—anything—but this room was designed so that you *have* to stare at the wall.

There's a loud bang behind me.

I angle my chair just in time to see Charlie and Jesse smirking through the door's narrow glass pane. I'm about to flip them off when the little elderly ISS lady orders, "Turn yourself around." I return my gaze to the gray brick wall, and it feels like I'm back in the refrigerator box.

When I was in the fifth grade—the same year I became Julian's reading buddy—there were two kids with ADHD in my class: me and Darren Holt. I didn't see much similarity between us, since he played alone and was constantly doing weird things like using strips of Scotch tape to collect tiny bits of debris from the floor.

One morning, when we got to class, a refrigerator box was standing in the corner, and Darren's desk was missing from its row. Mrs. Nethercutt explained that Darren preferred peace and quiet to do his work, meaning he and his desk were *inside* the box.

A few weeks passed like that, then one day Darren didn't come to school. I was pissing Emerald off by swinging her braids like double-dutch jump ropes when Mrs. Nethercutt suggested I try working in Darren's *little room*.

It didn't occur to me to say no, so I went into Darren's box and sat at his desk. The cardboard walls were taped with magazine photos and computer printouts of different kind of insects, and in one corner were dozens of balls of Scotch tape. It was creepy, but even worse than that, it was boring.

I pitied Darren for all the days he'd spent like this. I vowed to never be *off task* again. I would stop pouring glue on my hand and pretending it was an old-man-hand. I would stop trying to deconstruct Emerald's perfect hair. I would take a vow of silence and do my freakin work.

Needless to say, when I told my mom how I'd spent my day, she did not take it well. The following morning she walked me into class, a protective arm around my shoulder, and demanded to know if Mrs. Nethercutt had locked me in a box.

My teacher started to stutter that the hyperactive child thrives in such a situation. They could focus without all the overwhelming stimuli of windows and bright colors and other children. They were happier this way.

"Happy?" Mom shouted. "My child was traumatized!"

That was an exaggeration. I was bored, definitely, but it wasn't like I stayed in there all day. I got out for lunch, recess, the bathroom, and a million other times to ask questions.

Mrs. Nethercutt looked panicked. "It was an experiment."

I think that was a poor choice of words as far as my mom was concerned. I remember her saying something about the Stanford Prison Experiment, and then she said a lot of other things neither of us is proud of, and Mrs. Nethercutt started to cry. In front of the entire class.

When Darren got back to school the next day, he was pissed at me because the principal had confiscated his little room. But I didn't get why he was so upset. Why would anyone want to spend their day inside a box?

JULIAN

My hidden room is darker than usual. It's drizzly and gray outside, so very little sun makes it through the porthole. It's quiet, the echoey kind that throbs inside your ears, and it will stay quiet since Miss Carlisle took back our dolls today. I pull my peanut butter and jelly sandwich from my backpack and take a small bite.

All morning I'd been planning my answer for the question I knew Adam would ask: *Anything interesting happen today?* But when I went into the hall to meet him last period, he wasn't there. I kept waiting, counting time. Ten minutes. Fifteen. Twenty.

Then I saw Dr. Whitlock striding down the hall. "I'm so sorry," she said. "I assumed if you didn't see Adam, you'd come on your own." She explained that he wouldn't be coming at all today, but she wouldn't tell me why.

I take another bite of my sandwich. My father used to pack them in my lunchbox every morning. It seems like they'd be easy to make, but now they never taste right.

It's strange how many ways there are to miss someone. You miss the things they did and who they were, but you also miss who you were to them. The way everything you said and did was beautiful or entertaining or important. How much you mattered.

When I was little, thoughts would always fill my head, because I knew as soon as school ended, my mom or dad would want to hear them all. When you know you're going to tell someone everything, you see your day through your eyes and theirs, as if they're living it alongside you.

But when you don't, it isn't only not seeing double—it's not seeing at all. Because if they aren't there, you aren't either.

SIXTEEN

JULIAN

"JULIAN?" DR. WHITLOCK'S careful tone catches my attention. "Would you like Adam to join us today?"

While Adam and I walked from my Art class to her office—slower than normal, because he was limping a little—he told me he'd been in ISS on Friday. He said it wasn't all that bad, since after an hour or so the teacher warmed up to him. "Do you want to go back?" I asked, and Adam said, "Do you mean am I going to intentionally get myself thrown into ISS so I can spend the day playing poker for Oreos with Miss Agnes?" I nodded. "You're funny, Julian." He laughed, but he never answered my question.

And I haven't answered Dr. Whitlock's yet.

Of course it would be much better if Adam were in here, but Dr. Whitlock is watching me with such intensity that I don't know what answer to give. I don't want to hurt her feelings, and Adam probably won't want to come in anyway. So it becomes awkward, because neither one of us is speaking.

"It's fine," she finally says. "I just thought you might prefer it."

"Okay."

"Okay?"

"He can. If he wants."

She nods and leaves the office. A couple minutes later he bounces inside and starts digging through the games. "Yes!" he cheers. "Jenga. Wanna play this?" He's already grabbing it and kneeling down in front of the bright purple coffee table.

"How do you play?"

"You've never played Jenga?" Normally a statement like this would embarrass me, because it's usually followed by some kind of insult. But his smile is good-natured and doesn't feel mean.

He dumps the box on its side and dozens of small wooden blocks tumble out. I slide off the couch to kneel down by the table like he is.

"We can play Sorry next," Dr. Whitlock says a few minutes later. "I know how much you like it." I don't like Sorry. I've never liked Sorry. But I can see she's trying to be nice.

"I like this game." I peek up, hoping I haven't offended her.

She doesn't look offended. Her smile is as big as Adam's.

SEVENTEEN

ADAM

ON FRIDAY, INSTEAD of taking the normal route to Whitlock's, I veer off course. We trek the upstairs hallways, head back down, then up, then down again in the most ridiculous, complicated route imaginable.

I keep waiting for Julian to ask why. I'm not sure what I'll say, because I sure as hell can't tell him that I'm now officially getting class credit for being his friend. It's kind of sweet really, Dr. Whitlock telling me to just walk and talk with him the whole period. Well, except for the part where I'm supposed to report back anything *concerning*. Which, obviously, I won't do. But the other part, the part where she wants him to have friends—even if they are assigned friends—is sweet.

After about thirty minutes of looping around the school, we head into the courtyard. "Smells like someone's burning leaves," I say. Julian shivers even though it's not that cold. "I love that smell. Makes me want to carve a jack-o'-lantern or something."

"Adam?" He's holding his arm in that weird sore-shoulder way.

"Yeah?"

"I don't want you to get in trouble."

"For what?"

"For not taking me to Dr. Whitlock's." Finally. "I don't want you to get fired."

I burst out laughing. "You're funny." I eye the brick wall, wondering if I could do that thing where you run up a wall and backflip. "I won't get in trouble. She said we could just hang out." I take a leap and end up falling on my ass. "Ow." I lie here while Julian cautiously sits on the wooden bench. "What are you doing later?"

"What do you mean?"

"Like tonight, this weekend."

"I'm not sure. What are you doing?" he asks it carefully, like a kid who's just learning correct phrases like *please* and *thank you.*

"Going to a concert. You like concerts?"

"We never went to concerts." Julian hardly ever talks about his parents, but whenever he does, it's like this. Like if something didn't happen while they were alive, it never would. "My . . ."

After a while I realize he's not going to finish, so I prompt, "Yeah?"

"My mom loved music."

"I know."

"She could play every instrument. She could sing anything. But we didn't go to concerts. I don't know why."

"Do you want to come tonight?"

"What do you mean?"

"Do you want to come to the concert?"

"I don't have a ticket."

"I can get you a ticket." I think I can, anyway. "I can text you as soon as I get it."

"I don't have a cell phone."

"Seriously? Everyone has a cell phone." He looks embarrassed. "Doesn't matter. You can just meet me at my house at six."

I'll have to prepare my mom first. Julian had been with us for eight months when, out of nowhere, a social worker took him. It turned out there was a relative, sort of—Julian's godfather/uncle by marriage. Mom and I thought we'd be able to at least *visit* Julian, but then she got a notice from the woman handling his case. The uncle said Julian needed to adjust to his new home and that he believed seeing us would *harm the process* somehow. I remember Mom carefully folding that letter before tucking it into a drawer as gently as if it were Julian himself. Losing Julian—for Mom, for me—it was like a death.

"So do you wanna come?" I ask.

He smiles, wide and happy like a kid about to blow out the candles on his birthday cake. "Yes."

EIGHTEEN

JULIAN

FOR THE FIRST time in four years, I'm standing on Adam's front porch.

But I can't make myself knock.

I have a strange, dizzy feeling, like the time Mom and I went on a hike and had to cross a tall suspension bridge. I remember being right at the edge and how it felt to peer over the side—terrifying and incredible all at once.

I take a deep breath, then I knock.

A moment later, Adam opens the door, saying, "Hey, come in." The house is just like I remember: yellow and cluttered and alive like an electrified current. "I'm almost ready." He darts off toward where I remember our room was.

There are still a ton of photos of Adam everywhere. Adam as a naked toddler in a bathtub with a soap beard. Adam proudly holding a badly carved pumpkin. Adam at a roller-skating party with dozens of other children when he must have been five or six.

I step closer to a photo framed in black—it's me. I'm nine years old, and I'm smiling as I stand on that wooden box I used to pretend was a stage. I scan the crowded wall of pictures and find my face again. In one photo Adam is carrying me on his back. In another I'm holding his hand.

"Hey," Adam says, appearing behind me. "You ready?"

I nod and try to smile, but it probably comes off more like a grimace.

He doesn't seem to notice, and tells me to come on. I follow him through the swinging doors. Standing in the center of the bright yellow kitchen, a rolling pin poised over a mound of dough, is Catherine, Adam's mother. She's pretty, just like I remember, and I feel a particular type of pain—the same squeezing heart I get every time I open the trunk. Suddenly I have this thought that I should have dressed up, the way you would before you enter a church. Instead I'm wearing my too-short jeans and too-small shirt with the holes in the armpits and along the collar.

She steps from behind the island, reaching out both hands as if she's going to hug me, then she glances at Adam and lowers her arms. "How are you, Julian?" There's a certain inflection to my name, the same tone people use to say *honey* or *sweetheart*.

"Fine." It seems wrong to give an automatic response like *fine* to her, but it's all I can say. No one starts filling the silence and it's awkward until I hear a bass pulse from outside, so loud it rattles the copper pots and pans hanging against the wall.

"Sounds like Camila's here," Adam says. Catherine smiles at him, sparkling and entertained like every word he says is worth hearing. "Gotta go, Mom." He kisses the side of her head.

"Julian?" She stretches out one hand, almost but not quite touching my shoulder. "You're welcome here anytime."

I nod, then follow Adam back through the swinging yellow doors. From the living room window, I see carloads of older kids disembarking and spilling across the lawn. That's when I realize it won't just be Adam and me going to this concert.

While he's shrugging on his jacket, I bolt out the back door, setting off a motion sensor light. "Hey." He's followed me into the backyard. "Where are you going?"

"I'm sorry, but I don't think I can go. Thank you for inviting me."

When I take another step, he hops over to block my exit.

"Why?" He follows my gaze to all the strangers filling the house. "My friends are cool."

And that's the problem. They're cool and I'm me and I won't know what to say and he'll realize that soon enough.

"Come on, I'll introduce you."

That sounds terrifying and I regret ever coming here.

It's as awkward as I could imagine. Not because they aren't nice, but because I don't know what to say. I'm annoyed with myself for being so bad at things that everyone else can do without trying.

After a long, uncomfortable ride in a girl named Camila's car, everyone grabs blankets and joins the thousands of other people milling around the giant field. I'm still a little queasy from the drive, and the loud music is giving me a headache. Adam and his friends talk and laugh and pile onto each other like puppies or children. It's uncomfortable watching people who know each other this well, like how it might feel to invade a stranger's Thanksgiving dinner.

It's even worse when Adam disappears into the crowd.

A few minutes later, someone asks where he is. The tall blond boy named Charlie answers, "Where do you think? Running up and down the field." Everyone nods as if they know what this means. Charlie sees me watching them and scowls. He doesn't like me, which isn't so unexpected, but it still stings.

I sit on the grass and pull my knees to my chin, trying to keep warm while everyone else sits on the quilts and talks. After a while Adam comes back and says hello to me, but then he races off again, smiling and chatting and hopping.

As it gets darker, the temperature drops. Soon I'm so cold I start to shake.

I'm startled when a figure wrapped in a blanket sits down beside me. It's dark; maybe she didn't know I was here when she decided to sit. Now that she realizes, she'll want to move.

But she doesn't. Instead she looks right at me and says, "I haven't seen you in a long time."

"You haven't? I mean . . . you remember me?"

When I lived with Adam, sometimes Emerald would visit. She always wore dresses, and she was pretty like an angel or someone's mother. I remember walking along a blue-green lake, and Emerald saying something about my blue-green eyes. I remember that whenever my legs got tired, Adam would kneel so I could climb onto his back, and when I wasn't tired anymore, I would walk between them, holding their hands.

"Of course I remember you," Emerald says. "You were like Adam's little brother." A look flashes over her face, one that's uneasy. I must have said or done something, but I don't know what. As we sit without talking, I expect her to leave, join the others.

Instead she smiles and says, "I'm glad you're here."

NINETEEN

JULIAN

AFTER THE CONCERT, Saturday and Sunday are silent.

Monday is like all Mondays. Like I'm sitting at the bottom of a pool, listening underwater to people living up above.

On Tuesday I see Adam, and after so much silent drowning, I can breathe. But after a few laps around the school and a few minutes in the courtyard, it's over.

Then there is a long invisible Wednesday and an even longer Thursday.

In the middle of the night between Thursday and Friday, I wake to a dark silhouette in my doorway. Sometimes when I'm afraid, I think I see things that aren't really there.

I find my flashlight, shine it, and say, "Russell?"

No answer.

But it *is* Russell, his eyes full of some emotion I can't name. We watch each other without speaking until he turns and walks away.

Now it's Friday, and I'm hiking the halls with Adam again. He's brimming with energy and smiling at sad teachers as my stomach clenches tighter with each step. I need this to keep going. I need to keep circling the school. I'm afraid for it to be over, and I'm embarrassed for being afraid.

Adam glances over at me and plucks the wrinkled paper from my hand. We both cringe when he sees the grade. I make a weak attempt at taking my essay back, but he just keeps walking, which doesn't seem like the best idea, since he often trips even when he isn't trying to read and walk at the same time.

"You write essays in Science?" he asks.

I nod.

"Weird." He flips the paper over and halts. "Now this is just mean." I guess he found Miss West's comments at the end. "I thought they couldn't take off points for spelling."

"Why?"

"You have dyslexia. Aren't you supposed to get—what are they called—accommodations?"

"No. I don't think so. I don't have dyslexia anymore."

He gives my paper a suspicious look. "You don't have Reading Improvement or anything?"

"No."

"Maybe Dr. Whitlock could test you for it."

"I don't think I have it." I'm just not smart.

"Well, if you *did* have it, it's fixable. There are exercises, homeopathic drops. . . ."

"Drops?"

"Yeah, there are remedies for everything. That's how I got off my ADHD meds."

I follow Adam as he flies into the courtyard. Once outside, he's like a dog let off his leash. I sit on the bench while he kicks a pile of leaves, then swan-dives into them. He peels off his red hoodie and uses it as a pillow. Lying on his back, he lifts my essay over his face and reads it again.

"It's good, you know," he says after a couple of minutes. "You were always a good writer—stop shaking your head. It's true. Sometimes people get too impatient. Your teacher can't read your handwriting, and you can't spell, so she just gave up. But it doesn't mean you're not good."

I look at him closely, trying to read his face. He looks like he really means it. I think of my trunk full of stories, and my heart speeds up. Maybe someone could read them. Maybe someone could *like* them.

"People get so impatient, you know?"

I nod. I know.

"When I was younger, my ADHD was sort of out of control. It drove my teachers freakin crazy. I wasn't trying to aggravate anyone, but it was like a physical impossibility to sit still and do work. In sixth grade I was failing every single class—seriously, *every* class—so Mom took me to a doctor and I got on meds.

"It worked, sort of. I mean I could sit in my chair without going insane, and I was quiet, so my teachers were happy. But then I got sick, like hospital sick. I was throwing up all the time. I couldn't sleep. I was losing weight."

I don't want to picture Adam being sick.

"Finally my doctor said everything was a side effect of the medication. He told Mom he could switch me to something else, but she was like, hell no. That's when she got really into nutrition and homeopathy. She'd do anything to make sure I'm well."

"Are you well?"

"Yeah. I feel great."

"So you're passing your classes now?"

"A's and B's."

"But don't you . . ." He looks up, waiting for me to finish. "Don't you still have ADHD?"

"I don't know. Maybe I do. But I get good grades and I can function and I'm happy."

"That's good, Adam. I wouldn't like it if you were unhappy."

He lifts his shoulders off the ground, flashing a sort of smile I can't decipher, then crawls out of the leaves and returns my essay to me. It's even more crinkled now, and smudged with soil. "Next time you have to hand something in, just tell me. I can proofread it or whatever."

I nod, but I know I won't. If he's being nice enough to offer, I should be nice enough to never do it. The wind picks up, but instead of putting his sweatshirt back on, he just fits the hood over his head. As he walks forward, it billows behind him like a cape.

TWENTY

ADAM

IT'S THE LAST day of November and so freakin cold I don't bother taking off my in-class-Siberia-layers when I'm walking to the van after school. I'm about to hop inside when I notice Julian standing totally still at the top of the back steps.

"Hey! Julian!" I call. He looks up like he's been snapped out of a trance. I wave him over, and he approaches, slowly. "You miss your bus?"

He makes the suspicious face he makes sometimes, like he's trying to come up with a story. "Yes."

"Get in. I'll give you a ride."

"It's okay," he says. "You don't have to. It's not that far."

"Where's your house?"

"Wicker Street. By the water tower."

"That's like ten miles. Get in."

"No really. It's—"

"Julian, get your ass in the car."

He quickly hops into the front seat, then looks around in awe. "It's a spaceship."

I'm chuckling when Charlie rips open the front passenger door and orders, "In the back." I consider protesting, but Julian's already climbing out. As soon as Allison, Jesse, Camila, and Emerald pile in back next to him, I peel out of the parking lot, and we all start talking about the birthday party Emerald's having at her place tomorrow.

"Exactly who's coming?" Camila wants to know.

"Well, us, of course," Emerald says, "and Kerry and Mason and that group, and—"

"Wait, *theater kids*?" Camila sneers.

"Careful, Camila." Charlie laughs. "Adam was almost a theater kid."

"Yeah, maybe if I wasn't so lazy." I glance in the rearview, catch sight of a very pale Julian, and shit, I didn't exactly forget about his car phobia, but I guess I thought he didn't have it anymore.

"Julian, would you like to come?" Emerald asks.

He flat out doesn't answer, and the van goes quiet.

I check the mirror again to find Allison watching him with a concerned, motherly expression—the same one she gave me when I twisted my ankle.

Finally, I hear a small voice say, "Yes."

The girls whisper something about *adorable*, which probably embarrasses the hell out of him. Lucky for Julian—but no one else— Jesse plugs his phone into my car, and the speakers start to shake with screaming guitar.

When we get to Julian's street, I'm happy to have an excuse to turn the music down. "Which one?" I ask.

"The fifth house on the right."

"This one?" I ask, surprised.

"Yes."

"Wow. It's really nice."

It's a huge white stone two-story with two long rows of square windows, and tall peaking points at each end like towers. It's nice, but it seems weird. You just assume that anyone who owns a house like this could afford to buy a kid a cell phone and clothes that fit.

TWENTY-ONE

JULIAN

THE COLD METALLIC taste of winter is in the air, the kind that excites your senses and snaps away the haze. I pedal my bicycle faster, skidding over patches of ice. Sometimes I'm tempted to ride it to school, but I know people would make fun of it since it's so small, and that would kill me. My dad gave me this bike.

Wide-awake and freezing, I knock on Adam's door, holding a small box wrapped in pink paper. He lets me in, and we walk into the living room where Emerald, Camila, and Allison are talking.

"You brought me a present?" Emerald asks.

"It's your birthday," I say.

Her smile is gentle as she carefully peels away the tape. Everyone is watching, and I'm embarrassed. I thought mine would be one present among a hundred others. She looks happy and expectant, and it makes me even more anxious, because it's not a great gift.

"I love it!" She smiles down at the ceramic butterfly. "How did you know?" I'm not sure what she means. "Thank you, Julian."

Someone turns up the music, then the three girls force Adam and me to sit. They disappear down the hall only to reappear wearing different clothes.

"Take mental notes," Camila orders. "Tell us which outfit's the hottest." After a few spins, they run off to change again.

"It's like they're all on drugs." Adam laughs.

Catherine comes in the living room while the girls are gone. She smiles when she sees me and gives me a cookie that tastes like fresh-cut grass.

The girls return and demand opinions. I can't remember what they were wearing a few minutes ago, so I have to lie. After four outfit changes, they sit on Adam's yellow couch and stare at me.

"Julian," Emerald says delicately, "we need to talk about your wardrobe." I glance over at Adam to find him watching with amused sympathy. "Take this . . . ensemble, for instance."

There's an embarrassing sting at the back of my eyes. I really tried to dress nicely for her party. I even snuck into Russell's room to borrow one of his button-down shirts.

"You're fine," Adam says to me, while shaking his head at Emerald.

Camila hops up. "We're taking you shopping!"

My stomach tightens. I can't just go out and buy clothes, but I can't tell them that. "These fit so—"

"We're not taking no for an answer," she interrupts, and the girls start scanning me up and down.

"Ladies," Adam says, "you're freaking him out." He turns to me. "I probably have some old clothes if you want them."

"Let's see!" Allison says, and they all fly down the hall toward Adam's room.

"Now?" he calls after them.

"It's my birthday," Emerald calls back. "Julian, come here."

Adam gives me another sympathetic smile and shrugs. "It's her birthday."

When I get to his room, they're yanking things out of his closet. His room is different than how I remember it. Instead of two twin beds, there's one big one, and most of his superhero action figures and posters are gone. But the fish tank, now empty, is still here. When I lived in this house, Catherine read me the story where Elian meets a privileged alien girl, and she shows him her massive bedroom. Along one wall the girl had a floor-to-ceiling red curtain, but when she pulled it back, instead of sky, there was a whale-sized creature— swimming. It wasn't a window at all, but a giant aquarium. I loved that scene. I wanted a room just like it, so Catherine bought that fish tank for me.

"Come here," Camila orders, and the girls take turns holding up shirts in front of me.

"This looks like it might actually fit," Emerald says.

"I don't understand why so many guys want to wear shirts that look like nightgowns," Allison adds.

Camila tugs it off the hanger and pushes it at me. "Try it on." Then she just stands there as if she expects me to change in front of them.

I feel a rush of panic. "Um . . ."

"We've seen nipples." Camila winks.

"Not *his* nipples," Adam says, stepping inside. He pushes aside a row of hangers, grabs a pair of dark jeans from the back, and hands them to me. "Clear out, ladies. He's not a stripper."

"Emerald!" Camila hops two feet off the ground. "We have to hire a stripper!"

The girls are laughing as Adam forces them out of the room. As soon as he shuts the door behind him, I quickly change. The shirt and jeans both fit. I can't remember the last time I wore something that really fit.

I open the door, startled to find everyone waiting right outside. The three girls burst into applause, then order me to spin around. Adam laughs and shrugs, so I do it.

When they all clap again, my mouth spasms into a smile.

"Is there going to be a magician?" I ask. The last birthday party I went to had a magician.

Adam shakes his head, smiling as if I said something funny. I glance around Emerald's living room. It doesn't *look* like a party. There aren't balloons or streamers or a piñata or anything.

Adam and I take a seat on one of the long couches, and soon the house fills up with seniors. I recognize a few from the concert, but most are strangers.

Some girls walk through the door, carrying four-packs of pink glass bottles. Beside them a group of boys hold up their huge boxes of beer, and everyone cheers and hands them cash.

"I don't have any money," I whisper.

"It's cool," Adam says. "I'll cover you." But he looks uncomfortable, like maybe he really doesn't want to. That expression intensifies when I grab one of the cans. It only takes one swallow for me to realize it's disgusting. I don't want any more, but I'd feel bad not finishing since Adam is paying for it.

Camila's eyes zero in on me as if she knows what I'm thinking. "Gross?"

"No, it's good," I lie.

"Have this, much better." She hands me her pink bottle. There's lipstick on it, which is kind of gross, but I don't want to offend her, so I take a small sip.

She's right. It is much better, like carbonated Kool-Aid. "It's good." She hands me one from her cardboard container. "I'll pay you back," I tell Adam, even though I have no idea how I'm going to do that, since I spent my savings on Emerald's gift.

"Those actually have more alcohol than the beer," he says, loud enough to be heard over the music someone just turned on.

"They do?"

"Yeah. You should probably just stick with the one beer." He takes my unopened pink drink and returns it to Camila.

"Can I just have soda?" There are a few three-liter bottles that some kids are pouring into red plastic cups.

Camila starts laughing. "Stop babying him, Adam."

"He's *fourteen*."

"I'm almost fifteen."

"Your birthday's in July." He laughs.

Camila seems to lose interest in the conversation and wanders away.

Adam grabs a cupful of soda and hands it to me, then he's off too, weaving in and out of different groups. I wish I had the ability to talk with people that way. Talking is a talent; he probably doesn't realize it, but it is.

I watch as the crowd swells and whirls around me. There is a cluster of dancing girls. In one corner a boy and girl are kissing. In another some kids are passing around a pipe—it's red, like the toy bubble pipe I had when I was little. I see Adam. He takes a puff from the pipe, passes it, then disappears into another crowd.

Minutes tick by and I keep sitting on the couch alone and drinking my soda, feeling so awkward I want to leave, but feeling so lonely that I can't.

I'm finishing my third cup when suddenly everyone fills the living room, squeezing onto the couches or sitting on the floor. They argue for a minute about whose turn it is, and eventually Camila wins.

As she looks around the room, it gets tense and quiet. Then she says with a smirk, "Charlie." Allison is sitting in Charlie's lap, and she pets his back when his name is called. "All right, let's see . . . take off your shirt, then—" The words are barely out of Camila's mouth before he has his fists at his hem and he tears it off, looking very pleased with himself. "*Then* take off Adam's shirt, then—"

Charlie's smile becomes a scowl. "Oh, hell no."

"Come on, Charlie." Adam gives him an exaggerated wink. "Get your sexy abs over here."

"Hell. No."

But everyone starts calling Charlie lame and telling him he has to do it, so in the end, he pulls Adam's shirt off and endures the screeching and whistling while he presses his palms to Adam's chest as ordered. Then, looking thoroughly disgusted, he puts his shirt back on and crosses his arms.

The next dare also involves some level of nudity and embarrassment, and I realize it's only a matter of time before I'm forced to do something awful or someone is forced to do something awful to me.

I don't want to take off my clothes. I can't do it. But if I refuse, everyone will get annoyed and tell me I'm being lame.

Adam hops up from the floor and sits on the couch beside me. "Julian is under my protection," he announces loudly, making me squirm. "He gets to watch us act like idiots, and that's it." When no one protests, I start to relax.

After almost everyone has been forced to do something horrible, someone turns the music up again and they all drift off into corners, into shadows. I'm left sitting alone, thinking about getting more soda, when Camila falls onto the couch beside me. Her neck is swaying like her head is too heavy. She leans in close.

"You've got pretty eyes," she says.

"Thank you."

"What color are they?"

"I don't know."

She slumps over, arms loose like noodles, and pours vodka from a giant glass bottle into my cup. "But Adam—"

"—is bossy." She pokes out her bottom lip. "And he isn't your dad. You don't have to listen to him."

Camila taps a long red fingernail against the side of my cup. I take a swallow and cough. "I like the other kind better."

"This'll help." She grabs the soda and sloshes some into my cup. I take a sip. "Better?"

I nod. It is better, but still not good. I keep swallowing until it's gone.

When a new song begins, everyone cheers like it's their favorite. It's fast and loud, and they all begin to jump. Camila grabs my sleeve, jerking me into the crowd of leaping bodies. I feel a soft hum in my limbs and everything is slower, calmer.

I dance, and pressed so close together, I'm anonymous, just one cell in the body of swirling figures. I'm dizzy. I'm here. I'm alive.

ADAM

It's after 3:00 A.M., and everyone's gone. Allison and Charlie were supposed to give me a ride, but I guess they took off. I'm looking for

Julian, but instead I find Emerald, half-sitting with her eyes closed on that fancy couch in the off-limits formal living room. Her eyes spring open when I trip over the Persian rug.

She smiles, looking wrung out, shoulders slack for a change, instead of squared like a soldier. "You know what movie you make me think of every time you walk into a room?" she asks.

"I don't know." I fall down beside her. "There're about a million movies where the lead does this slow-motion-sexy-walk, so it could be—"

"*Bambi.*"

"*Bambi?*"

"You know that scene where it's Bambi's first winter and he steps out onto the ice?"

"Not cool, Emerald," I say when she starts laughing. She leans onto my shoulder and the weight feels good, like her head's *supposed* to be there.

"And with your eyes and eyelashes and cheekbones, it's even more perfect."

"I have Bambi's cheekbones? What does that even mean?"

"You know . . . the sort of angular face. High cheekbones. And you have big brown Bambi eyes."

"That's awesome, Emerald. Just what every guy wants to hear." She laughs again. "So you're officially eighteen. Do you feel different?"

"You'll find out soon enough."

"I don't want to wait three more weeks. Tell me."

"No," she sighs, still resting on my shoulder, "I don't feel any different." She scoots down a little till her ear's against my chest. "When I was younger, I thought I would. Didn't you? When you were a little boy, didn't you think that once you were an adult you'd be smarter? And stronger?"

"I don't know."

"I did. I used to think about it all the time. As soon as I turned eighteen, I'd move out and be one of those strong, independent women who never cries."

"You're already one of those people who never cries." I mean, even when she won the spelling bee in middle school and Amy Flowers got jealous and poured her milk over her head, Emerald didn't cry. If it weren't for those red blotches that broke out on her neck, I wouldn't have even known she was upset.

"I do cry. I probably cry once a week."

"Seriously?"

"Well, not in front of anyone, but yes. Why are you so shocked? Everyone cries, Adam."

"Not me." She looks up and grins the way she did when I said I got into a fight with Marcus. "I'm not trying to be a badass. I just don't. My mom told me that even when I was a baby I didn't. She said I was always happy."

She lowers her head again, and I feel her soft laugh against my chest. "That sounds about right."

"So what'd you get from your mom?"

"I don't know yet. I won't see her until tomorrow. She's with her boyfriend."

"Seriously?" My mom would go insane if she couldn't see me on my birthday.

"It's fine. The people I wanted most were here."

"Well, except for Brett, right?" Apparently he had some flight test he couldn't get out of. "Sucks that he couldn't come."

"Yeah . . . I don't know. I know it's not *really* long distance, but sometimes I'm not sure it's worth it."

If I were with someone who was beautiful and brilliant and amazing, an hour drive would be nothing. "If someone really matters to you, it's worth it."

She shifts away from me and leans back against the couch.

"I probably need to go," I say. "I told my mom I'd be home by two, and I'm already an hour late. I can't even call her, because I lost my freakin phone again." I hop up. "Have you seen Julian?"

I open the sliding glass door in the living room, zipping up my coat against the cold, and finally find him outside on Emerald's trampoline.

"You gonna jump or just lie on that thing?" I ask, climbing up and hopping a couple times. He starts laughing in a way that tells me he's drunk. "Hey, I thought I told you—" He looks up at me with giant worried mouse eyes. "Forget it."

Emerald steps outside, wrapped in a thick gray blanket. She climbs up to sit next to us, and I mouth the word *drunk*. She laughs.

"Julian." I nudge him. "Time to go."

He starts to hum, but other than that he ignores me.

"I can walk you home," Emerald says.

"Walk us home?"

"It's a nice night."

"It's snowing."

"I don't want my birthday to be over yet." A few strands of her hair have come undone and are falling into her eyes. I want to touch them, push them back into place.

"Okay." I hop to the ground and give her my hand. "Walk us home."

I jostle Julian's shoe. "Julian," I say. He blinks up at me. "Let's go."

For once he doesn't flinch away when I come too close, doesn't seem to mind that Emerald and I loop our arms with his to keep him upright. Soon the three of us are sliding down the snowy sidewalk together.

"You should just carry him," Emerald suggests when he stumbles for the third time.

"No," he mumbles. "Wanna walk."

"You heard him," I say.

He trips again, makes me lose my balance, and my feet slide wide apart—like Bambi on ice. I manage to pull them back together while Emerald laughs, a sound that echoes likes a bell. Linked and tripping over moonlit ice, I feel a rush of happiness so strong my legs fill up with energy and I just want to run.

"Do you see?" Julian whispers.

"See what?" I ask.

"My breath." He exhales heavily. A small cloud fills the air. "Do you see it?"

"I see it."

"I'm real."

"Yes," I agree. "You're real."

We tiptoe into my dark house, and at this point we're practically dragging Julian to my bed. He topples over onto his back and starts humming again while I tug off his cracked sneakers. Emerald looks down at him with amused affection. She and Julian both have snow-flushed cheeks and wet hair.

"Wait," Julian says, his eyes just foggy slits as I throw a blanket on top of him. "You didn't ask."

"Ask what?" I say.

"How many. You didn't ask how many."

"Okay, how many?"

He smiles and closes his eyes. "Ten . . . thousand . . . stars."

TWENTY-TWO

JULIAN

I WAKE WITH a start, still dressed in Adam's clothes. My head aches and feels a little bit cloudy, but I try to shake it away. *Russell.* If he came home last night . . .

And if he knows I didn't . . .

I find my sneakers on the floor, tug them on as fast as I can, and rush into the hall.

I hear the shower running. It's probably Adam, but there isn't time to wait. I have to go now.

I hop on my bike, a sick wintry feeling in my stomach as I pedal. I skid through a patch of ice, and the bike begins to wobble. I lurch to one side, but somehow manage to right myself and pedal even faster. My lungs begin to burn as I suck in too much freezing air.

When I get to the house, I'm sweating despite the cold. Russell's car isn't in the driveway. I feel a flash of relief, but then the fear amps up again. That doesn't mean he never came home. He might still know. And if he does . . .

Think good thoughts.

I park my bike in the garage and go to my room, the silence ricocheting off all the walls, the cold air from the fast ride still in my lungs. I change into a clean shirt and sweatpants, but I'm too nervous to do much else besides sit in the center of my bed. Then slowly, slowly, my muscles loosen, and I let myself lie on my back until the light begins to change.

The thought of sunset brings a fresh wave of nerves. I don't remember much of what happened last night after Camila poured vodka into my cup, but I remember sleeping deeply.

I wish Adam could sleep over.

Or that I could sleep at his house again.

But I know neither thing can happen.

I climb out of bed, calm enough now to open my trunk and fish out an Elian Mariner book. The glossy cover is smudged and cracked from so much handling. There's a white line right through the center of the lilac people—the aliens with lilac skin and feathery manes, all tall and slim and androgynous like lilies. The ones who could escape their frozen planet if only the shadow man—the towering monster with insect wings and mouths full of sharp teeth at the tips of all his fingers—would let them go.

I sit on my bed and turn to the first page. It begins the way every Elian Mariner book does, with his mom and dad tucking him in, then shutting off the light. In the dark you can still make out his bed and his toys and the ship in a bottle on his dresser.

Turn the page and the bottle starts to shake.

Turn again and the glass disappears.

Soon the ship starts to grow, so big the room has to expand to fit it. Somehow Elian's parents never discover what's happening, but he's not dreaming—it's magic.

Elian climbs aboard, and the ship floats like a ghost through the ceiling, into outer space. He sees the stars and a tiny earth and it's so beautiful until—

I hear a noise.

Someone is opening the back door. My stomach starts to hurt and my ears tingle as I listen. The jingle of Russell's keys. His footsteps on the hardwood floor.

My wildly beating heart is so loud, it's hard to hear anything else as I wait for him to either go up the stairs or come down the hall.

TWENTY-THREE

ADAM

I'M WALKING AND texting my way through the hall on Monday when I spot Mom coming out of the main office. For a second, I get a PTSD-style flashback of her menacing my middle school principal.

"Mom?" I say, and she gets this suspicious, caught-in-the-act look on her face. "What are you doing here?"

She straightens, her expression fierce all of a sudden. "Meeting with Mr. Pearce."

"Oh—I swear that whole intercom thing wasn't me." The Game might've gotten a little out of hand during first period. But Allison totally didn't have to accept the dare just because she's an office aide with access to the PA system. Okay, maybe she did, but—

"What?" Mom looks completely confused. "No, about Julian."

"Julian? Why?"

"I just wanted to see how he's been doing, and *that man*"—she means Julian's uncle—"changed his number—not that he'd take my calls anyway—and Mr. Pearce won't talk to me either. Confidentiality and everything." She's getting all worked up and not even bothering to put on the creepy-fake-happy smile.

"Mom, everything's cool. You just need to take some anxiety drops."

That suggestion goes over the way it usually does, with her being mildly offended at first, then saying, "Maybe you're right," with a sigh. "I need to get back to work." The bell rings. "And you need to get to class," she adds, scolding all of a sudden, like she's not the reason I'm late.

"Okay." I bend down to give her a hug. "See you at home."

TWENTY-FOUR

JULIAN

"WHAT IS HE—YOUR DATE?" Charlie mutters as Adam hands me my shoes.

When Adam asked me to go bowling this Saturday, I didn't realize Charlie would be coming too. It's been a week since Emerald's birthday, and I've been getting a ride home from Adam almost every day since. Jesse and Allison and everyone else talks to me, but I think Charlie hates me.

I pretend he isn't glowering and tell Adam, "I can pay you back."

"It's cool," he says. "It's like two dollars."

I'm sitting on a bench in front of our lane, taking off my sneakers, when Charlie asks me loudly, "Do you shave your legs?" Now both he and Adam are staring at the strip of visible skin between my socks and too-short jeans.

"Yes?" I answer.

"Why?" Adam asks. He doesn't look like he's joking.

But to confirm: "Are you joking?"

"I'm totally serious. Why do you shave your legs?" They're both squinting at my shins. I wish I wore Adam's jeans again, even if they are dirty.

"Because we're supposed to. Don't you?"

"No," they say together.

"But you have to. You'll get sick. Body hair carries germs. It isn't sanitary."

"Who the hell told you that?" Charlie is looking at me like I'm crazy.

"My uncle."

"Russell told you you'd get sick if you didn't shave your body hair?" Adam's voice deepens, clearly concerned for some reason.

"But that's stupid," Charlie adds. "You've seen guys' legs before, right?"

I know that some men keep their leg hair, but Russell says it's a disgusting habit and they're going to get sick.

"What about PE?" Charlie says. "Don't you see the other guys in the locker room?"

"I never had PE."

"Never?" Adam asks.

"When I was really little, but not in years."

Adam looks suspicious. "But it's a required class."

"I don't know. I never had to take it," I say.

"You should still know this stuff," Charlie grumbles. "Everyone took that puberty class in sixth grade."

I didn't. Russell never signed the consent form, so when the boys and girls were split up to watch the video, I was sent to the library.

"So . . ." I say, "you really don't shave?"

"I really don't," Adam says. "Guys don't shave their legs. Except swimmers, because it's supposed to make them faster—which I don't get, because how much can leg hair slow you down? But no, it's just something girls do."

"But why just girls?"

"Because," Charlie says, "no one's gonna go out with a girl with hairy legs and pits— Wait a minute!" He grabs my sleeve. "Does this mean you shave your pits?"

I pull away.

"Quit it," Adam says, moving to sit on the orange plastic bench between us. "New topic. Do we need to get the bumper rails for you, Charlie, or do you think you can handle it without them?"

"Right," he says, "as if you will *ever* beat me at bowling."

Adam grins over at me as if we're in on a joke, and I smile back.

TWENTY-FIVE

JULIAN

WHEN MY ALARM goes off at six on Monday morning, I see the twenty-dollar bill beneath my shell. Through slices of pain, I walk to my attached bathroom, whimpering as every movement pulls the cuts on my legs. Tears sting my eyes, reminding me how much I embarrassed myself last night. Russell never gets mad at me for crying, but it's still humiliating.

I use the toilet, then consider showering, but everything hurts too much. For a moment I stand in front of the floor-length mirror on the back of the bathroom door, looking at the horizontal red lines from my collarbone to my waist. He's never done that before, never the front. It makes sleep impossible. I can't lie on my stomach. I can't lie on my back. But I have to, and it hurts.

I turn around to see the long red stripes from my shoulders down the back of my legs. The legs that are pale and skinny, and according to Adam and Charlie, strangely hairless. I know Russell is just worried about my health, but I don't want to shave anymore, not if no other boy does it.

I feel another surge of regret knowing he's gone to work and I'm home. I hate that I keep doing stupid things. I hate it when he's mad at me. I hate that the proof of how he feels is still all over me.

I turn around to face the mirror again and look into my eyes. When I was in the third grade we had to do a genealogy assignment, and my mother told me that no one in our family had eyes like mine. The only person I knew from Mom's side of the family was her sister, Russell's wife, but she died when I was five, so I barely remember her. My mom never spoke to any of her other relatives. I knew something had happened, some falling-out with her parents, but she never wanted to talk about it, and at the time I wasn't curious enough to ask.

My father didn't have any brothers or sisters. His parents were old by the time they had him. He said they called him their miracle because they didn't think they could have children. I don't remember either of his parents, since they both died when I was still a baby.

It hits me all of a sudden—my parents lost their parents. But they always seemed so happy. Was it real? I can picture them looking at each other, smiling right into each other's eyes. Hers were bright blue. His were faded green. Mine are both, and sometimes when I look in the mirror, I can see both of them looking back at me.

TWENTY-SIX

ADAM

"HAVE YOU HEARD from Julian?" Dr. Whitlock asks the second I get to her office on Wednesday.

"No. But he doesn't have a phone or a computer, so I never hear from Julian."

"He's out again today." She frowns, obviously worried. I don't tell her he's probably just skipping. I mean, is she forgetting the first weeks of school when he dodged her? "This is the third day in a row. I've called home, but I haven't heard back from anyone."

I guess three days is weird, even for him. "I could go by his house."

She perks up. "Would you? That would be very helpful."

"I can go now if you want." Anything's better than sitting in this office doing nothing. I can tell she's about to say no, so I add hastily, "I've got lunch next period, so I won't be late to class or anything."

"All right. You can go"—her eyes shoot from side to side, and she whispers like her office is bugged—"but don't tell *anyone* I said that."

"No problem, Dr. Whitlock." Everyone worries too much.

☆ ☆ ☆

JULIAN

I ignore the doorbell. It's always a UPS man or a salesman, never anyone I want to see. When it rings again, faster and more insistent, I slowly climb out of bed, wincing. I take careful steps to the front door, then peek through the fish-eye.

"What are you doing here?" I ask when I open the door.

"Manners, Julian," Adam scolds, sweeping right past me. "Nice house." Then he squints at me. "What's wrong with you?"

I retreat a little, afraid he might try to touch my shoulder. "Nothing."

"You look like hell."

The pain has dulled to something bearable, but I'm congested and my head aches. This happens a lot after a punishment. Just as the marks begin to fade, I get sick.

"It's just a cold. Or maybe the flu."

"You go to the doctor?"

"No."

"Well, what have you been eating?"

"Uh . . . peanut butter and jelly."

He shakes his head as if disappointed, then scans the house again. "Is your uncle really anti-technology?"

"Why?"

"No computer. No TV. What do you do here all day when you're sick?"

"Nothing."

"That sucks," he says sympathetically.

He starts jogging through the house the same way he does through the courtyard at school. I'm terrified he's going to break something, or that Russell will be home at any minute. Russell might be gone for two days or he might come home right now.

"Where's your room?"

"It's the last one on the hall. But I—"

He starts jogging in the opposite direction and stops in front of the china cabinet. "What is all this?"

"No one can touch that!"

But he's already opening the glass doors and poking at everything on the shelves—five antique cameras, dozens of first-edition books, delicate dishes, and an old silver gun.

"This is weird," Adam says, picking it up. "Who mixes their weapons with their china?"

"I don't know. He doesn't like people touching them. He doesn't like people in the house at all." When Adam puts it back and carefully closes the glass door, I exhale in relief.

But I get nervous all over again when he bounces into the kitchen and tears open the refrigerator. "Is this all you have?" he asks.

I nod.

Adam frowns as he studies the jar. "Now if this was a halfway-decent brand of jelly it would be one thing, but it's all *processed*." He says it like it's a curse word. "Full of sugar and preservatives." Those are curse words too.

"I'm feeling a lot better. I'll probably be back at school tomorrow."

"Want me to hang out?"

"No," I say quickly, listening for Russell's car. "My uncle really doesn't like people to be over."

"But you're sick. He wouldn't want you to be by yourself when you're sick."

"He won't care what the reason is."

Now Adam looks at me so intensely that for a second he reminds me of Dr. Whitlock and Mr. Pearce and everyone else who tries to read my thoughts.

"Okay," he says, still looking uncertain. "I guess I'll go."

TWENTY-SEVEN

JULIAN

WHEN I GET to first period on Thursday, the door is locked. It takes me a second to notice the sign that reads CLASS IN LAB ROOM 202. By the time I get there I'm late, but it looks like almost everyone else is too.

"I told the class yesterday where to go," Miss West says when she sees me. "Is that so hard to remember?"

"I'm sorry. I was absent yesterday."

"It's always something with you, isn't it?"

I sit at the empty table in the back and drop my head onto my arms. A minute later, a throat clears behind me. I open my eyes to find Kristin, Alex, and Violet standing over me. "Would you mind if we took this table, since it's big enough for three people?" Violet asks. Her eyes are round and black and kind.

"Okay."

I'm grabbing my backpack when Kristin adds, "Unless you're waiting for all your friends."

"No . . . I'm not waiting for anyone."

The three of them exchange a look, then Kristin smirks. "Yes, Julian. We know."

"Julian!" I hear Adam call out from inside a classroom. I halt and find him grinning at me from his desk. "Come here!" His class is noisy chaos, so I continue to hover in the hallway. "Come on."

Cautiously, I make my way inside.

Allison and another girl—I can't remember her name—are standing in the front on a raised platform. Some kids are sitting in their desks, ones that are scattered instead of in rows, and the rest of the kids are standing or walking around.

Adam taps the empty desk beside him. I sit down and ask, "What class is this?"

"Theater. Where were you going?"

I shrug.

"Skipping?"

I shrug again.

"You're going to get caught eventually."

He's right and it scares me, but I had to. When I got to Child Development, Miss Carlisle said we'd be doing group work. "I told my teacher I was going to the nurse."

"Are you still sick?"

"No."

"So you were faking?"

"Well . . ."

"You're the reason Grumpy Nurse is so suspicious!" He points an accusing finger at me.

"I should leave. Before your teacher gets back."

"She's not here. She's running lines with some kids for the show."

"Oh. So who's in charge?"

"Me." Then he pitches his voice louder. "All right, everybody, listen up." Everyone stops talking and watches Adam pull a slip of paper from the small metal box on top of his desk. "Hypochondriac at the doctor's office. Go!"

Allison and the other girl on the platform whisper into each other's ears, then the girl clutches her knee and wails. The classroom fills with laughter as the scene continues.

When Adam's phone beeps, he yells, "Time!" Then it's someone else's turn. After several performances, he looks at me. "You want a turn?"

I quickly shake my head. "No, thank you."

"How 'bout you, Stef?" he says to a girl I didn't notice until then.

Stef looks embarrassed and pulls at her wild, frizzy hair. "I'm not sure. . . ."

"Come on," Adam says, hopping out of his seat. "I'll be your partner."

I know he's just being nice. All of Adam's friends are so pretty, but she's like me, one of those people you aren't supposed to talk to if other people are around to see.

Stef blushes as they walk to the front of the class.

"Julian," Adam says, "read one of the prompts."

Everyone looks while I pull a strip of paper from the box. "H-hiring a . . . private de-detective."

Adam grins and whispers in Stef's ear. She blushes again and keeps trying to control her hair. Their performance is really funny, and I find myself laughing along with the rest of the class. If this is what school is like for him, I can see why he likes it.

When the timer goes off, Adam grabs Stef's hand and pulls her into a bow. He looks happy. Not acting nice or feeling sorry, but genuinely happy, as if he likes her as much as he likes everyone else.

TWENTY-EIGHT

ADAM

IT'S FRIDAY NIGHT and we're all piled into Jesse's living room. Suggesting The Game was totally strategic on my part—any excuse to turn off that music no one can dance to.

"Okay . . . *Jesse*," Charlie says, looking at him in a way that makes him fidget. "I want you to lick Camila's . . ." He pauses, and Jesse grins nervously. ". . . *purse*."

Disappointment falls over his face. "Seriously?" We all watched the documentary in Ms. Fry's class this week claiming purses are dirtier than toilets. "But I might get sick."

Charlie smirks. "Do it anyway."

After a lot of harassment from everyone, Jesse gives in, revolted, then chugs his beer as if the alcohol will sanitize his tongue.

"My turn," Camila says, sticking out her chest and tossing back her dark hair.

"How's it your turn?" Jesse protests. "I'm the one who had to—"

"I just had to sit back and watch someone rub their disgusting mouth all over my purse." Jesse looks hurt. "Definitely my turn."

She points a sharp red fingernail at me. "Question." Seeing my naked ass must be losing its appeal, because lately, instead of giving me dares, my friends've been making me answer questions. I think they're hoping that eventually something will embarrass me, but it hasn't happened yet. "Describe the first time you got naked with a girl. In detail."

"Okay," I say. "I was in kindergarten."

"No. Doesn't count if your mom put you in the bathtub together."

"No, this counts. It was in a sexual context."

"You're disgusting."

"But it counts. So, okay, her name was Charlotte."

"Charlotte King?" Allison asks.

"Yeah."

"We were in Brownies together," Natalie adds.

"Can we get back on track?" Camila's glare silences the room.

"Okay," I say. "Charlotte and I were the only two kids who took the van from school to our day care. We'd sit in the very back row where the driver couldn't see us, and play this game where basically you could ask to see any body part you wanted. I'd ask to see her vagina. She'd ask to see my feet."

Everyone bursts out laughing, so I have to explain that this was an actual problem. I wasn't great at tying my shoelaces—I used to have coordination issues—so getting my shoes and socks on and off was freakin exhausting. Sometimes I wasn't sure if seeing her vagina was worth all the trouble.

"Oh my god." Charlie cackles. "I bet she's totally still into feet. She's probably one of those girls who likes to suck toes."

"That doesn't count," Camila says, and I'd say she's pouting, only I don't usually find pouty faces intimidating.

"There was the time I got a massage," I say. Charlie shoots me a dark look that means *shut up*, and then pretty much everyone says that definitely doesn't count. "Well, that's all I've got." There's a moment of silence after I've basically announced my virginity to the entire room.

"But what about Kelly?" Emerald asks, blue eyes really intense all of a sudden.

Kelly's another girl who left town shortly after being intimate with me. "It never got that far."

"But she took off her purity ring."

During sophomore year Kelly and I got as far as no shirts, but me touching her bra-covered boob filled her with so much shame that she tore off her ring and said she wasn't fit to wear it. Guilt-fueled nausea is not the expression you want to see on a girl after you inquisitively squeeze her nipple.

"I've answered the question," I say, because it's not really my secret to tell. "Now my turn." I aim a devious smile at Charlie, and he cringes.

"Oh God."

It's two in the morning when I head out to my van. "Can I get a ride?" Camila calls out. I turn around. Her eyes are gleaming in the dark like a panther's.

"Where's Matt?"

Her four-inch heels clack down the long driveway. Everything's curvy and bouncing.

"He left me behind." She makes another one of those scary pouts, and I feel sorry for her brother.

"Okay, sure." We hop in the van, then I glance in the rear-view mirror. "Damn, we're blocked in. Let me see if Sean can move his car."

"Wait." She grabs my arm.

"What's wrong?" Suddenly her lips are smashing against mine, while she tangles her hand into my hair and tugs. "Ow."

For some reason she takes this as a sign to pull my hair again and kiss me even harder. It's not exactly surprising that she kisses with as much aggression as she does everything else, but it's more painful than hot—at first, anyway. After a few minutes of fingernails and biting mouths, we're both panting.

"Adam?" She lowers her sharp fingernails to my zipper. "I don't want to look at your feet."

TWENTY-NINE

ADAM

AT SCHOOL ON Monday, the girls are acting weird. Even sweet, motherly Allison, who normally stays out of conflicts, is on edge. Camila and Emerald won't look at me, and the other girls keep glaring at me like I'm evil. What the hell?

"So how long's this fight gonna go on, ladies?" I ask, and the entire lunch table goes silent. "It'd be better if we just got it out in the open. Full transparency. Right?"

Camila is studying the same sharp nails that left scratches down my neck.

Emerald flushes, pink blotches high on her cheekbones. "Camila knows what she did," she finally says, and the look she gives the other girl is chilling.

"Oh my God," Camila hisses. "I've apologized like a thousand times. I was drunk! And besides, he's not your property."

Everyone holds their breath, waiting for Emerald's response like she's the star witness who's finally taken the stand.

At least I get it now. "So this is about Brett." I sigh. "You can't let some guy come between your friendship. Girl power, right?" That must've come off more insulting than encouraging, because now everyone's looking at me like I've lost my mind.

"That's not . . ." Emerald starts, and everyone leans forward in tense anticipation. "It's nothing." With perfect poise, she gathers her things and leaves the table.

"Julian, let me explain something to you," I say as we head up the stairs on our convoluted route to Dr. Whitlock's. "Girls are crazy."

He looks at me doubtfully.

"It's true. I was *raised* by a woman, okay? I was raised to be a feminist. But then I realized this fact: they're *insane*."

"Did something happen?"

"None of them are speaking to me! Half of them aren't speaking to each other, and Emerald isn't speaking to anyone. We have a field trip to an art museum on Thursday, so that should make for a fun bus ride."

"The girls in your grade don't like you?" He looks at me with so much sympathy that I want to laugh. "The girls in *my* grade like you," he adds quickly, obviously trying to cheer me up. "They always talk about you."

"Seriously?"

"Yeah, they talk about your, um . . ." He looks down, embarrassed.

"My what?"

"Well . . ."

"Jesus, what, Julian?"

"Your lips."

"Oh, I thought we were going in a totally different direction for a minute there."

"I didn't even know boys could have pretty lips. You don't wear lipstick."

I have no idea how to respond to that. "They're just crazy," I find myself repeating.

"Crazier than Charlie?"

He has a point. "Okay, a different sort of crazy. Charlie's just a pissed-off person, so you get it, but with the girls I have no freakin clue. I mean, we should all be happy today. A bunch of us got our letters, but instead everyone's just . . . I don't even know."

"Your letters?"

"Yeah. College acceptance letters. It's not a huge deal. We all knew we were getting in, but still."

"Which college?"

"Risley. About an hour from here." He doesn't look particularly impressed. "Yeah, I know, but I never really wanted to go somewhere far away. My mom's here, and all my friends are going there, so yeah."

"Will you live at home?"

"No, the dorms. Part of the college experience, you know? What about you?"

"Me?"

"Do you have any idea where you want to go?"

"I'm not going to college."

"Why not?"

"My grades aren't good."

"Not everyone who goes to college has amazing grades."

"You do."

"But do you want to go?"

"Does that really matter?"

His question startles me for a minute. "Does what you want matter? Of course it matters."

We head back down the stairs and out into the courtyard. It's cold, so I hop up and down for a minute to warm up while Julian leans against the brick wall.

"Leaving," he says, "does sound fun. When I was younger I always wanted . . ."

I wait for him to finish his thought, but the thing with Julian is sometimes you can wait, but sometimes you have to push. "What?"

"Adventure?" He looks wary, like he thinks I'm about to make fun of him.

"Yeah, I can totally see that." I nod enthusiastically enough to keep him talking.

"I really liked movies and books about people exploring new places. When I was little, I never wondered how I'd do it. I just knew one day I would go everywhere. But when you get older, you realize wanting isn't the same as having. There are all those places you *want* to go, but it doesn't mean you can actually get there." He takes a breath. "When I was little . . . in our backyard . . ."

"Yeah?"

"We had a forest, a bamboo forest, and I'd pretend . . . I'd pretend to be an explorer." He grabs his skinny bicep in that broken arm stance. "I miss my house."

Sometimes Julian says things that are like a sucker punch to the chest. I wish I could buy his house and give it to him, but it would still be sad because it would be empty, so I wish I could change that too—that I had time-travel-world-spinning superpowers and could undo everything.

"We should go there," I suggest impulsively. It's something I think

I'd want if I were him, but then again maybe it'd be too painful, like walking through a cemetery.

"I do."

"You do? You know the people who live there now?"

"No. I mean . . . I don't go inside or anything."

And now I'm picturing Julian standing outside the house where he lived with his parents, watching, but never going in, and . . . Jesus.

"Well, we should go introduce ourselves. I bet they'd let you inside."

"I don't know. . . ."

"Is this Julian-shyness, or do you really not want to go in? Because if you really don't, I'll shut up."

He looks at the ground.

"Well?"

"Shyness."

"So you want to go inside?"

"Yes."

"Then we will."

THIRTY

JULIAN

"TURN HERE," I tell Adam.

"Okay."

I feel sort of empty and absent as I touch the vent on the dashboard. "This looks like a robot face."

He chuckles. "I know."

"Turn right at the stop sign. It's the third house on the left."

"The green one?"

"Yes."

Adam hops out, and slowly I follow.

This is my house, my *real* house. For the most part it looks the same as it always did, but there are small differences. A mailbox that isn't ours. A wreath on the door. Red curtains in the window.

We're halfway down the path that leads to the front door when I halt. "Maybe we should . . ."

"What?"

"Leave."

"Do you really want to? We can if you want."

I don't know what I want.

Adam stands there fidgeting until a girl with a blond ponytail opens the door. "Can I help you?" she asks.

Adam wheels around. "Brittany!" He knows her, of course. They hug, and she tells him she's taking a year off from college and she'd love to hang out sometime. She looks curiously at me. "Oh, this is my friend," Adam says. "He used to live here. Can we come inside?"

She says, "Sure," as if it isn't an odd request at all.

Adam looks back at me and waits until I cross the threshold.

Right here in the entryway there should be flowers. The scent should be strong, almost overpowering. Instead it's spicy, peppery, the smell of food that burns your eyes. Below my feet there should be flat green carpet. But it's gone, replaced by red-brown tile. Just two steps farther into the entryway is where my mother's piano should be, and above it one of my father's paintings. But they're gone. Everything is gone.

Without a word to Adam or the girl, I cross my old living room and step out into the backyard. I take in a deep breath, and blink back tears. This is my yard, my *real* yard. And it's closer to what I remember, but it's still wrong. It's smaller, as if the fence has been squeezed in on all sides. The bamboo forest isn't a forest at all, just two dozen waxy green stalks, most of them not much taller than me. I remember getting lost in them.

I walk the perimeter of the fence, and try to summon what I used to feel back when I thought I could bend time and spoons. I touch the red grains in the wood. I have a vague memory of doing that.

I freeze at the triangle-shaped garden in the corner. There are no flowers since it's winter, but it's still framed with red brick exactly as it was. I kneel in the grass and press my fingers into the cold soil.

I remember.

Waking up early on Saturday to the specific scent of morning and pure unfiltered joy. Grabbing a gardening shovel, eager to get outside, then being here in this exact spot. Black dirt on my fingertips. The sun and air clinging to my skin and my clothes. I remember looking over my shoulder, and there was my mother, still in her nightgown, standing on the back porch shielding her eyes from the sun.

"Are you okay?" Adam asks as we're driving away.

I don't really want to talk, and for once I don't want him to talk either. I'm trying to capture more of the memory. What came next? Did she step off the porch? Did she say something? What did we do that day?

But the rest won't come. I have just that moment, her on the back porch, me kneeling in the grass and feeling a sort of happiness I didn't remember I could feel.

"Yes," I finally answer. And even though it's not enough, I add, "Thank you, Adam."

THIRTY-ONE

ADAM

THE BUS RIDE is quiet—boring. Everyone scatters in a million different directions the second we get to the museum, so I have to wander around alone—also boring. Then an elderly security guard yells at me for stomping. So basically this field trip sucks.

I explain to the old man that I wasn't stomping, but my feet fell asleep and I was doing that thing where you jump around to wake them up. We end up talking and I find out his name's Gus and he has four kids and nine grandkids. He shows me a private exhibit of swords that's closed to the public, so okay, maybe things are looking up.

Gus and I are saying our good-byes when I spot Charlie and convince him we should go outside and find that labyrinth our teacher kept telling us about—the one modeled after the eight-hundred-year-old Chartres Cathedral in France, the most intricate labyrinth design ever created.

After a twenty-minute cold gray hike, Charlie and I reach our destination. "Well, this sucks," he says.

I agree, the labyrinth is a little disappointing. I was expecting something from *The Shining*—you know, a complicated maze of tall green hedges with plenty of corners to hide in. Instead it looks like a massive pagan crop circle, only the swirls are made of red and black stone tiles winding until you reach the center.

"It's not even a real maze," he whines. "There's only one way to go." He's right. There aren't options, just a single path. After a minute of looping around, he yells, "This is dumb!" and stomps over the lines.

"Cheating!"

"I don't care. I'm going back in. It's cold."

I ignore him and keep walking the maze. It's impossible to tell how far I am from the center. As soon as I think I'm close, the path forces me back down and around again.

I hear soft footsteps behind me, and glance over my shoulder. Emerald. She doesn't look at me and keeps walking, her shoulders back and her strides long. Maybe this is why she's always fascinated me. She seems so perfectly contained, while I feel like I'm spilling out of every pore.

The two of us weave in and out—at one point she's only a line away—but we still don't talk.

It takes a while, but finally I make it. I stand in the center, looking out over the vast field and foggy sky. When Emerald joins me in the middle, she glances around, a brief flicker of triumph in her eyes before they fill with hurt. Whatever Brett did, he's an idiot.

She turns, already leaving.

"Wait," I say. "Don't go yet." She pauses. "I haven't seen you in a while. I mean I've *seen* you, but we haven't talked. It feels like a divorce or something. Like we're all gonna be sent to different families."

"And which side will you be on?" she asks.

"What do you mean?"

"If it's a divorce, I guess you'll be on Camila's side."

"Why would you say that?"

"I know what happened between you two, Adam. I *saw* you."

"You saw us kissing?"

"It looked like more than kissing." It probably would've been if Camila hadn't puked on the floor of my car about five seconds after shoving her hand down my pants. "Are you two going out now?"

"No."

"But you liked kissing her?" Her tone's way too intense, and even though she hasn't moved, I feel like I'm being driven toward the edge of a cliff.

"Well, yeah, of course I liked it. Why are you—"

"She knows I like you!" Emerald never does anything undignified, but here she is, shouting so loud it echoes.

"Wait, *what*?"

"Camila knows, and she kissed you."

"But you're going out with Brett."

"Oh God. You don't get anything!" She spins around and I follow, landing in front of her so we're still face-to-face.

"I don't get what?"

"There is no Brett."

"There is no Brett?"

"No."

"But Brett has such a detailed backstory. I feel like I know Brett."

"There is no Brett!" Her eyes shine with tears, her chest is heaving, and bright blotches of color stain her cheeks. This is the most emotional I've ever seen her.

"Why didn't you just tell me?"

"This is humiliating."

"What is?"

"I was trying to make you jealous, but you're incapable of normal guy feelings."

"Wait . . . does Camila know there's no Brett?"

"*Everyone* knows there's no Brett! Can you please focus?"

"So you like me?"

She looks at the ground. "Yes."

"Really like me?"

The blush spreads from her cheeks down her neck, so dark I can barely see her little moles. "Yes."

"Since . . ."

"Forever. Since forever." She makes eye contact, and she's so beautiful, my chest hurts like asthma or a heart attack.

Her eyes widen, a perfect startled blue, when I press my lips into hers. Not very smoothly either. She presses back, just as clumsy. For a minute it's like that—rough and messy like we're doing this for survival instead of fun.

Then I'm touching her hair and slowing down, and it becomes something softer and deeper. She pulls her head back just a little, so our mouths are no longer touching. Her eyes darken, steady laser beams on mine, and it's as if she's about to tell me the most important thing I'll ever hear. She takes a breath. Exhales. But doesn't speak.

I cup her cheeks with my palms and kiss her again. I wish there were tall green hedges with lots of corners to hide in, but this time for entirely different reasons. We keep kissing and I can feel her lips smiling against mine.

THIRTY-TWO

JULIAN

MISS WEST IS sitting silently at her desk, staring at nothing. I can tell she's upset, but I'm relieved, because it looks like I won't get called on today.

A couple of boys start to whisper, daring each other to ask her a question about the assignment, but neither of them actually does it. A couple minutes later a different boy asks if he can go to the nurse, and she snaps at him so viciously that no one tries it again. Other than that everything is quiet, and Miss West just keeps staring.

When the bell finally rings and the room clears, I approach her desk, my heart pounding hard against my ribs. "Miss West?"

"What?" Up close she's even scarier, with eyes that glow and skin shiny like wax. "*What?*" she repeats.

"Are . . . are you okay?"

Her dark ink-eyebrows rise up. Her chin quivers.

Then she starts to cry. I don't know what to do, and I'm afraid anything I say might make her yell again.

"It's my son's birthday," she says.

And immediately, I understand. "I'm sorry."

"He was twelve. Only twelve."

She looks younger and frailer now, but I'm still not sure what to say. My father never really talked about what happens when you die. I remember one vague comment that you go somewhere else. Sometimes I wonder if my mother and father haven't stopped at all. Haven't stopped reading or drawing or singing. They're just doing it *somewhere else*.

I pull a tissue from the box on her desk and hand it to her.

She wipes her face, smearing the makeup below her eyes.

The second hand of a clock ticks loudly on the wall. The bell rings, but no more students rush to fill the room.

"You'd think it would get easier," she says. "It's been eighteen years. I remember being pregnant with him, and now he'd be thirty. Can you believe that? Thirty!"

My mother once said that the planet was like an enormous womb, and every single one of us was a fetus. Death was nothing to be afraid of. It was just birth to another world, and someone would be waiting for us there. Sometimes I try to see this, my mother and father as two newborns holding hands and ejected into this other world. There they are just beginning.

"They're—he's okay," I say. "I think he's okay."

"Yes." She nods, wiping her face again. "It was meant to be. We each have a mission on this earth, and we don't die until we complete it. I may not understand it, but he completed his mission."

I've heard people say things like that before, but I still want to ask her what she means. What sort of mission? How is she so sure that he finished? How does she know he didn't die in the middle?

Miss West looks almost peaceful now, but if she has an idea where her son is, she doesn't say. That's the thing I wonder about most—not why they're gone, but *where*. Sometimes when I can't sleep and I'm trying to think good thoughts, I imagine that magical place between worlds, the place in the flash where Elian's ship disappears before it reappears again. In that split second maybe time slows down, and he can see all the invisible places. And maybe, sometimes, he sees *them*.

THIRTY-THREE

ADAM

I'M STILL GRINNING like my face is broken. I can't turn it off. Emerald and I have become that annoying couple that kisses in public and can't stop staring at each other and makes everyone else feel both nauseated and suicidal—according to Charlie, anyway. Yesterday at school he told me to take some meds and calm the fuck down, but I couldn't. I *can't*. I'm happy. And I see no reason to pretend I'm not.

Though I will try my best not to annoy him this afternoon. The second I step inside his house, I'm ordered to stand on a rock resistant to space acid (aka throw pillow) while I wait. Today, all his brothers and sisters are aliens struggling to survive on a dying planet. Upstairs is the safety zone, but getting there is treacherous since the ground floor's acidic. Most of the kids have already lost a limb and are dragging themselves around on couch-cushion lifeboats.

After a few entertaining minutes, Charlie stomps downstairs, ignoring the kids' warnings that his shoes will melt and he'll die.

We hop into the van, and I modulate my smile. A couple minutes later Charlie demands, "Why are you turning this way?"

"I have to pick up Julian."

"What?!" he screeches about as loud as one of his little sisters. "He's seriously tagging along again?"

"He's not tagging along. He's invited."

"You don't see me bringing Carver."

"Carver's eleven."

"I don't get it. Julian's weird—he doesn't talk, and he just stares at everyone! It's fucking creepy."

"Julian's not creepy. He's, like, the nicest person ever."

Charlie sighs deeply. "You and Emerald have been together every second for the past two weeks, and now you're bringing Julian. It's never just us anymore."

For a second I'm too stunned to react. Then I laugh out loud, which is the wrong thing to do right now. I think he may actually punch me in the face. When I catch my breath, I say, "I'm sorry. You're totally right. We need a night out just the two of us." He looks suspicious. "I mean it, baby. You pick the restaurant and afterward . . ." I waggle my eyebrows suggestively, and Charlie does punch me, a painful blow to my bicep. "Ouch. Ouch. Ouch."

When we get to Julian's street, he's waiting on the corner, almost hidden underneath a tree. "See?" Charlie says. "Weird."

It *is* a little weird, but I'm not going to agree with him. "He's just polite. You could do that instead of always making me go in to get you."

Charlie looks hurt. "I thought you liked coming in."

"I'm kidding. Jesus." But seriously, even Emerald doesn't make me go to the front door to get her.

Julian steps up to the van, but his smile quickly falters. I follow his gaze to Charlie's scowl—the one that turns all freshmen into frightened mice. I smack his huge shoulder with the back of my hand, but his expression becomes only microscopically less menacing.

JULIAN

Charlie keeps sending me bruising glares as we join the long line for laser tag. I think he's mad because Adam paid for me again, and it was a lot of money: twenty dollars.

Just as we're nearing the front, a staff member tells us there's only enough room for two more players on the Red team. One of us will have to join the Blue unless we'd rather wait forty minutes for the next game.

"How about I go with Julian this time?" Adam says.

"Whatever," Charlie answers, looking angry.

We're all allowed into what looks like a little locker room full of equipment. Everyone begins swiftly suiting up. I lift the red gear from one hook, and mimic them by lowering it over my head. It looks like a football player's safety pads, only it has a rifle attached by a wire. Beside me, a man kneels in front of a smiling boy and helps him put on the gear.

A flame-haired worker shouts, "Attention!" Everyone gets quiet while he goes over the rules. "No physical contact allowed! No sitting or lying in the arena! You earn ten points every time you shoot your opponent in the kill zones . . ." He taps his head and chest. ". . . and *one hundred* points by shooting the signal over their home base! If your gun starts flashing, you're out of ammo! Go back to your home base to reload! If you're shot, you *must* return to your home base to recharge! Is everyone ready?"

The players all cheer, shaking their rifles in the air.

"You get all that?" Adam asks me, and Charlie mutters something about babysitting.

"I think so," I say, but it's a lot to remember and I've never done this before, so I probably won't be good at it.

The staff lets the Blue team in first, then the ten of us on the Red team gather in a tight passageway where the walls and floors are completely black except for glow-in-the-dark swirls. Adam's fingernails and teeth are glowing. I stretch out my hand. My fingernails are glowing too.

An alarm sounds. A speaker overhead announces robotically, "The game will commence in three . . . two . . . one!"

On lightning legs, Adam immediately darts out of base.

Much more cautiously, everyone else cascades from the room until I'm left standing alone. I don't want to leave, but it's kind of scary waiting here by myself. Suddenly Adam leaps back into the little room, startling me.

"Come on," he orders. I follow him down a dark hall. He's swift and confident. He must know the maze well. "Duck!" Someone is shooting at us.

We dive into another passageway, pressing our backs against a black wall. My heart is pounding fast.

"We've gotta get to their base." Adam says it so seriously that I start to laugh. All of a sudden this feels fun-scary, like when my dad and I used to play hide-and-seek in the dark.

Adam grins at me with glowing teeth. "You ready?"

I nod.

The second he jumps out, a little girl in blue fires at him. His chest plate beeps. "Damn it! Gotta recharge." He disappears.

I stand here alone for a moment, then duck into a narrow passageway. I don't see anyone, but they must be nearby. My heart starts beating faster now that I'm alone.

Where's Adam?

I creep down hall after hall until somehow I'm standing right in front of the flashing blue base signal. For a few seconds I just look at it. Then I take aim and shoot. I feel a jolt of surprise when I hit it.

Behind me there's an electric gunshot noise. I duck and sneak down a hallway. I'm trying to find my home base, but every path looks the same. The hall begins to fill with white vapor so thick I can barely see. I start to feel the vague dread that comes when you're blind and you know someone's right beside you and you could get away if only you could see.

I freeze, waiting for the fog to clear.

When it does, there's a figure in front of me. Charlie. Huge in the ice-blue helmet and gear. For a moment neither one of us moves. Then slowly he raises his rifle and shoots me in the head.

THIRTY-FOUR

ADAM

MOM'S SHOUTING ANSWERS at the TV when I get home—she likes to feel superior to all the contestants on *Family Feud*. When she sees me, she smiles and grabs Connect Four while patting the couch next to her.

"You've been busy these days," she says after I take a seat. I'm pretty sure this is her way of fishing for information about Emerald, so I give a noncommittal "yeah." She seems to get that the subject is off-limits, so she asks how Julian's doing instead.

"Good. He totally kicked ass at laser tag last Saturday." This makes her smile. "But he was really sick a few weeks ago. I mean, he's sick a lot, but I guess I've never seen him sick in person like that."

"You never told me that! What's wrong with him?"

"Don't freak out," I say, but it's too late for that. "He just gets the flu a lot."

She hops up, forgoing the final round, which is saying something, and starts riffling through the cabinet full of homeopathic remedies. "Take these to him."

"Okay, I'll give them to him at school on Monday."

"You know you can't bring these to the school."

She's right. Teachers tend to get suspicious when you carry around little brown glass bottles full of liquid. "All right. I'm about to pick up Emerald, but we can drop these by his house first."

"Wait—you're going out again? You just got home."

"I was with Matt and Joe and Eric and those guys. Emerald's been studying all day, so we haven't hung out yet." She's obviously disappointed, so I say, "Why don't you call Denise or something?"

"It's Saturday."

"So?"

"So I'm sure she has plans with her husband," Mom says stiffly. "But it's fine. Really." She places the remedies in a paper sack and hands it to me.

"Thanks." I kiss her cheek before I go.

My fist is poised to knock on Julian's door again when it swings open. The suited man standing there is big—practically Charlie tall—but a lot more built. His dark eyes look a little impatient, like maybe I interrupted something.

"Hi," I say. "Is Julian home?"

"And you are?" He has one of those anchorman voices—deep and without a trace of any accent.

"Oh, sorry. You must be Julian's uncle. I'm Adam."

I pause for a second, waiting to be invited in, because it's freakin cold out. Instead he takes a step forward, his wide shoulders and stance filling the entire door.

"I just wanted to drop these off for him." I raise the paper sack in the air.

He takes it and peers inside. "What is this?"

"Liquid chlorophyll and astragalus root. All-natural remedies—great for colds and flu. He didn't look so good when I stopped by the other day. And since he's always coming down with something—"

"You stopped by?"

His tone freezes my smile. I remember Julian saying his uncle didn't like it when he had people over. Now I've probably gotten him in trouble. "Well, yeah, but I was in and out. He wasn't at school, so I wanted to check on him."

"You go to school with Julian?"

"Yeah."

"You're in the same grade?" He gives me a suspicious squint, which I get. I'm obviously not a freshman.

"No, a senior."

"A senior."

"Yeah—yes. Sir."

"And you're spending time with Julian."

"Yes."

"Adam, is it?" I nod. "Adam, I hope you understand, but I don't want Julian getting mixed up with the wrong people."

I don't even know what to say to that. I'm pretty sure no one in my entire life has ever looked at me and figured I'm the *wrong people*. "Well, I mean, I'm not getting him into trouble, if that's what you're thinking. I don't even use pharmaceuticals." I point to the paper sack.

"I'm just trying to understand what someone your age sees in a boy Julian's age." An uncomfortable feeling starts creeping down my spine. "What is your *interest* in him?"

"My interest? We're friends."

"Yes, I can see why you'd want to be friends with someone like Julian." He smiles, flashing a row of tiny white teeth, but there's an edge to his tone, almost like he's being sarcastic.

"Why wouldn't I want to be friends with Julian?"

"He needs friends his own age. Apparently, so do you." He pushes the bag into my chest and shuts the door in my face.

"Not everyone's going to like you, Adam," Emerald says after I get back into the warm car and tell her what happened.

"He didn't just not like me. He accused me of, like, *molesting* his nephew."

"He said that?"

"He didn't use those exact words, but he implied it."

"What did he say?"

"It's not just about what he said. It's a feeling. Like in nature videos, when the deer's ears perk up even though they can't actually see the hunter. They can just *feel* that something's off."

Emerald cracks up.

"I'm serious. And he wouldn't even invite me in. Like I'm a vampire or a Jehovah's Witness or something."

"Maybe the house was messy."

"I really doubt that. You should see that place."

When I pull up to Emerald's curb, she hesitates, her fingers flipping the robot-face vent, flashing heat up then down across her cheeks. "My mom's staying with Rusty again."

"Yeah?"

"She's been there for almost a week."

"I can't imagine my mom leaving me alone for a week." I laugh. "I don't think she trusts me that much."

"Why don't you sleep over?" she offers suddenly.

"Uh—"

"And I'm not suggesting whatever it is you're thinking."

"I'm not thinking anything."

She raises one perfect eyebrow.

An hour later, she's leaving the shower, dressed in a long white cotton nightgown like some Victorian-era maiden. It probably shouldn't be a turn-on, but it is. Her skin's showing through the wet fabric on her stomach and thighs. Her hair's still damp and loose around her shoulders. All that's a turn-on too.

She crawls into her bed next to me, and rests her head on my chest. "I'm glad you're here," she says.

"Me too." I lean down to kiss the little mole under her eye.

"It's too quiet at night."

I kiss the one on her cheek.

"I don't like it."

I kiss the one on her shoulder.

"Adam?"

"Yeah?"

"I love you."

I get that feeling—air loss and a heart attack. "I love you too."

THIRTY-FIVE

JULIAN

RUSSELL IS STANDING in my room. He's smiling, but something is wrong, something I can sense more than see. "Where have you been?" he asks.

"The library."

"The *library*." He picks up the battered Elian Mariner book I forgot to put back in my trunk. "To read something like this?"

When I nod, he laughs. "Do you know who stopped by earlier?"

"No."

"Adam."

I feel sick, like I'm in a speeding car instead of standing still.

"He said he's been here before. That he came inside." His smile goes wide and artificial like the face of a clown. It's a smile painted around a sneer.

"I . . . I told him to leave."

"You mean he forced his way in?" Russell pulls his cell phone from his pocket. "Should I call the police?"

Slowly, I shake my head.

"So you let him in."

I fiddle with the hem of my sleeve.

"Answer me."

When I nod, the thick vein jumps in his throat. "What did you tell him?"

"Tell him?"

"That's what I said."

"About what?"

"About why you were home."

"Nothing."

"Really? Nothing at all?"

"I just said I was sick."

"Do I give you too many rules?"

"No."

"Maybe I do." He puts a hand under his chin like he's seriously contemplating this. "Remembering things isn't easy for you. I know that." A little laugh. "But this isn't really a case of forgetting, is it? You told him to leave, so you knew he shouldn't be here. Isn't that right?"

"I don't know."

"You don't know," he repeats, wearing that same strange smile.

"I don't know."

There's a sudden blur, a moment of blank empty space, and then pain so intense it knocks the breath from my lungs. I'm on the floor and my cheekbone throbs and my stomach heaves as I roll over and push myself up with my hands.

Above me, Russell is holding my conch in his fist. He's never hit my face before. Never. Another blur and this time the shell crashes into my mouth. Lips tearing on teeth, I fall onto my side. Stunned, I hold my face and watch the blood spill through my closed fingers.

My eyes flick back up. Russell looks even angrier, his whole body expanding and contracting like an unstable molecule.

He lifts the shell high into the air.

I cover my head with my arms.

Hear a splintering crash.

I peek beneath my arm to see the dent in the wall and my shell—shattered into sharp pieces on the floor. But I don't move, not until I hear Russell's heavy feet leave my room, not until I hear his car start and drive away.

I'm not sure what time it is or how long I've been standing here. I know that my hair is wet and my legs are numb and that every cold breath burns my nose and lungs. I'm straddling my bike across the street from my real house, but I'm not really looking at it. It's there, but just an out-of-focus, hazy green.

Mostly I'm watching my breath as it emerges in light smoky crystals. If it were a list, it would just be numbers. *One. Two. Three.* A list of proof that I exist.

I'm still counting when a car slows to a stop. I barely notice it. So many cars have driven past while I've been standing here in the dark. Then I hear my name, and I cough a wet cloud.

"Julian?" the voice repeats, full of concern, then a door's slamming and Adam is standing in front of me. Before I can ask him why he's here, he says, "Brittany called me. What are you doing?"

It's too dark to see much of his face, but I can hear the worry in his voice. "Jesus, Julian, it's freezing. How long have you been out here?"

Maybe I could answer if time were measured in exhales, because I've counted all my breaths. He watches me with shrewd eyes for another minute, then straightens as if he's come to some decision. "Come on," he says. "Let's go."

He opens the passenger door, spilling light onto us both. "Jesus," he gasps. "What happened to you?" He looks from my face down to my T-shirt. I follow his gaze and see that it's splattered with blood. "What happened?" he asks again, but I'm still staring at the blackish-red droplets on my chest.

Adam raises both hands like a criminal proving he's holding no weapons. Then, slow and cautious, he touches my shoulder, maneuvering me off my bike and into the car. I stretch my cold fingers, realizing I never released my tight grip on the handlebars, not the whole time I was standing there.

Adam moves quickly like he always does to toss my bike in the trunk, then he hops into the car. He pulls my seat belt across my chest, and turns up the heater. A circle of red light appears like a glowing robot mouth, one that's open wide in shocked horror. Adam is making the exact same face.

Instead of going to my house, or even to his, we pull into Emerald's driveway. Like before, he opens the passenger door as if I can't do it myself, and he guides me inside.

Emerald is dressed for bed and sitting on a chair in the living room. She leaps up, eyes filling with alarm, and suddenly she's standing right in front of me, asking the same thing Adam did.

"What *happened*?"

I feel like I've been caught standing in a roomful of clothed people, only I'm completely naked and completely flawed. Adam takes me by the shoulders and pushes me onto the couch. He kneels to peer at my face, but I'm too ashamed to look him in the eye.

"Did your uncle do this?"

Adam's question catches me off guard. Why would he think it was Russell? Anything could have happened. I could have fallen. I could have been burglarized. Some kids from school could have done it. But he sounds so sure, as if he *knows* it was Russell.

Without deciding to nod, I nod.

Adam bolts to his feet, yanks his phone from his pocket, and starts punching numbers.

I panic. "W-who are you calling?"

"The police."

"No, don't!" I plead.

"I'm reporting this." All the muscles in his face are tightly coiled. "That asshole is going to jail."

"No!"

"What do you mean, no?" he yells back. "We have to!"

He's angry, I realize, a little stunned. I didn't know he was capable of getting angry.

Emerald is still standing, troubled eyes flashing from Adam to me. Then she walks to the couch and sits down beside me. She squeezes my hand and says, "Calm down."

I'm not sure if she's talking to me or to Adam, but neither one of us calms down. I begin to shake, and he looks even angrier.

Ignoring Emerald, he demands, "Why? Why don't you want me to call?"

"Because I don't want you to." Which isn't really a reason at all, but I don't know how to explain. Yes, Russell got angry, but that doesn't mean I hate him. Just the idea of him in jail is making me feel sick. "You don't know how much he's done for me," I finally say, hoping that maybe Adam will understand, even though he probably can't. He doesn't know what it's like to be raised by someone who doesn't have to do it. "He's not good with kids, but he still let me live there even though it's hard for him to have a kid in the house. Especially one like me."

"One like you," Adam repeats coldly.

"Yeah. I'm not . . . You know how I am."

"How are you?"

"You know. I'm hard to be around. You *know*!"

"He told you that?" His facial muscles twitch as if they aren't used to forming frowns.

"Adam . . ." Emerald's voice is coaxing. "If he doesn't want you to call, you can't call. It should be his choice."

For a moment he just looks at her, then he wheels around to rip open the door that leads to the backyard. He goes out, leaving it open and letting freezing wind into the room. A minute later, he reenters and starts pacing.

"Adam, stop," she orders, sharply. "You're scaring him."

He goes completely still, face twisting in guilt. He rakes his hands through his hair, then kneels in front of me and taps my bouncing leg. "Hey, I'm not mad at you."

I nod. I know.

"But we have to report it."

There's so much that Adam can't understand. He told me once that he never met his dad, so he can't possibly understand that fathers do things differently. Most of all, he can't understand what it's like to have nowhere else to go. But instead of trying to explain all that, I just say, "Please."

He takes a deep breath. "Okay. Okay."

He rises and walks away long enough for me to wonder if he's coming back. Then he reappears, this time kneeling in front of me with a wet cloth. He wraps one hand around the back of my head, and with the other he dabs my lip with the cloth. Warm water spills down my chin, and my eyes sting with tears.

"Am I hurting you?"

I shake my head, blink, and the tears spill over my cheeks. I feel Emerald's hand begin to rub small circles on my shoulders while Adam continues to gently scrub the blood from my face.

Nothing they're doing hurts, but it feels as if something is tearing away the center of my chest. The cold is dissolving. Their hands are soft. Everything is quiet except the tears that are climbing from somewhere beneath my ribs. I've cried in pain and I've cried in fear, but these tears are different, deeper, like I'm breaking apart.

The noise should drive them away, but Emerald's hand stays, and Adam's hand stays, and he keeps washing my face long after it has to be clean.

Eventually, all the tears are gone, and I'm empty, but it's a good sort of empty. Like I'm lighter, and if Emerald's hands weren't still on my back and Adam's on my head, I might just float away.

I hear my slow, hitching breath, and suddenly I'm too tired to keep my eyes open. I can barely see as Adam helps me stand and steers me down the hall into what must be Emerald's room. There's a feminine scent, like the way it used to smell after my mother took a shower, and on every surface are porcelain butterflies.

I'm swaying on my feet until Emerald tells me to sit, gesturing to the flowery comforter on her unmade bed. I sit, and vaguely hear Adam ask me to lift my arms. I do, and he peels my shirt over my head and dresses me in one that's clean and warm. I'm so tired, a cell-deep exhaustion like nothing I've ever felt before.

My eyes fall closed, then one of them, either Adam or Emerald, pushes me to lie down. One of them pulls off my shoes. One of them presses an ice pack to my cheek, and I'm tired, so tired. One of them pulls the blanket up to my chin, and the scent of my mother is stronger. Then one of them presses lips to my forehead, and I'm asleep before one of them can turn off the light.

ADAM

"I can't just not call," I tell Emerald once we're back in her off-limits living room. She takes my hand, pulls me to the couch.

"He doesn't want you to."

"I don't care what he wants."

"Adam."

"I'm serious. I'm not sure he's the best judge of what we should do. That guy should be nowhere near him."

"People make mistakes."

"Mistakes?"

"I'm just saying, sometimes parents do bad things. Not everyone's family is perfect, you know."

What are we even talking about? It's like we're having two completely separate conversations. "Julian's uncle hit him. He was freakin bleeding."

"What do you think will happen if you do call? What? Maybe his uncle will go to jail for a couple of nights. Then what? Julian will be right back with him, and things might be even worse."

I've heard my mom say the same thing a million times about other abused kids, so Emerald might be right, but I don't care. I want her to say that maybe it won't do any good, but that we still have to try. "I can't just do nothing." I pull my hand from hers.

"Adam . . ." Her eyes fill with hurt. "Don't be mad at me."

"I'm not mad at you." I'm really not. Anger is such a waste of time. "I just don't know what to do."

We sit without talking, without touching, till she says, "It's late. . . . Are you tired?"

"Yeah."

She picks up my hand again, and we walk to her room. For a minute we stand in her doorway watching Julian sleep, the ice pack still resting against his face.

Suddenly he cries out like he's in pain or he's scared.

I cross the room and touch his shoulder. He goes quiet. Once his breathing is nice and even again, Emerald and I crawl under the covers, on opposite sides of Julian.

PART
TWO

THIRTY-SIX

ADAM

SPRING BREAK STARTS in—I glance at the clock—guh, forty more minutes. All day the teachers have been totally checked out. As soon as we got to seventh period, Ms. Fry let Charlie stick in a DVD he brought from home—one about this guy with a vendetta who keeps stabbing people with his machete. I'm pretty sure it's not school-appropriate, but I guess it doesn't matter since Ms. Fry hasn't looked up from her computer.

"This is boring!" I finally have to shout.

"Shut up." Charlie wants to punch me, I can tell. "It's good."

The killer—I still don't know if he's supposed to be a hero or villain—pulls his blade out of some guy's stomach and wipes it across his sleeve. "Why do they always do that in movies?" I ask.

"Do what?"

"After they stab someone, they take their knife and wipe it on their shirt. Why? So the next person they stab doesn't get an infection?"

"Adam," Charlie moans, "stop *talking*."

This sucks. I tap my foot, watching the clock till *finally* the bell rings. I leap into the hall, get yelled at for running, then burst outside, where Julian's waiting by the van holding a *Hamlet* script. Even though I just saw him this morning and even though it's been nearly two months since his uncle hit him, I still spend a few seconds just looking at him.

When he got back to school a few days after it happened, his lip was swollen and his cheekbone was bruised. "Dr. Whitlock's gonna wonder about your face," I told him. He didn't have real appointments with her anymore—most of the period we just walked around—but he'd check in with her for the last five minutes or so.

"So I won't go to Dr. Whitlock's," he said.

"Maybe I should tell her."

Desperation filled his face, making him look half-crazy. "If you do . . ." He was clearly struggling to come up with a threat. "If you do, I won't be your friend anymore." That was something I hadn't heard since elementary school, back when it was common to withdraw or offer your friendship as some sort of bargaining chip.

Julian's threat might have been childish, but it didn't shock me to hear him say it. He's only four years younger than me, but I feel so much older, or maybe he feels so much younger. I used to think struggle was what aged you, but if that were the case, Julian should've been a hundred years old. Now I wonder if the opposite is true. Maybe instead of accelerating your age, pain won't let you grow.

Eventually, I promised Julian I wouldn't say anything, and we haven't talked about it since, but I've thought about it. A lot. I've debated telling Dr. Whitlock even though I said I wouldn't. I've thought about telling my mom. I've considered confronting Russell, pictured charging into that huge house and telling him to keep his fucking hands off Julian.

But in the end I didn't do a thing.

I tilt my head toward the script in Julian's hand. "Wow. The play's coming up soon, huh?" He nods, climbing into the backseat. "Have they assigned the parts yet?"

"Yes. I'm the Gentleman. He's the one who tells Hamlet's mom Ophelia's going crazy."

"You got a speaking part?"

He nods.

"That's awesome!"

"It's only a few lines."

"Yeah, but out of like four hundred kids you got a speaking part. That's amazing!" He makes that face, the one that's embarrassed and happy at the same time.

A minute later Charlie, Jesse, and Allison get in the backseat while Emerald slides into the passenger seat. She's beautiful, hair up to expose her pale neck, wearing a short dress to expose her long legs. I smile my broken-face-smile, and kiss her while Charlie pretends to vomit. Jesse shoves his iPod into the auxiliary, filling the van with a song we actually know and like, so we have no choice but to sing at the top of our lungs.

Once I've dropped everyone off, I look at Emerald and she looks at me and gives me this secretive smile I have to kiss. I feel giddy, like I've been injected with caffeine and pixie sticks. She laughs like she feels it too, like we're both thinking about our duffel bags hidden in my trunk.

I told my mom I was going on a hiking trip with Charlie. I don't think she'd care that I'm really going with Emerald, but she'd ask a lot of nosy questions and offer embarrassing advice and no one needs that. Not that anything's going to happen that would require advice. If I even think about sex, Emerald calls me out on it with psychic-level accuracy.

"So what cover story did you give your mom?" I ask.

"She won't notice." She says it in the flat, almost-professional way she says most things. She's fiddling with the ring on her index finger—the one her grandmother gave her for her birthday. As far as I know, it's the only present she got from anyone in her family.

Maybe Emerald will never be the type of person to just come out and tell me her deepest, darkest secrets—she seems to think it's more dignified to hatch an elaborate scheme that forces you to figure her out all on your own. But now that we're spending every free minute together, I've picked up on things, and one thing I know is that the cold voice pretending not to care is a lie. Maybe she really does believe parents just make mistakes, but it still hurts her that her mom doesn't seem to know she exists.

"Emerald?"

"Hmm?"

"I see everything you do."

She looks over at me. Blue eyes watery, she squeezes my hand.

We drive. Out of town to a higher elevation, to wider roads and a bigger sky. It's sunset by the time we reach the cabin. I'm excited to see that it's even nicer than it looked online, small but secluded among the most massive trees I've ever seen.

We spend the first day hiking, never crossing paths with anyone. It's like we're alone on our own planet where everything is giant. That makes us miniature, but since it's all ours, we're also larger-than-life.

We spend Day Two running through woods till we come across a lake enclosed by mountain-tall rocks. We jump in the green water in our underwear. We kiss underwater, which isn't nearly as hot as I'd always thought it'd be, since I choke on the water and can't even really feel her lips. We swim behind a waterfall and find a cave that smells like moss and something ancient. Kissing here is much better.

On Day Three we're miles into the forest when I stumble over a tree branch. Luckily I don't break anything, because it would suck if Emerald had to carry me out of here. While I'm recovering on a fallen log, she tells me formally that she's ready to have sex whenever I am.

I nod and suggest we return to the cabin immediately.

Emerald is lying on her back, her hair fanned out on the pillow like a mermaid. I've been obsessed with her hair since I can remember. It's always done up in complicated ropes and knots like she has a team of people preparing her for the ball. But down and loose like this, in a way that no one ever sees, is how I like it best.

It's more than a little surreal that she's stretched out naked in front of me, and that I'm not only allowed to look but looking is expected. She's not making any attempt to hide her body, but she's lying there rigidly as red blotches stain her cheeks, neck, and chest.

"You're embarrassed," I say, the second I realize this.

"Of course I am." She pulls the thin sheet up to her chin. I try to tug it back down, but she's stronger than she looks.

"I'm naked, and I'm not embarrassed."

"Well, you don't feel things like normal people." Now she pulls the sheet up over her face, muffling her words. "You don't get nervous or shy or jealous. Nothing affects you like that."

"I feel things." Maybe I don't get worked up the way some people do, but I can *feel*.

She lowers the sheet just below her eyes. "That's not what I mean. I'm not saying it right."

I crawl into the bed, propping up my head up on one hand, waiting for her to say more.

"It's just . . . you're sort of unbreakable."

I laugh. "Unbreakable?"

"I mean, nothing ever bothers you. I guess that's why everyone loves you. You're so comfortable with yourself, you make everyone else feel comfortable too. And you're strong, like what hurts most people can't hurt you. But sometimes it seems like you don't *need* people. Like if this—us—works, you'll be fine with that, but if it doesn't, you'll still be okay. You won't break. Not the way I would."

It's like we're back in the center of the labyrinth—that magic place where she doesn't stand like a soldier and she's compelled to tell me the truth about everything.

"Emerald." I touch her cheek, poking at her scattered moles like a game of connect-the-dots. "However you're seeing me, it's not true. I need you as much as you need me."

She doesn't believe me—I can tell—but she wants to. Her hand moves to my neck, squeezes. My hand moves down to her sheet. This time she lets me pull it away.

THIRTY–SEVEN

ADAM

EMERALD AND I walk hand in hand across the parking lot after school. We stayed in the cabin a total of five days—not nearly long enough. She keeps looking at me with soft-shoulder contentment. I kiss her, then unlock the van, and we wait for it to fill up.

Jesse's first to hop inside, and immediately he grabs the auxiliary cord to plug in his iPod.

"Hey, man," I say to Charlie a couple minutes later when he joins Jesse in the back. "Why didn't you drive today?" He finally saved up enough to buy his own car—a black Jeep.

"What's that supposed to mean?" he growls just as Camila slides into the van, forcing him to the middle.

Emerald and I exchange confused looks. Normally this would be when Allison would give his back a comforting pat, but unfortunately, she and Charlie are currently *off*.

"I just figured you'd be pumped to drive. You've been complaining about my car for two years," I joke.

He glares at his phone. "Text your mom. When you don't answer her, she texts *me*. She did that the whole spring break, and lying for you got really fucking annoying." He scowls through the window at Julian, who's headed our way. "You're seriously giving him a ride? Again?"

I see Julian's worried face, and I get pissed off. "You know what, Charlie? If you have a problem with Julian, you don't have to ride with us."

The van goes quiet, and Charlie looks at me with high-level betrayal, like I just slept with Allison or something.

"Whatever." He grabs his backpack, but he's too freakin tall to make a smooth exit, so there's a lot of angry unfolding and shuffling. He shoves past a scared-confused Julian.

"What the hell?" I ask.

Emerald pats my back.

JULIAN

"Anything interesting happen today?" Adam asks on Tuesday as we're walking down the hall.

"Not really." But I am relieved school has started again. Spring break was the longest, loneliest week of my life.

"How's the play going?"

"Miss Cross is unhappy that no one memorized their lines."

Adam laughs. "Did she really expect people to study over spring break?"

"Yes."

He laughs again. "Well, how are yours coming?"

"I almost know them." The first sentence isn't so hard, but after

Hamlet's mother responds, I have ten uninterrupted lines, ones that don't make any sense. When I studied over the break, I thought I could at least *read* them. Then I got to English, opened my mouth, and watched the words on the page slide together. After stuttering and stuttering, Miss Cross told me to just practice when I got home.

"Adam?"

"Yeah?"

"Have you ever heard of Alma, Colorado?"

"No, I don't think so."

"What about Village of the Sky, New Mexico?"

"Nope. Why?"

One of the pages in my mother's notebook is a list of cities. She never mentioned them, not that I can remember, but they have to mean something. Why would she write them down unless they meant something? Maybe they were places she'd been, but I don't know all the places she'd been.

"Planning a road trip or something?" he asks.

"No. I don't have a car. And I don't know how to drive."

Adam chuckles. "I know."

"But I would go there. I think they must be nice places."

We turn a corner, and there is Miss West. I flinch away so fast that I step onto one of Adam's red high-tops, making him stumble. By the time he's righting himself, she's gone.

The very next day after Miss West and I'd talked about her son and missions, she was the same as she'd always been: volatile and unhappy with a hatred that spewed out of her like missiles. I thought I understood why. She must have hated us for being alive when her son was dead.

Lately the class has been turning against her. They're openly hostile, and they whisper plots for revenge. It seems unfair, the way unhappiness flows out of a person, just to ricochet.

"Adam . . . do you think we have missions?"

He looks at me with a confused expression. "What kind of missions?"

"Things we're meant to do."

"I don't know. Do you think you have a mission?"

I shrug, disappointed. If Adam doesn't know, then I guess no one does.

A girl turns onto our hall, eyes red and sad, and as she passes, Adam sends her a smile. Her whole face brightens and she sends him a smile back.

Hate ricochets, but kindness does too.

THIRTY-EIGHT

JULIAN

KIDS ARE CIRCLING beneath the black iron ladder that leads to my hidden room. I'm afraid that any moment one of them will get the idea to climb it, then someone will shove around the furniture and discover the crooked boards. Someone will pull them back, and then a hundred more kids will jump inside and my room won't be mine anymore.

It's Monday, less than a week until the play. Everyone with a speaking part has to stay after school to rehearse in the auditorium. At this point even the kids with substantial parts know their lines. But not me. I'm still struggling just to read them.

"Speak up," Miss Cross and the other English teachers keep telling me, but then it's just louder stuttering. I want to disappear or teleport, but instead I'm on a stage, more visible than I've ever been.

Finally, at six o'clock, the teachers tell us we can leave. Instead of following the crowd, I look both ways and dart up the ladder into my room.

I wait here long enough for everyone below to be gone before

I climb back down. I'm alone backstage with all the props and the piano, and I'm tempted to sit down and play it. Only I never really learned, even though Mom tried to teach me, because reading music was too hard and I gave up.

I'm stepping toward the curtain when I'm startled by a voice. "He's going to ruin the entire production!"

I peek around the large wooden castle and see a flash of orange hair. Kristin is standing across from Alex, who's playing Hamlet. "I mean, really, in three weeks you can't memorize *thirteen* lines?" She whispers something, then leans in close to him, touching his arm. He pulls back a little, then her fish eyes dart over to find me watching them. "Yes, Julian," she says, "we're talking about you."

It's raining cold, wet bullets and my hair is plastered to my head when a black Jeep squeals to a stop right beside me.

"Need a ride?" Charlie calls through the window.

I hesitate before opening the passenger door.

"You're getting water all over my new seats," he says as soon as I sit down. Charlie's never friendly, but tonight his expression is different, scarier.

"I'm sorry. I can get out."

"It's fine," he snaps, pulling into the street. "So? You didn't ride with Adam today?"

"No, I had rehearsal. You didn't either?"

"Adam's an asshole."

"No he's not."

Charlie clenches the steering wheel like he might tear it off, then he takes a sudden angry turn. For a second we're airborne, then we skid though a deep puddle in the shoulder. My heart is tripping in my ears, and I'm afraid I'm going to be sick. "Um . . . it's all right, Charlie. You can let me off here."

"I said I'd give you a ride, so shut up and let me give you a ride."

He slaps a lever, turning the windshield wipers to a higher speed, and swerves back onto the road. I grip my stomach, willing the nausea to pass.

"I'm sorry," I say after a few blocks in silence. "I know I annoy people." I'm not sure why I'm talking. I can tell he doesn't want me to speak. "That's why I don't ride the bus."

He gives me a sharp look. "Some people are bothering you?"

"Just one boy. Since I started school."

"He's been bothering you all year?"

"No, since I started school. In kindergarten."

"What's he been doing?" For some reason Charlie sounds even angrier now than he did before, and he folds his lips into his mouth.

"He hits me sometimes. But it's okay. I know—"

"How's it okay for someone to *hit* you?"

"He's just unhappy."

"Unhappy?" Charlie is so scornful that I start to stutter.

"N-no one wants to hurt anyone. They d-do it because they're unhappy."

"Or maybe they're just dicks."

I watch the steady clip-swipe of the windshield wipers. They can't move fast enough to keep up with the rain.

"Charlie . . . are you?"

"Am I what?"

"Happy?"

He looks stunned for a minute, like I've voiced the most personal question he's ever been asked. It's raining so hard I can barely hear him when he answers, "No."

"Why not?"

"I don't know."

We slowly wind through wet gray streets. "I'm sorry."

"Yeah. What do you care?"

"I do care. I want you to be happy."

His expression flickers between anger and something that looks like shame.

By the time he pulls up to my house, it's pouring even harder. I have my fingers on the handle when he speaks.

"If you ever need a ride . . ." He's looking down at the steering wheel, his fingers slowly tightening and loosening around it.

"Thank you, Charlie." Then I open the door and run through the rain.

THIRTY-NINE

JULIAN

AFTER SCHOOL I jog to catch Adam just as everyone is piling into his car. Charlie is in the back, so I guess he isn't angry with Adam anymore.

"Hi, Julian," Jesse says, and at the same time Adam asks, "You don't have rehearsal today?"

"Um . . . no."

"Really? The play's in like two days." He keeps looking at me as if he suspects I'm lying and is considering kicking me out of his car.

"I kept messing up," I finally admit, too embarrassed to look at anyone. "Miss Cross had to give the part to someone else."

"You should've told me." He puts the car into drive. "I would have practiced with you."

I glance up to find Emerald watching me, her eyes full of sympathy, and I have to look down again.

"It's not a big deal," Charlie says. "Did you even really want to be in the play?"

"No." But I did, mostly because Adam seemed to think it was so amazing that I was cast in the first place. "I guess not."

After Adam drops everyone else off, he drives to his house instead of mine. Once we're inside, he heads straight to the giant computer on the desk in the living room. "I'm pulling up the script," he says as he sits down. "Let's go over your lines."

Even if it weren't too late, I wouldn't want to embarrass myself by trying to read in front of him. I'm not a second grader anymore. "No."

For a moment he looks surprised by my refusal, then he pushes out the chair next to him. "Julian . . ." For Adam, it's an incredibly firm tone. "Come on."

My feet begin moving all on their own until I'm sitting at the desk. Frustrated, I drop my head onto my outstretched arms.

"These lines *are* kind of hard," he says after a minute. "Sit up. All I want you to do is read them, all right?"

"I can't."

He tugs the back of my collar just hard enough to make me look at the screen. "Try."

So I try, and I actually do okay until I get to line three. "Sp-spruns evnee—see? I told you I can't!" I drop my head back down.

"You can. You were doing fine. Sit up."

I do what he says.

"Read this word again." He brackets it between two index fingers so it's all I can see.

"Sp-spruns."

"Spurns," he corrects.

"Spurns."

"And the next word?"

"I don't know."

He brackets it just like he did before.

"En-enviously?"

"Right. Now start that line from the beginning."

"Spurns enviously at s-straws; sp-speaks things in doubt." I glance at Adam. He nods, so I keep reading.

"See?" He smiles. "You know it. It was one word tripping you up. Now do it again."

ADAM

Instead of going to lunch, I head to the English Hall. Ms. Cross is eating a sandwich with one hand and typing with the other. I knock on the doorframe.

"Adam!" She smiles, and it totally transforms her face. "How's my all-time favorite student?"

"You say that to everyone, don't you?"

"No, I do not," she says seriously.

I pull a chair up in front of her desk and take a seat. "Since I'm your all-time favorite student, I was wondering . . ." Her eyes narrow in exaggerated suspicion. ". . . if I could talk to you about Julian Harlow."

"I can't believe this." She sets her sandwich down firmly on a napkin.

"What?"

"Is this about him being reinstated as the Gentleman?"

"How'd you know?"

"You are the third person to speak to me about this today."

"Seriously? Who else?"

"Emerald, and another boy who has asked to remain anonymous."

"Oh, come on. Tell me."

"Charlie Taylor."

"Charlie?" I laugh.

"I'll tell you what I told them. Julian is a very sweet boy. I gave him the part to begin with because I . . . My point is, it's just too difficult for him."

"It's not."

"We've been at this for nearly a month and he still—"

"He just gets stressed, but he memorized it completely last night." I can tell she's considering this, so I press on. "Please? He was really disappointed. Can you just give him a chance to show you he can do it?"

"Oh, all right! All right! But honestly, Adam, if he can't do it, he can't do it. I don't want him getting up on that stage and embarrassing himself if he can't."

"He can."

JULIAN

I take a seat on an overturned crate in the hallway that runs alongside the auditorium. The corridor has been blocked off with a few partitions and is serving as a dressing room since we can't all fit backstage. At least fifty yelling kids are getting dressed and putting on makeup around me.

Yesterday Miss Cross told me she'd thought it over, and she was willing to give me another chance. And I could actually say my lines! I was so . . . relieved, but now that the play is about to begin, I'm just nervous. I can hear families crowding into the lobby outside the theater, and every minute or so, a boy or girl appears to deliver carnations to a different actor. Parents can buy them for two dollars and have them sent backstage before the show.

Suddenly, a panicked voice shouts loudly enough to be heard over all the chaos, "Why are the seniors here?"

"What?" someone else yells.

"Seniors! A big group of them." A crowd of ninth graders run to the partition and peek around it.

"Oh shit," one boy moans. "They're gonna do something to us. I know it!"

"Oh god, it's *them*." Kristin sounds horrified. "Why are they here?"

Curious, I get up and peer though their necks, but it's too congested for me to see anything. Then I hear my name. The kids part just enough for me to see Adam grinning and waving me toward him. Everyone in the entire hallway stares at me. I pretend not to notice as I ease through the crowd of ninth graders into the even bigger crowd of families.

Adam and Emerald are smiling and holding hands. Beside them are Charlie, Allison, Camila, Matt, Jesse, and a lot of Adam's other friends.

"What are you doing here?" I ask.

Adam gives me a look, a cross between amused and exasperated. Charlie is wearing a harsher version of the same face. "Why do you think?" Adam says.

"I don't know. You said the plays are horrible. You said students never come."

"We're here to see you, stupid," Charlie says, but he's actually smiling.

"Oh."

"Don't you need to put your costume on?" Adam asks.

"Yes."

Charlie points back toward the dressing area. "Go!"

"Okay. Bye!" I wave, then weave back through the swell of people. The sick nervous feeling I had just a minute ago has disappeared. Instead I feel something warm spread through my body. People I love will be watching me. Their eyes like safety nets, I can't fall.

ADAM

The play is as awful as they ever were, so about five minutes in, I'm fidgeting.

Charlie stomps on my foot.

"Asshole." I wince, but this just seems to make him happy. Five seconds later, I'm squirming again, not intentionally trying to piss him off, but it's a nice side effect.

As each terribly executed scene drags on, I get a little more agitated. I can't stop thinking about what Ms. Cross said, how she didn't want Julian to publicly humiliate himself. Maybe I made a mistake in pushing him. If it doesn't go well, who the hell knows what'll happen?

Then *finally*, in act IV, Julian steps out onto the stage. He's wearing a puffy velvet jacket, little pants that end at his knees, and god-awful purple tights. Charlie laughs, and it's my turn to stomp on *his* foot.

I hold Emerald's hand as Julian says his first line. Easy part down.

Hamlet's mother responds, then I squeeze Emerald's hand harder, reciting his lines in my head as if I can send them to him telepathically. Julian answers, maybe not with the best projection, but all his words are correct and clear.

As he's exiting stage left, I break into noisy applause, totally inappropriate for the somber scene. Emerald looks at me with a startled laugh, then she claps too, and soon Charlie, Camila, and every other senior we dragged along stands and cheers.

FORTY

ADAM

JULIAN AND I are on our convoluted walk to Dr. Whitlock's when he says, "Do you want to know where I eat lunch?"

I glance over at him, surprised. "Sure."

"I can show you, but . . ."

"What?"

"It would have to be a secret."

"Okay, now I'm really curious."

"You couldn't tell anyone."

"I won't." He still looks uncertain, so I repeat, "I won't."

"Okay." He smiles suddenly. "Follow me."

We head into the auditorium, and I follow as he flies up a ladder backstage into the prop attic over the theater. He heads behind an old bureau, and slides back two loose boards like a magician.

I bend, peering into the dark. "There's another room!" I say, amazed. But I don't see how you could get there without risking a deadly fall. There are too many missing floorboards above thirty feet of darkness.

Julian squeezes into the narrow space and steps onto a plank. When he gets to the end and bends his knees like he's going to jump off a diving board, I say, "Julian, *wait*!" But he's already leaping through the air.

He lands in the other room, then turns around, looking a little worried now. "Maybe you shouldn't," he says. "You'd have to jump and . . ."

"And what?"

"You fall down a lot. Even . . . even during normal walking."

If anyone else said that, I'd think they were being a smart-ass. Coming from Julian, it's totally sincere concern. I gauge the distance, and really it's only a couple feet.

"I think I've got this."

He doesn't look convinced, but he steps back enough to let me jump through the narrow passageway. When I make it, Julian's wearing this hopeful smile, so I say, "This is cool." But it's not cool. It's practically a closet, one that was burned and rebuilt but still smells like it's rotting. "You eat lunch here every day?"

He nods.

That's even more depressing than this room. We've been up here for less than two minutes, but already I'm feeling bored and caged. I pace the floors, look out the little window, then pace some more and end up stubbing my foot on something—a stack of composition notebooks stuffed into the corner.

"What's this?" I say, crouching down to pick one up.

"Oh . . . nothing . . . well, just . . ."

I open it and find Julian's hieroglyphic-style handwriting, but it's neater than it used to be and not *that* hard to read if you try.

Walking toward the little round window, I start to read. Then, even though this room's too dim and way too cramped, I find myself sitting on the floor and turning page after page.

When I glance up, Julian's watching me, chewing on his thumb.

"How do you do it?" I ask.

He gives me a worried look. "Do what?"

"Write stuff like this. How do you think of it?" Reading his story—it's like how I used to feel when I read Elian Mariner books. How much I loved them, and how it felt to suddenly find myself in another world. Julian's looking even more worried, so I realize I need to clarify. "It's good, Julian. Really, really good."

For a minute his face freezes completely, and then he smiles a wide smile.

I stand and hand the notebook to him.

The bell rings, a much more distant sound than usual. "Are you hungry?" I ask, struck again with the image of Julian having lunch up here in the shadows.

"Yes."

"You should eat in the cafeteria. I mean, why eat alone when you have friends?"

JULIAN

I feel the curious eyes of my classmates as I enter the cafeteria for the first time.

The giant room is full of people and Adam is walking so quickly, I'm afraid I might lose him in the crowd. I jog to keep up.

When we get to his table, it's awkward trying to find a seat where there isn't really room, and right away he starts talking with Emerald, so I'm not talking to anyone.

Then Jesse asks me if I want to listen to his iPod. Without waiting for an answer, he pushes his headphones against my ear.

"It's nice," I say.

While we're talking about our favorite music, Adam tells me to drink half his green juice. Camila tells him to leave me alone, but I drink it anyway, then Adam says something funny and I laugh along with everyone else, and it feels just like dancing at Emerald's party— the same electric connection.

That feeling follows me all day, and I imagine I can see it the way you can see the golden glow that surrounds angels in paintings. It's still there when I enter the house after school, a safety net, a trail of gold, happiness.

It takes a moment to register him. Russell. Standing in the corner of the kitchen, dark as a shadow and statue-still except for the insect pulse in his throat.

FORTY-ONE

JULIAN

"IT LOOKS LIKE the bus got you here early today," Russell says.

"Yes."

He stares at me like if he looks hard enough he can see the truth written there. "What are you wearing?"

"What?"

"What part of that question was confusing to you?"

"Nothing, I just . . . it's just a shirt."

"I know it's a shirt." He smiles. "Where did it come from?"

"A friend from school."

"A friend?" A small, disbelieving laugh. "And by friend, you mean Adam?"

". . . Yes."

"So first he's coming into my house, and now he's dressing you in his clothes?"

"He hasn't been coming to the house."

"He's never been in this house?"

"I just meant he only came inside that one time. He hasn't come back."

"Why would this boy give you clothes?"

"I don't know."

"What are you giving him?"

"I haven't given him anything."

There's a frightening blip in the vein in Russell's neck, like on the night he broke the shell. "That's a lie."

I take a step back.

"What are you doing for him?"

"I don't know."

"You don't know what you've been doing?"

"I mean I haven't been doing anything."

"You must be doing something. People don't just give you things for no reason."

"I'm sorry."

"That's not an answer."

"I don't know the answer."

"Were you complaining, lying about me?"

"No."

"Then *why*?"

"I think he just thought my clothes were too small."

"So you *were* complaining."

I shake my head.

"You must have been. Do you think I believe for one second that just out of nowhere this boy took special notice of *you* and your clothes?"

"I don't know."

"Julian . . ." My name is a sneer. "Why would he notice your clothes?"

"I don't know."

"What are you not telling me?"

"He was just being nice. He's my friend."

"I've known you for your entire life." His mouth twists to the side in an almost smile. "You don't have friends."

Tears spring to my eyes, but I don't feel sad. I feel—

"*Why* is he giving you clothes?"

—angry. "He thought I needed them."

"Why?"

Fury curls in my stomach. "Because mine don't fit."

"And how would he know that?"

My hands curl into fists. "Because he can see!"

I don't think I've ever seen Russell look shocked before. But he is, mouth slack and eyes wide—shocked. For a minute neither one of us speaks.

Then his face unfreezes and turns red. "Go get it."

"W-what?"

"Don't ask me *what* again. Go get it."

"But I didn't do anything!"

"That boy Adam, he's been planting things in your head! You never used to talk to me this way." Russell strides to the cabinet, yanks open the bottom drawer, and grabs the switch. "Take off your shirt."

Behind my eyes, I see the fury on Adam's face the night Russell hit me with the shell. My heart's a fist, opening and closing and growing with every beat. "I did nothing wrong!"

The switch blurs. Red slashes of pain. Pain that isn't right or mine to take. I fall, kneeling inside Adam's anger.

☆ ☆ ☆

When I wake, I'm stiff and sore. I glance at the dresser, but there's no money and no shell. Whatever courage I felt last night is gone. All that remains is regret. I have a long walk to school, so I need to get ready.

Every movement is slow. Every movement hurts.

I've just finished pulling on my sneakers when Russell appears in my doorway. "I'm taking you today." He has never, not once, driven me to school.

"Thank you," I say.

As we zip through the streets in silence, my stomach lurches. I'm afraid I'm going to be carsick, and I can't imagine how furious he'd be if I threw up on his leather seats. I wrap my arms around myself and think good thoughts.

The parking lot is full of kids when we get there, but instead of dropping me off, he pulls into a space. "We're going into the office, and you're withdrawing."

"Withdrawing? I . . . I'm not going to school anymore?"

"Nora's agreed to let you stay with her."

I don't want to live with Russell's sister. I don't want to move far away now that I've made friends. But it's finally happened. I pushed him that far.

"I've tried with you for almost five years, but you're still *spoiled*."

While Russell signs forms and waits for my school records in the main office, I close my eyes. If I concentrate, I can bend time and spoons.

But somehow we're back in his car and I haven't changed anything at all.

As Russell is turning the key in the ignition, I ask, "Can I say good-bye to Adam?" I'm afraid he's going to hit me right here, he looks that angry.

Suddenly he laughs. "You really think he's your friend, don't you?"

I don't answer.

"Adam's the same boy, isn't he? The one you lived with?"

I nod.

"This is the boy who didn't think enough of you to call you in, how many years? The same boy who begged his mother to make you leave so he could have his room to himself again? He's not your friend. You need to remember who's actually been there for you all these years."

I gaze out the window. The bell has rung and now the parking lot is empty.

"Do you know his number?" Russell asks.

I nod, warily.

He pulls his cell phone from his pocket and hands it to me. "Make it quick."

That wasn't what I meant; I want to go inside and say good-bye in person. But wanting isn't the same as having.

I find the notebook in my backpack with Adam's number written in it, and I dial. I don't expect him to pick up at this time of day, and he doesn't. It goes straight to voice mail and a robot voice tells me to leave a message.

"Hi, Adam," I say while Russell watches. "I just wanted to let you know I'm moving in with Russell's sister and . . . I just wanted to say good-bye."

"Wait here," Russell says when we pull into the driveway. I stay in my seat, looking forward, but not really seeing. After a while I count the minutes as they pass. Ten, twenty, thirty.

Russell knocks on the passenger window and aims his long, skinny thumb backward, indicating that I should get out of the car.

Does this mean he's letting me stay?

I follow him into the house, into my bedroom. My trunk is open and empty, all its contents stuffed into two cardboard boxes. He points to a suitcase and says, "Pack."

Numb, I take the clothes from the closet.

I'm zipping the suitcase closed when he returns and leans against my doorway. "You've lived here for a long time. You had no one, and I took you in."

I nod.

"I wanted to do the right thing for you after your parents died. I was only a little older than you when my father died."

"I know. I'm sorry."

"When you were younger, sometimes your parents brought you into this house."

"I . . . I remember."

"They didn't care how you behaved, how many messes you made, how loud you were. They'd *smile* when you interrupted them." Russell's eyes glow with fury. "And they expected me to be subject to the whims of a child. To stop everything because you wanted to *sing*." He's getting angrier and his body is getting bigger. "None of you was satisfied unless everyone's eyes were on you." The vein in his throat starts to pulse. "You were *spoiled*."

He takes a breath.

"But with me . . ." His voice is softer now. ". . . you began growing into something better. I'm not sure what happened this year." He pulls something from his pocket. "But I don't think it's too late." A lock, heavy, shining silver. "I think I can still teach you."

"Teach me what?"

He looks at me the way you'd look at a painting or a statue or anything that can't look back. "Get in the trunk."

"What?"

"Get in the trunk."

"But . . . I . . . I'm going to Nora's."

"No, Julian. You're not."

FORTY-TWO

JULIAN

I LOOK FROM Russell, to the trunk, to the door. He seems to know what I'm thinking, because his face twists into something terrible. "Stop. Fighting. Me."

I try to think of anything to say that will make that expression disappear, but instead a memory from Miss West's science class flashes in my mind. A diseased brain. Something blocking the space between neurons so no messages could pass.

"I'm trying to give you a chance here." Russell's voice is so close to gentle that it shocks me into really looking at him. "Would you rather I sent you away?"

"You . . . you don't want me to leave?"

"No," he answers. "I don't want you to leave." My eyes flood with tears, a collision of relief and reliving rejections. "Do you want another chance?"

I nod quickly.

"One more chance. That's all I'm willing to give."

"Thank you."

☆ ☆ ☆

I kneel until my face is pressed into the cold metal floor of the trunk, then I angle my knees to the side in an awkward contortion. I think wildly for a second that I need to turn over, find a better position, but too quickly the lid has closed over me. I hear metal scraping against metal as the lock slides into place. It sounds very far away.

I shift, try to pull my hands from where they're pinned beneath my chest, but there's not enough room. It's too dark. I can't move. Already I'm sweating, from the heat, from the fear. The sound of my breath is louder in the trunk and coming too fast. There won't be enough air.

I try to free my arms again, but I smack my elbows against the walls. The awkward angle of my hips is already hurting, but there's no way to straighten.

It's too dark.

I can hear my heart pounding in my ears, so fast and loud that I wonder if I'm dying. Then a muscle in my shoulder rips and somehow I'm moving, turning over just enough to see it. Light.

When I was nine years old, only a few hours before I left for camp, I found my package of glow-in-the-dark stars, and I stuck them all to the roof of this trunk. Why did I do that? It wasn't as if I'd ever see them.

My stuttering laughter echoes inside the trunk. My breath comes easier now. I look up, watching the lid expand higher and higher until it isn't there at all. I'm lying beneath an infinite star-filled sky.

ADAM

I get tired of pacing outside Julian's classroom after about two minutes and just knock. His teacher peeks her head out. "He's absent," she says, then shuts the door. Awesome. That means a boring hour of sitting in Dr. Whitlock's office.

My phone buzzes—a pissed-off text from Charlie. His Chemistry teacher's out to get him again. While I'm messaging him back, I stumble into a trash can and fall on my ass. As I'm getting back onto my feet, I notice I have a voice mail.

"It doesn't make sense," I say to Dr. Whitlock for the third time. "Julian would've told me if he was moving."

"I don't know what to tell you, Adam." She's sitting at her yellow desk, flipping through a thick file folder. "His uncle signed the paperwork this morning."

"So he decides to have Julian move when we've got, what, a month left of school? Does that make sense to you?"

"No," she agrees, "it doesn't."

JULIAN

I awake to throbbing pain. My elbows and shoulders and knees ache, worse even than the stinging cuts on my skin. I'm thirsty. I'm hot. I don't know how much time has passed. My breathing is still ragged and heavy, the way it is when I have a cold. The stars look dimmer, or maybe my eyes are just blurring.

No, definitely dimmer.

And then I remember. They have to absorb light to glow. I stare up, neck bent at a painful angle, as they fade, slowly, terrifyingly, into nothing.

It's too dark. I can't breathe.

I want to scream, but Russell might hear. I claw at the metal. I need out!

Then my fingers find it. A small round hole.

Instead of feeling relieved that I'll be able to breathe, I imagine Russell drilling holes into the trunk my parents gave me, and I feel sick.

I pull my knees to my chest a little tighter. I need to pee. Soon that's worse even than all the cuts and sore joints.

Just when I think I won't be able to hold it anymore, there's the unmistakable sound of the lock being opened. The lid lifts and I launch upright, taking gulping breaths. A cold glass of water is pushed toward me. I grip it with two shaking hands and drink, then I say, "Bathroom."

Russell is watching me with a sort of detached curiosity. When he nods, I move in a stumbling jog that reminds me of Adam.

After I use the toilet, I sink to the floor to rest my face against the cold tile. The walls and floors and lights are brilliant white. I can stretch my arms and legs, and it's cool, so cool.

Russell's tall shadow falls over me. "Get up."

I don't ever want to leave this room, but I lever up with my palms and stumble toward my bed.

"Where are you going?" he asks.

I cough. My throat is dry. I wish I drank more water. "To sleep?"

He shakes his head, and points to the trunk.

"I'm sorry." I start to cry.

"You're fighting me." He turns and leaves the room. I fall onto my bed, but moments later there's stinging pain across my shoulders and back.

"Stop! *Please!*" I try to lift my arms, but the muscles won't work, so it hits my face. It keeps falling. "I'll go to Nora's!"

The switch stops abruptly, and the expression on Russell's face is the scariest I've ever seen. "You want to leave?"

"No." I shake my head. "No."

He's still holding the switch with a frozen shattered expression. "After everything? You want to leave?"

"No." I shake my head again, but he doesn't seem to hear me. Suddenly the switch descends with dizzying speed. "I'm sorry." I rise and stagger to the trunk.

He's still hitting me as I lower myself inside.

FORTY-THREE

JULIAN

THERE WAS LIGHT before, two pencil-thin rays through two air holes, but now it's completely dark. I'm hot. I'm thirsty. I'm hungry. I feel a sudden jolt of panic and the urge to scream.

Think good thoughts.

If I think good thoughts, I can breathe. I imagine Elian Mariner. I'm standing on his ship, and his ship can go anywhere.

My breathing gets easier and soon I'm so calm I'm half-asleep. More thoughts drift in and out of my head. My mother . . . my father . . . Emerald . . . Adam.

How much time has passed?

I don't know.

After a while, I can only think of one thing: I need to pee. I count to sixty, and then I do it ten more times. Ten minutes. Twenty. Thirty. Forty. Fifty. It's not a decision. There's no choice. I can't hold it anymore.

You can't always control what you remember. Like the look on Mom's face when I got angry and said I loved Dad more. Or the look on his face when I got angry and said I loved *her* more. It's as if those kinds of memories are all tied together on a single string. You look at one and you can't stop seeing them all. Every bad thing you ever did.

Like the time we went for a walk and I found the baby frogs. Mom wouldn't let me bring them into the house, so I hid them in my pocket. And the time I found the robin's nest with three eggs still in it. Dad told me not to touch it, but I snuck it to school for show-and-tell.

When I took the frogs out of my pocket, they were dead.

When I got to school, my teacher said the mother bird wouldn't come back to the nest, even if I returned it to the tree. The birds would never be born.

I didn't mean to kill the frogs. I didn't mean to kill the birds.

Mom and Dad told me not to cry. He picked me up, saying, "You'll give yourself a headache." But I already had a headache. He rubbed my head with his rainbow-colored fingers while my mom said, "It was an accident, just an accident." But *accident* wasn't a word for when something died—for when you *made* something die.

The memories for *accident* are on the same string too. The accident I had at school in second grade when Mom had to bring me clean pants. Accidentally spilling red paint on the couch. And the social worker who told me about my parents. An accident, just an accident.

I think I hear the lock. Sometimes I think I hear it and it turns out to be nothing, but this time it's real. The lid opens. Russell must be standing right above me, but all I can see is light so bright my eyes start to tear. But bright light is good. It will activate the stars. The longer the trunk stays open, the better.

When a cool glass of water is thrust into my hand, I gulp it down. My vision clears, and I see Russell's lips curl. He sniffs the air, disgusted, and I cringe in shame. All he says is, "Shower."

My arms and legs hurt even worse than before, but the water feels nice. I pick up the soap, scrubbing my stinking body and hair. The water is running cold by the time I climb out.

My mouth tastes stale and fuzzy. The bathroom door is wide open, and I don't see Russell. Hurrying now, I don't waste time putting the toothpaste on the brush; I squirt some directly into my mouth. It's so sugary and solid, so close to food, that before really thinking, I've swallowed it.

I'm coughing when Russell's shadow falls over the floor.

I turn away, but I can feel his eyes on my back. He tosses a pair of sweatpants onto the ground. I pull them on, then stumble straight to the trunk and climb inside. I look up at him to say, *See? I'm doing it. I am.* But there's nothing to read on his face. Cold, blank, he shuts the trunk again. When I look up, the stars are glowing bright.

FORTY-FOUR

JULIAN

HOW MANY DAYS have passed?

I don't know.

There's a pattern. Waking up to the beams of light. Being hungry, getting water, then using the toilet. Sometimes I make it before he comes.

Sometimes I don't.

The trunk opens, and my eyes blur at the brightness.

"Good," Russell says. Today I've made it.

After I use the bathroom, I slide to the floor. I'm still kneeling when he sets a plate on the floor beside me. A ham and cheese sandwich. My eyes blur, this time with emotion. I can't remember him ever making food for me before.

I try to say thank you, but the words won't come out, so I just nod, hoping he'll understand. It tastes good, but suddenly my stomach seizes up and I gag.

The approval on his face vanishes. "Slow down."

When I take another bite, I gag again. He moves to take the

sandwich, and without thinking, I've pulled it to my chest. The vein pulses in his neck as he rips the sandwich from my hands and throws it in the trash.

I've done it again. Fighting. Fighting. Stop fighting.

I get up, shaking, and crawl to the trunk, only to find it closed. With two hands, I lift the heavy lid and climb inside. Soon I hear the lock. Looking up into the darkness, I start to cry.

A memory, so clear. Me, lying on my mat during nap time at preschool, missing my parents in the deep, painful way you miss someone who's died. I began crying and calling for them. I must have been only three or four years old, and I remember believing that when I said their names, they could hear me wherever they were. I could see my thoughts rushing through clouds and outer space like magic to find them. They could hear me calling and would come for me.

I know it's pointless, but I find myself doing it now. Projecting thoughts and whispering names. Trying to send out a message that will never be received.

ADAM

"What's going on with you?" Emerald asks. We're lying in her bed under her butterfly blanket. Her head rests on my chest, and I run my fingers through her long loose hair, down her bare shoulder. "Did you take your drops today?"

"Yeah. Why?"

"You're acting, I don't know, antsy."

"I'm always antsy." But I know what she means. It's definitely more intense than usual, but it doesn't feel ADHD-fidgety, it's like—

"Are you nervous?"

"No." She knows I don't get nervous.

"You seem nervous."

I kiss her, wanting to distract both of us from whatever this is.

"Oh yeah," she says a few minutes later. "Why didn't you answer me today? I texted you a hundred times."

I groan and cover my face with my hands.

"Not again, Adam. Tell me not again."

"Okay, so I was in the van. I plugged in my phone, and I forgot I had a glass of water in the cup holder. I mean, I never do that. It's always bottled!"

"So you dropped it in the water."

"My mom said she's done. She's not replacing this one."

"Can you blame her?" She laughs. "This is what, the tenth phone this year?"

"Fourth," I correct.

"Try rice."

"What?"

"Stick your phone in a bowl of rice. It's supposed to absorb the moisture." She kisses my chest and lays her head back down. "You memorized my number, right?" She keeps insisting it's vital since I lose and break so many phones, but I suspect she really just thinks it romantic—me knowing her number by heart.

"Yeah."

She kisses me again and for a few minutes neither of us talks. Then she asks, "You still haven't heard from Julian?"

"No. It's so weird. It's been over a week, and nothing."

"He called you before he left, right?"

"Yeah . . ."

"Maybe he just got busy. Moving and everything."

"Maybe." But I don't think so. I have this persistent bad feeling, like a throbbing toothache you can't get rid of. "I'm going to his house tomorrow. I'll get his aunt's number."

Emerald sits up and looks at me. "Do you think his uncle will give it to you?"

No. He probably won't just out of spite. "I'll make him."

She looks worried and amused at the same time. "I'm going with you."

"No." I don't want her anywhere near that guy. "I'll be fine."

JULIAN

I remember having a toothache once, the world reduced to one inch of pain. Nothing else existed outside of it. It was the sort of pain that defined you, and you knew you could be free of it, if only you could rip it out of your skull and toss it away.

I feel that now, on the right side of my back under the rib cage. Everything hurts, but it all seems to converge there.

Slowly, slowly, the points of pain multiply so I don't know which one is worse. For just a second there's a thought outside the pain, but then it's gone. It's like a song stuck in your head, but one without lyrics. A steady percussion, drumming beat, painpainpain. You can't turn it off. You can't pull it out.

Russell opens the trunk. "Shower," he says. "You stink."

I hurt too much to move.

"Now."

I unlock my limbs. I don't have the strength to scream, but I hear it anyway, ricocheting inside my head.

Tears streaming, I pull off my pants and crawl into the tub, but actually turning the knobs is impossible. Russell sets a razor on the ledge beside me, then leaves. I can't pick it up. It hurts just to sit. So I let myself fall over.

I'm lying on my side against the cold porcelain when I hear the doorbell chime.

FORTY-FIVE

ADAM

IMPATIENT, I RING the bell again. Russell's flashy car is in the driveway, so I know he's home. Finally, the door swings open. Julian's uncle looks like he's seen better days. His clothes are wrinkled, he's got several days of stubble, and dark, sweaty hair hangs into his eyes.

"Yes?" he asks with a strained smile.

This is the man who hit Julian, this grown man who's big enough to make Charlie look puny. I bite down on the fury boiling up inside me and open my mouth to ask for the phone number, but this comes out instead: "Can I grab something from Julian's room? I loaned him a book, and I need to get it back."

He laughs like that's a huge joke. "You loaned Julian a *book*."

"Yeah."

"He took all of his things."

"He told me he forgot to pack that. He said he left it in his room."

"He told you?" His dark eyes narrow. "When was that?"

"Uh . . . a couple of days ago," I say. He glares like he knows I'm lying. "I think I'll just check." I try brushing past him, which is stupid. It's not like the number's going to be taped to the wall or something.

Russell muscles me outside and slams the door behind him. "I said"—he gets right into my face, baring a row of tiny white teeth—"it's not *here*." I'm really glad Julian isn't living with him anymore, because he's pretty freakin terrifying, and he's got to be even scarier to Julian.

I take a step back, holding up my hands. "Okay, I get it. I lost his aunt's number. Just give me that, and I'll go."

"You *lost* her number." He has this way of repeating everything you say like it's so unbelievable that you start questioning yourself.

"Yes?"

"He has your number, correct?"

"Yes."

"Then I'm sure if he wanted to talk with you, he'd call you." And just like before, he slams the door in my face.

JULIAN

I thought I heard Russell talking to someone, but now there's only silence.

"What are you doing?" he yells when he comes into the bathroom. "You're just laying there!"

I try to answer him, but I can't. I hear the knobs twist, then water pours down on me, ice-cold like the time Charlie picked me up in the rain. Russell continues to yell, telling me to bathe, to shave, to wash my hair. I try to lift my arms, but they hurt and I start to cry.

"If you're not going to wash yourself, you can just get out."

Every movement is slow and painful. Pulling on pajama pants

is excruciating. So is climbing back into the trunk. When it closes, darkness surrounds me.

Think good thoughts.

Elian. I'm on his ship. I can go anywhere.

But the image breaks.

The trunk shrinks, and it's as if I'm shrinking too, then fading to somewhere else. The place between worlds. The split second before Elian gets from where he is to where he's going. The long stretch of ocean that Inuit sailors fear between shores.

It's the place you disappear.

FORTY-SIX

JULIAN

MY LAMP, THE one with a pedestal shaped like a crescent moon, must be broken or the bulb must have blown, because my room is completely dark. My father is sitting on the edge of my bed; he must have heard me crying. He pushes back my sweaty hair. It's too hot. Why is it so hot?

It's summer. . . . We saw the fireworks today. We walked on the beach. I found the biggest seashell I'd ever seen. Mom called it a conch. She said, *Put it to your ear. Listen.* Air echoes through its chambers, and it sounds like the ocean.

But it's too hot. I feel sick. I have a headache. I want a cold cloth. I want my TV on. I want Mom. I try to tell Dad all of this, but he says, "It's time for sleep now."

"I can't."

He ignores me the way he always does when I tell him I don't want to sleep. But this is different. I'm sick. I'm in pain.

My father is asking me something: "How many stars?"

"I don't know."

"You know the rules." His voice is gentle. "How many?"

I look up at the pitch-black sky. "I don't see any stars."

FORTY-SEVEN

JULIAN

HOW LONG? NO light streaming through. Did I miss it? Or is it too soon? How long have I been inside this shell? I'm echoing back and forth through the chambers for eternity. I'm not real.

I'm wet. I'm hungry. He's not coming back.

It's dark.

I'm scared.

I'm never getting out.

I scream and claw at the walls of the shell. There's a bright explosion of pain, a snap of bones, but I keep hitting.

Then I'm falling.

My face slams into something cold. Metal.

My fingers find two holes. I try to push one finger through, but it hits something smooth, hard, and cold. I've turned over my shell. I need to get it upright again or I'll drown. I slam my shoulders against the wall, but it's too heavy. Fighting against metal and gravity and waves, I'm so tired now.

Deep ragged breaths.

I can hear the ocean inside the shell.

ADAM

I wake up flailing. I've already forgotten whatever the nightmare was about, but I remember the feeling—like suffocating. I hop out of bed, too awake to sleep now. I slip out of the house quietly so my mom doesn't wake up, get in the van to go to Emerald's. . . . Then it occurs to me that she's probably asleep too.

Nothing's open, so I drive aimlessly till I find myself pulling up in front of Julian's house. The streetlamp reflects against the two rows of square windows, making them shine like teeth. No lights are on in the house, which makes sense, since it's after midnight. Russell's car isn't in the driveway, but it could be in the garage.

I head to the front door and ring the bell. As it echoes through the house, I get an apprehensive twinge. Russell's probably going to kick my ass for waking him up. But whatever, I've gone this far, and I'm not leaving till he gives me the phone number.

Only no lights come on, and no pissed-off asshole comes to the door. It's pretty obvious no one's home, but something is stopping me from getting back in my car.

What I do next is so colossally stupid that I immediately start planning my defense for when the police arrive. I'm off my ADHD meds, I'll say, and impulsivity is the hallmark of my condition. It's not my fault I kicked in my friend's window.

When no home invasion alarm sounds, I slide my hand through the broken glass, trying not to cut myself, and turn the locks. I slide the window up and slither in, making a lot of noise when I fall inside.

I'm not doing this whole breaking-and-entering thing properly, I know that.

I scramble to my feet, ready for Russell to burst into the room and scream at me for being in his house. Or maybe he'll think I'm a freakin burglar and charge in with a gun. I freeze.

The house stays totally silent.

I take a deep breath, inhaling the gross, stale odor of what has to be Julian's room and flip on the light. There's a suitcase against the wall.

"Julian?" I yell, even though if anyone was home they would've heard my fantastic entrance. I stride past his dresser and trunk into his bathroom, out into the living room, then back into the bedroom. I lift the suitcase—heavy, still packed.

I start pacing again. There's nothing here, but something's wrong—I know it. I pull out drawers, looking for something, but I don't know what. I kneel down to open the trunk.

It's lying on its side, so I heft it upright, grunting. It's a lot heavier than I expected. For a second I just look at it, puzzled by the huge padlock and round holes drilled into the side. Then an idea forms . . . an idea so terrible, my hearts shoots up into my head and starts pounding, the noise replacing all thoughts.

I tug on the lock, but it won't give. A silver glint catches my eye. A key on top of the dresser. I grab it. My fingers fumble as I slide it into the heavy lock. It falls open, and I lift the lid.

FORTY—EIGHT

ADAM

MY EARS RING like a sonic blast just split the air. All frequencies interrupted, everything goes white. I'm deaf. I'm blind. My pulse has gone so slow and cold, I can't move.

Julian is inside the trunk.

His body's contorted into an impossible position. There are shiny red welts and purpling bruises up and down his arms and back. Blood is caked under his nose and mouth. Every rib in his back is visible. His shoulder blades are sticking out, sharp like wings.

Inside the trunk, the stale sick odor of the room is stronger—a combination of sweat and blood and urine. He doesn't move, not even a little flicker when the light falls over him. There's no sign that he's breathing.

Then, under the sharp shoulders there's a movement so small, I don't know if I just imagined it. Then a sound, a tiny rasp.

He opens his eyes.

Relief hits me so hard, I feel weak. He's alive, but he doesn't seem to see me. He blinks, tearing up like he's looking into the sun.

He makes a lurching move to rise, but he can't. I try to lift him, but he cringes away, folding himself back to the bottom. The terrifying thought suddenly strikes—Russell. He did this, and he could come back any second. I reach into my pocket for my phone and then remember—shit—it's still on my bedside table sitting in a bowl of rice.

I start talking, saying Julian's name over and over, trying to sound soothing even though I'm panicking. I reach for him, and this time he lets me lift him out. I try to avoid touching any part of him that looks bruised or cut, but that's impossible. My hands are under his frail arms when his legs give out, and he crumbles to the floor.

"Open it," he says. "Please."

"Julian, you're out. You're out now."

"Open it . . . for the stars."

He's not making any sense. "Julian."

He slides on his stomach along the floor, tries to open the trunk again, but his arms flop uselessly.

"It's okay. You don't have to get back in."

But he keeps pulling desperately at the lid, saying something about stars. I try to grab him, but he cringes and holds his arms over his head.

"Julian!" I'm terrified Russell will be back any second. "We have to go *now*."

He blinks at me. Something seems to register. "Adam?"

"Yes."

"You can see me?"

"I can see you."

He nods and closes his eyes.

I lift him easily. I'd like to believe it's because of my fear-fueled adrenaline, but I suspect he really is this light.

We're on the street when he goes totally limp, and I'm pretty sure he's stopped breathing.

I jog through the automatic emergency-room doors, carrying him with the steady accusing thought that I'm doing this all wrong. His head is flopping around like a doll's—I should slow down, keep his neck stable, but he's so still, and his skin's ice-cold and clammy like a reptile's.

I stop for a minute, scan the empty white expanse of the room. Where are the crowds of crying, bleeding patients? Where are the screaming women clutching their bellies as they're wheeled off for labor? Where are the fucking doctors?

Through a small glass window on the opposite side of the ER, I spot a woman calmly typing at her computer. I start jogging again and call out, "A little help?" She clearly sees me—we're making eye contact—but her face has no expression. She stands—slowly—and turns away, exiting through a back door behind her glass partition. "Hey!" I spin around the empty room.

A minute later, a pair of double doors creak open, and the woman and a bearded guy slowly wheel a bed to us. Maybe their almost sedated calm is supposed to calm me, but it's having the opposite effect.

"He's really hurt," I tell them.

They take him from me and lay him down. I follow as they roll the bed through the double doors with the same casual indifference as they did when it was empty. As we walk, I try to answer their questions, but it's like I'm drunk. All my explanations are nonsensical and thick-tongued.

They push Julian into a tiny room where the lethargic lady wraps a blood pressure cuff around his skinny arm. When it beeps, she murmurs something to the bearded guy, and suddenly no one's casual anymore. Seeing them morph from bored to frenzied is terrifying.

A dozen hospital workers seem to appear out of nowhere and move in tandem, somehow never bumping into each other, speaking fast in a shorthand I don't understand. I flatten against the wall, trying to stay out of the way.

One woman plunges a needle into the top of Julian's hand and tapes it down while someone else attaches an oxygen mask to his face. A tall man in black scrubs rolls a giant square machine into the room, then quickly covers Julian's chest with round white stickers. Each circle has a silver nipple that he attaches to a wire that runs into his machine. Someone else takes the long dangling cord from the blood pressure cuff still attached to Julian's arm and connects him to a different machine. Another nurse tapes a white clothespin to his index finger; from the tip runs a long, thin wire.

In under five minutes he's efficiently tethered to a dozen machines by a hundred wires. He's a cyborg. A science experiment.

Abruptly, everyone parts for a young man in blue scrubs. He leans into Julian's face, peels back his eyelid with his thumb, and shines a light into one eye. Julian blinks, opens his mouth like he's going to speak, then passes out again.

The doctor addresses me while still looking at Julian. "What happened to him?"

My story's a little more coherent now: *A trunk. I found him in a trunk.* Then he asks for details I can't give. *I don't know how long he was inside. I don't know when he last ate or drank. I don't know how he got all the cuts and bruises.*

The man in black plucks the wires from Julian's chest, leaves the stickers on, and pronounces the EKG normal.

"What's that mean?"

"His heart," the doctor explains, "looks fine. But his blood pressure is too low."

I follow the cords running from Julian's arm to a black screen with rows of flashing green numbers.

A small woman rolls in a cartful of test tubes. I get squeamish as she takes vial after vial of blood from Julian's arm. Then she's off, adding five full tubes to her collection.

A new woman arrives with a plastic bag of fluid that she swiftly attaches to the silver coatrack by the bed. She runs a narrow plastic tube from the bag to the needle in Julian's hand.

Julian. Jesus. He's always been thin, but now he's emaciated, every rib grotesquely pronounced, his heart almost visible through his skin.

"He's going to be okay?" I murmur out loud.

"We'll know more when we get the blood work back." The doctor's expression doesn't fill me with much confidence. "I'd also like to run a CT scan and an MRI."

"A CT scan? Why—"

Before I can finish, a nurse takes me by the shoulder and asks if I could step into the hall. Just outside are three police officers with crackling walkie-talkies. One of them, massive and scowling, marches toward me.

FORTY-NINE

ADAM

"ARE YOU ACTUALLY a cop?" I ask.

He glares and flashes his badge.

"So you're not about to rip all your clothes off and start dancing?" Why I just asked that, I have no freakin clue. Maybe I'm having a mental breakdown. Officer Clark—according to the silver tag on his lapel—looks more like a stripper than a real police officer, or maybe his uniform just shrank in the wash. If he wasn't pissed before, he definitely is now.

He crowds me against the wall, snarling, "Shut up, and hand me your ID." I pull my license from my wallet, and he scrutinizes it carefully like it might contain clues, then passes it to another cop. "You're the one that found him?"

"Yeah."

"I need you to tell me exactly what happened."

My story makes more sense this time around, but it still doesn't make a lot of sense.

"You broke into his house?"

"Yes."

"Because you had a bad *feeling*?"

"Yes."

"And why did you have this bad *feeling*?"

I tell him that a few months ago Julian's uncle hit him, so yes, I had a bad *feeling*.

"You report that?"

"No."

There's no obvious censure in his face—it's the same exact glare he's had all along—but I feel the criticism anyway. I should have reported it. I know that.

Then he asks: "Where are his parents?"

"Dead."

"Any other family?"

"No."

There's something painfully bleak about saying that out loud. He has no family. None.

Then Clark starts asking me questions I don't know the answer to:

"Where does Russell work?"

"I don't know."

"Where is he now?"

"I don't know. I really need to go back in there—"

"No, you need to answer my questions."

I squeeze my head with both hands, resisting the compulsion to rip out my hair. "I don't *know*."

He frowns even more severely—something I didn't know was possible. "Wait here against the wall." He and the other officers huddle like a trio of football players, voices too low for me to catch.

I see Julian in my head, limbs twisted inside the trunk like he was pushed from the top of a skyscraper. The trunk was tipped over onto its side. The air holes were covered, but for how long?

What if I never thought to lift it? What if I never came at all?

One of the cops, this one a little younger and leaner, looks up from the huddle. "Did you take something tonight?" he asks me.

"What?"

He crowds in just like Clark did, looks deep into my eyes, and *sniffs* me. "Why are you tapping your foot like that?"

"I'm nervous! And I have ADHD."

"Lower your voice. Right now."

"I'm sorry. This has been an insanely stressful night, and I just want to see my friend."

His dark eyes go semi-sympathetic. "Wait one more minute."

Clark struts over and slaps my license into my palm. "We'll be back later to talk to the boy."

Awesome.

I head back into the little room just as Julian's being rolled out. A nurse says they're taking him to Radiology and it'll be a while.

I stand in the now-quiet room, staring dumbly at the empty spot where his bed was a second ago. My legs are shaking and I remember freshman year, the time I passed out running cross-country in August. I remember the pounding head, the sick shaking body, the way the sky seemed to merge into a thousand black dots.

My legs go rubbery-weak, and I find myself sliding against the wall to land on the floor. Up close, the tile's grimier than a hospital floor should be. I should tell someone about this.

I'm not sure how long I have to sit before I'm able to get back onto my feet and ask a nurse if I can use their phone. There's only one number I know by heart.

It didn't occur to me that after I hung up with Emerald, she'd call everyone we know. Julian would freakin hate it, but seeing my closest friends rush into the emergency-room lobby wearing pajamas or hastily-thrown-on, wrinkled clothes sends an unexpected burn to the back of my throat.

Emerald, Charlie, Allison, Jesse, Camila, and Matt stand in a semicircle around me with wide-worried eyes, and again I have to explain what happened. This time I get through it like a professional, calmly bullet-pointing all the pertinent facts.

They seem to take my pausing for a breath as the signal to start crying. Emerald and Allison tear up, and—Jesus—even Charlie's eyes become suspiciously watery before he turns around with a furious scowl. My cheeks stretch up into what I hope is a reassuring smile as I tell them really, everything's fine. They should go home and get some sleep. I'm met with stunned glares, and then, in almost synchronized fashion, they take deliberate seats. That esophageal burn magnifies while I spastically nod.

I tell them I'll be back as soon as I check on Julian, and I return a few minutes later knowing no more than I did before. My friends all have the sick and grieving look of mourners at a wake. Emerald's still quietly crying, her face red and blotchy as she sits on one of the gray vinyl-upholstered ER benches. Jesse's slumped over nearby, his earbuds notably missing, tapping a steady, solemn beat on a tabletop with his fingertips.

Camila and Matt are actually holding hands as they sit together on another bench. They're both wearing red plaid pajama pants and

T-shirts, and I wonder if this is a thing they do—dress alike when they're at home.

Charlie's on the other side of the giant room, turning around in circles like an angry dog. Allison's a pale shadow behind him. Everyone looks traumatized, while I move from person to person like the host at the world's most depressing slumber party. I kiss Emerald's hair and hug Jesse and stuff vending machine snacks into Charlie's fists, but I'm not sure if anything I'm doing actually helps.

At four in the morning I head back to Julian's room for the thousandth time, and the doctor tells me his results are ready.

Mostly normal. No brain trauma. No organ failure. But he's depleted, dehydrated, not breathing well on his own, and his blood pressure's still too low. He's being admitted into the hospital and moved to a room where he'll stay till he's stronger.

When I report this to my friends, it seems like one of those moments where we're all supposed to leap into the air with overjoyed relief. Instead, everyone just looks exhausted and depressed, like we're all depleted now.

Emerald takes my hand and pulls like she expects me to leave with my mobilizing friends.

"I'm staying," I tell her.

"You need to get some sleep."

"I can sleep here."

"Adam . . ." She looks like she wants to say something, but she just kisses me before she joins the others.

I watch while everyone disappears through the automatic doors.

Julian's new room is totally dark except for a panel of fluorescent lights behind his bed, making him look like a strange museum exhibit, every cut and bruise perfectly lit. His right index and ring fingers are wrapped in bandages. He's wearing an oxygen mask and is connected to just as many machines as before. He has an antiseptic smell, like maybe they washed him before dressing him in the hospital gown.

I get a sudden rush of apprehension. Russell must've gone home by now, must've seen Julian isn't in the trunk. What if he tries to find him? What if he comes here?

I jump when a round nurse touches my shoulder and says she'll be taking care of Julian till her shift ends at seven A.M.

"What happened to his fingers?" I whisper, even though he's shown no sign of stirring.

"They're broken." I must look as sick as I feel, because she adds, "He's not in any pain. The doctor gave him morphine." Overhead, there's a noise, like a couple of bars of music from a creepy ice-cream truck. "A new baby."

"What?"

"That little lullaby plays all over the hospital whenever a baby is born." She smiles like it's sweet, but there's something twisted about it to me. I mean, everyone, everywhere in this hospital can hear it, but why? So when you're dying you can contemplate your own mortality and the circle of life?

The nurse points to an orange-and-yellow-striped recliner in front of the window. "That'll pull out into a bed," she says. "I'll get you some covers."

"Thanks." It's freezing in here, like even colder than school, which can't be good for sick people.

Soon I'm under a thin blanket on the hard twin fold-out bed.

Lying in the same room like this reminds me of when Julian and I were younger, only now each of his inhales and exhales are mechanical and amplified like he's breathing through a microphone.

I'm exhausted, but too keyed up to sleep. When Julian lived with me, sometimes he had trouble sleeping. I remember one time, being almost asleep and hearing him whisper my name.

"Adam?"

"Yeah?" I said.

"Can you see me?"

There was just enough light filtering through the mini blinds in my room. "Yes, I can see you."

"I'm scared."

"What are you scared of?"

"I don't know."

"Try and go back to sleep."

"I can't. I'm too scared."

"Just think good thoughts. Mom used to tell me to do that when I was little."

"You used to get scared?"

"Sometimes."

"What did you think about?"

I rolled over and looked at him. A vertical stripe of light from the blinds fell right across his eyes like a mask. "Spider-Man."

He squinted at me skeptically. "You'd pretend Spider-Man was with you?"

"Well, no, I'd pretend I *was* Spider-Man."

"And that made you not scared?"

"Yeah, I guess so. I'd think about the movies, sort of playing them in my head. Then I'd just fall asleep."

"But Spider-Man is scary."

"No, he's not. He's awesome."

"I don't like that one guy with all those metal arms."

"Doc Ock? Yeah, I guess he is pretty scary. Okay, so don't think about that. Think about something you like."

"I don't know what I like."

"Yes, you do. Think."

"Elian Mariner?"

"Okay, so think of your favorite Elian Mariner book, and go through the whole thing in your head and don't let yourself think about anything else."

He squeezed his eyes shut.

"Are you doing it?"

He nodded.

"Where are you?"

"In Elian's ship. I'm flying."

Now the machine version of Julian's breath echoes in the room. The burn in my throat intensifies. Something hot and wet streaks down my cheeks. I'm crying, hard but without sound, into the stiff hospital blanket. I want to stop, but all I can picture is nine-year-old Julian's face when I gave him my brilliant piece of advice—fearful and doubtful, because he must've already known the truth. Superheroes aren't real, and even if they are, they come too late.

FIFTY

ADAM

I WAKE TO the sound of whimpering. A nurse built like a wrestler is jamming a needle into Julian's skinny arm. How could they possibly need more blood?

A quick glance at the digital clock on his bedside table reveals it's only seven thirty. I must've fallen asleep, though I'm not sure how. I'd always figured hospitals were quiet, restful places. Instead they're full of medical machinery going off like car alarms, nurses coming in and out every few minutes, and the pitiful screams of sick people in pain.

I stand, my back aching. "Hey, Julian, are you okay?" He doesn't open his eyes, but he whimpers again when the nurse retracts her needle and jabs it back in.

"Do you have to be so rough?" I ask her.

The lady gives me a dirty look. "He has small veins." She grabs his other arm, ties a rubbery rope around it, then slaps it with the back of her gloved hand. Again, she digs in the needle. A couple of tears escape his eyes, rolling toward his ears.

"Julian?"

He's still out of it—groggy with meds, I guess—but obviously he can feel what she's doing. It must be so scary to be in pain but too incapacitated to do anything about it.

I rest my palm on his forehead like I'm trying to take his temperature. "She's getting it," I tell him when I finally see his blood being sucked into the tube. After gathering five vials, she rolls her cart from the room. Julian's cheeks are still wet, but his mechanical breath evens out. I drop back onto my fold-out bed, which is only slightly softer than the floor, and glance around the room.

I guess I couldn't see it last night, but now that it's daylight, I realize this is the pediatrics ward. The main wall's covered in a mural of jungle and farm animals all living together in perfect harmony under an enormous rainbow. It's a motif more appropriate for a four-year-old than a fourteen-year-old, and the cheeriness of it just makes me sadder.

"Adam?"

Mom's standing in the doorway.

"What are you doing here?" I ask.

She doesn't answer, just stares at Julian in shock and horror. I can see him through her eyes. The skeletal limbs. The cuts. The wires.

"I always check in on you before I go to work." She's talking to me, but looking at him. "It was hard for me when you started driving and I wasn't taking you to school anymore. Hard not seeing you off in the mornings." Her lips quirk up. "When you weren't in your bed today, I got so worried. I know it's silly, but my first thought was you'd been kidnapped. I used to worry about that all the time when you were a little boy. We'd go in the grocery store and you'd shout hello from the cart and try to talk to everyone we passed. You had no concept of *stranger*. I was worried, and since I couldn't call you, I called Charlie."

When tears start streaking down her face, I pull her into a hug. "He's going to be okay," I say.

She straightens, suddenly fierce. "Yes. He will."

Julian drifts in and out all morning. A nurse gives him more painkillers through his IV whenever he cries, and I fidget in a metal chair near the bed.

I'm picking at the lunch tray sent from the cafeteria when a tall, broad lady with smooth dark skin breezes into the room. She's wearing a purple blazer with shoulder pads, a matching purple skirt, and a floral scarf that flutters around her neck. She looks like she escaped the set of an '80s sitcom about women in the workplace. Somehow she's both regal and ridiculous.

"Adam Blake?" she asks, thrusting out a manicured hand.

"Yes?" I shake it cautiously.

"I've been appointed as Julian's guardian."

FIFTY-ONE

ADAM

THE LADY HANDS me a business card as if this makes it more official, and there it is: DELORES CARTER, LICENSED CLINICAL SOCIAL WORKER. "His guardian ad litem," she adds. "I've been appointed by the court. In a situation like this, someone has to make decisions until a permanent guardian can be named." She looks around the room, zooming in on the blanket on the fold-out bed. "Are you here by yourself?"

"Yes."

"Where's your mother?"

"I'm eighteen." She sniffs, obviously not impressed. "Julian doesn't need a guardian. I just talked to my mom, and she's going to contact the judge. She used to be his foster mom, and I'm eighteen, so we can make decisions about—"

"Hold on, hold on, take a breath."

I do, preparing my rebuttal if she tries to kick me out.

"I haven't met Julian, but I have no intention of keeping him away from his friends. That wouldn't do him any good."

I mumble, "Thank you," then sit back down, feeling oddly weak. Delores finds another metal chair. "They used to do that." Her voice is gentle but filled with deep strength, like someone who's seen it all.

"Hmmm?" I'm trying to pay attention. I know I need to seem responsible in front of this lady, but I'm jittery and tired.

"They kept people out. Banned fathers from delivery rooms, family from hospital rooms. They don't do that so much anymore."

"Why not?"

"Because people heal a whole lot faster when they're with someone who loves them."

My eyes start to water, and I feel a brief twinge of panic. Jesus, am I about to—? Yes, I'm crying again. And this time a woman I've just met is pressing my face into one of her purple padded shoulders.

I don't pull away.

Around five, Emerald arrives carrying a jade planter with a tall exotic flower I don't recognize. She looks perfect, of course, her hair twisted and coiled like she just stopped by on her way to prom.

She halts at the sight of Julian exactly the way my mom did this morning, staring at him without moving or speaking. I pry the plant from her trembling hands and set it on the dresser in the corner. I nod toward the hallway and she follows me. Out here is another mural, this one of an elaborate underwater sea party with smiling mermaids, sharks, dolphins, and fish.

"I didn't think he would look like that," she whispers. I nod. She doesn't have to explain what she means. "Matt drove me. He's with Camila downstairs. They wanted to come up, but they didn't know if it was okay."

I cross my arms and lean against the wall, next to the happiest octopus I've ever seen. "It's not. Not yet."

"You look tired," she says. "You should probably get some sleep."

"Yeah, I'll get right on that."

She flinches, her blue eyes looking confused and hurt, but I don't apologize. Her hair is perfect, and something about that bothers me.

"Adam . . ."

"I should get back inside."

She squeezes my hand. I don't squeeze back.

FIFTY-TWO

ADAM

THE SECOND DAY in the hospital passes a lot like the first. Julian sleeps. I pace, sit, and eat crappy companion meals sent from the cafeteria. There are long stretches of nothing, interrupted by visits from Delores and Mom, plus friends who venture no farther than the hall. Now the room's scattered with flowers, floating balloons, and stuffed animals.

I'm sitting in the metal chair by Julian's bed when he wakes up so suddenly, I jump. He claws the air, then tries to yank the tubes from his nose.

"No, leave them," I say, pulling down his hands.

He goes still and blinks like he's awoken from a nightmare. "Adam?" This is the first time I've heard him speak since I carried him into the hospital . . . was that only a day and a half ago?

"Yeah?" I hold him till I'm sure he's done flailing, and I hook my foot into my chair to drag it forward. "Are you okay?"

It's a stupid question. The bones in his wrists are grotesque knobs.

Liquid sugar runs through a bag and down a tube into his hand, spreading out into his veins. Machines pump oxygen into his lungs and measure his pulse and blood pressure.

Instead of answering, he whispers, "Is school out?" His tone's dull, voice scratchy like he has a throat infection.

"I don't know. I didn't go today." I glance over at the clock.

"For . . ." He looks down at the round white stickers pasted to his chest, then fiddles with the tubes at his nose. I'm about to tell him to stop when his arm thuds to his side like it's too heavy to lift. "For the summer."

"For the summer? No . . . we still have a couple weeks left."

He looks so confused and alarmed that I expect the heart rate monitors to start beeping wildly like they do in movies. "It's next year?"

I don't understand what he means. It's nonsense, like leaving the trunk open for the stars. "Next year?"

"I missed next year. I missed summer."

"No. It's still this year. We haven't had summer break yet."

He sinks a little and closes his eyes. "That's good. I always miss it." Then his eyes spring back open, looking wild and panicked again, while mine flit to the monitors. "But I must have. I was there for so long. I counted. But I couldn't count anymore. I was in a shell, then the shell disappeared and I didn't know where I was. I knew you'd be gone. Everyone would be gone."

"Inside a . . . ? You were in a trunk, Julian."

"A shell. I was all alone in a shell."

My fear and worry are ramping up and I think about getting a nurse, but I can't leave him. I don't want to upset him by getting upset myself, so I try to keep my voice calm. "It was a trunk."

He shakes his head, but it looks like he's working in slow motion. "You . . . sure?"

"I'm sure."

"How long?"

"I don't know. When I found you, it was nineteen days after you checked out of school."

His eyes close. His eyelids look pink and translucent. "Adam?" I lean in closer to show I'm still here, still listening. "It didn't . . . feel like nineteen days. It was like a thousand years . . . longer than my whole life before it. Why?"

I have to hold my face rigid, because it's happening again. The burning throat and the urge to cry. I went years without crying, but now it's like I can't stop. In spite of my decision to be calm and soothing, I have to blink and brush away tears, but then more stupid tears just refill my eyes like a faucet I can't turn off. I drag in a breath and try to answer his question.

"It must've felt like forever."

"But why?"

"Because it was so awful."

"But why can't good things feel like forever? It was all so fast . . . before they left. I want to spin it back . . . slow it down. Why is time like that? Why does it slow down in the places you don't want it to, but it speeds away when you're happy?"

I wipe my face again. "I don't know."

He gazes toward the window even though the curtains are drawn and there's nothing to see. Then his head drops in the jerky movements of a robot powering down.

FIFTY-THREE

ADAM

THE NEXT TIME Julian wakes up, my mom and Delores are both there. Delores is good with him, all things considered, trying to get him to eat something without being pushy about it. But he stays on edge till they stop talking to him altogether, then he aims his attention at the blank television screen.

"You want to watch something?" I ask, grabbing the remote control/nurse call attached to his bed. He doesn't say no, so I click it on and flip through the channels. He nods when I land on the Disney Channel. Some sitcom I haven't seen in years about a teenage girl with magic powers.

He's watching with absorbed concentration when Officer Clark and his friends fill the doorway. "We're here to speak with Julian Harlow."

Delores stands, looking tall and formidable in her bright pink power suit. She presses a business card into Clark's palm and tells him firmly that she won't be going anywhere. He looks impressed.

"All right," he says. "Everyone but the guardian, out."

Julian shrinks into his bed with wild-wide eyes.

Delores grows six inches taller. "He'll be more comfortable if they are allowed to stay," she tells him.

She and Clark argue for a while, then he points a finger at me. "You can stay as long as you're quiet and out of my way. Against that wall." Clark loves making me stand against walls. Mom looks irritated on my behalf but doesn't say anything.

"Son," Clark says to Julian, "I need you to tell us exactly what happened."

Julian looks small in his hospital gown, surrounded by cops who don't even bother to sit. I can see the impatience on Clark's face when, instead of answering, Julian starts to pick at the tape on one of his broken fingers.

"We have to know, so I'd appreciate it if you'd cooperate."

Julian gives a shaky nod, and for the first time he explains in quiet stutters about being locked inside the trunk. After a while I can't look at him, so I stare at the wall and focus on a smiling sheep.

When he stops talking, I feel sick.

"Do you know where your uncle is now?" Clark's tone is so unaffected, so compassionless, it pisses me off.

"Maybe at work? He works a lot."

"Your uncle hasn't worked in over a year," Clark snaps, as if he thinks Julian's lying.

I look away from the happy sheep to see Julian's eyes widen in confusion. "But he goes to work. He always—"

"If you know something," Clark says, "you need to tell me."

"But I don't know."

"Could you guys maybe give him a minute?" I say.

"Son . . ." Clark says *son* in the most condescending and grating way imaginable. "I'm gonna need you to wait outside."

Julian looks even more panicked now.

"He doesn't want me to go." I gesture to the obviously terrified kid.

"Are you refusing to leave this room?" The officer's deliberate tone sounds like a dare.

Delores stands as if she's going to intervene, but before she can, my mom steps in front of me.

Clark drops a hand to his holster. "Ma'am, I'm gonna need you to take two steps back." This has suddenly become a deadly serious game of Mother, May I.

"Yeah, because she's such a threat," I say. Furious, I cross my arms over my chest, and I almost want some sort of video to memorialize this moment when I'm completely not me anymore.

"If you don't stop talking"—Clark steps right into my face—"I'll arrest you."

"You can't do that," I sputter. "You can't arrest someone for talking."

He pulls his cuffs out with one hand and shakes them in the air. "I'll arrest you for interfering with a criminal investigation."

Mom disobeys the stay-two-steps-back order and grabs my arm. "Adam, just leave."

"Are you fucking kidding me?" I demand of Clark. "Look at him!"

Mom grabs my shirt. "Adam, go." And that pisses me off too. Where's the person who'd take on anyone? Julian's pale and shivering in his bed, and Clark actually smiles at me. I open my mouth, but Delores quickly shakes her head.

"I'll be right outside, Julian," I say. Seething, I go.

FIFTY-FOUR

JULIAN

WHEN I WAKE up, I find Adam asleep in the chair next to me, his mouth hanging open and a physics book across his lap. A tall nurse cheerfully greets me as she comes in, and she startles him awake. He rubs his face, somehow managing to knock his book, notebook, and pencil to the floor.

"I hear you're ready to take a shower," the nurse tells me with a proud smile, holding a pink plastic tub of supplies: a fresh gown, tiny shampoo, and body wash.

"Yes." I need to shower. I smell bad, like the trunk.

While the nurse unhooks me from the IV, she and Adam continue a conversation about her son that they must have started while I was asleep. She leaves the needle in my hand, wrapping it in plastic and gives me a warning not to get it wet. Then she reaches down and unties the first string on my gown.

"What are you doing?" I shrink back. She looks shocked, as if she has no idea what the problem is. "I can do it."

I'm blushing, but it's only one of a hundred embarrassing things that have happened while I've been here. They ask personal questions, touch you in personal places, and they don't care who is in the room to see it.

"I can help him," Adam offers.

"Don't let him fall."

"I won't."

For the first couple of days I had a catheter. Then I used a plastic bucket before graduating to walking to the toilet, but even that was closely monitored.

As soon as the nurse leaves, I shift my legs over the side of the bed. "I can walk," I tell Adam.

"I know." But he still stands right beside me until I enter the bathroom and shut the door. I'm a little shaky and I have to hold on to the silver bar attached to the wall while I pull at my hospital gown. It reminds me of my old karate top, the same folds and hidden strings to tie it all together. Karate was another thing I gave up when it became too hard. Now everything seems too hard. Untying strings. Breathing. Thinking.

The lightbulb flickers over my head with a staticky buzz. It sounds like it's about to blow out. My breathing starts to get heavy, but I'm not sure if it's from exertion or fear. I want to leave this tiny room, but I still need to shower. *You stink,* I can hear Russell say.

No one knows where Russell is. The police believe he's hiding, but I can't imagine Russell hiding from anyone. Wherever he is, he must be angry. I left the trunk.

I pull back the shower curtain. There's no ledge to step over or any sort of barrier, and I wonder what keeps the room from flooding. I step inside and stand near the bench attached to the wall. When I close the curtain, the light flickers again, and suddenly the space shrinks to nothing.

My pulse in my ears. My sweat in my nose. I can't breathe.

I tear at the curtain.

I fumble at the doorknob. Locked.

I start scratching, crying out in pain when I bump my broken fingers. I yank the door open, and fall out.

"What is it?" Adam asks, rushing to my side. "Are you okay?" My knees buckle, eyes looking up for something, for stars. He grabs my arm, steadying me. "What happened?"

"I don't know."

He nods as if this is an explanation. Still holding on to me, he gives me a towel. "You want to get back in bed? You don't have to do this now."

"I have to get clean."

"Would it help to leave the door open?"

"I don't know."

This time Adam walks inside with me and leans against the wall. "Just shower. I'll wait here."

I step back into the stall. I close the curtain. "Adam?"

"Still here."

I turn on the water. It's not ice-rain cold, but it doesn't get hot either. I wash quickly, starting to feel sick and dizzy. I hold on to the metal bar as my knees shake. I remember riding my bike. I was so fast. I could ride forever. Will I ever be strong again?

I wrap the thin towel around my waist before getting out. Adam gives me a clean hospital gown, but I want to put on real clothes. I lean on him all the way to the bed, then he hands me underwear and pajama pants.

He presses the call button to tell the nurse I'm out of the shower so she can reattach my IV and blood pressure and pulse monitors. Tears sting my eyes. I didn't want him to call her. I just want a few more minutes of being unplugged like a real person who can go anywhere. I want my body to be mine again.

FIFTY—FIVE

ADAM

I'VE LOST TRACK of how long I've been in this room. I left for a little while. . . . Was that only yesterday? Julian had nodded off, so I jogged down the hall to grab a pudding from the mini fridge in the visitors' kitchenette. I was on my way back when I heard him crying because he'd woken up alone. I haven't left the room since.

The cops still don't know where Russell is, which gives me that unsettled, deer-in-the-woods foreboding.

Julian isn't eating, in spite of the nurse scolding him last night like a pushy grandmother. Under her stern glare, he shrank back into his bed and mumbled, "My stomach hurts."

"You have to eat," she insisted. "We've got to get you back up to fighting weight."

He relented and drank another protein shake, but he wouldn't touch solid food.

It's past midnight now, and he's asleep, but the TV's on. I tried muting it sometime—yesterday?—but he woke up panicked, said it was too quiet. So it stays on all the time, tuned to Nickelodeon or the Disney Channel or some other network meant for kids.

I'm lying on the fold-out bed by the window, scanning all my texts on the new phone Mom brought me a few hours ago. She's convinced that Julian and I could've both died the other night and it would've been her fault since she didn't replace the phone immediately.

There're a million messages—mostly from Emerald and Charlie—but there are also a bunch from people who never text me. I don't know if they're genuinely concerned or just curious. Deciding not to respond to any of them, I turn off the phone. I pull the thin blanket up, close my eyes, and try to sleep under the extreme bright colors, high-pitched kid voices, and studio-audience laughter.

I wake up inside the refrigerator box. It looks exactly like I remember, only smaller—or maybe I'm bigger. Darren's glossy photos of insects cover every surface. Their prehistoric-looking bodies are grotesque, but they're sad too. Hard evidence of all the time he spends alone in here.

A picture of an enormous copper-backed beetle catches my attention. It has long antennas, black leathery wings, shiny black legs with a dozen joints in each one. I'm looking right at it when a single antenna twitches.

I jump back, hitting my head against the wall behind me, but the cardboard doesn't give. It's cold and immobile like polished steel. Breathing hard, I squint at the photo. It's just a picture—not real. But as I'm watching, both antennas straighten as if it can sense me. All at once a thousand black shiny eyes blink, and the box fills with noise.

Buzzing, chirping, grinding.

There are millions of them. Flying through the air. Crawling down the walls. They fill the box. They cover my skin.

Adam.

I kick and punch the walls, but they're made of metal. I scream, but no one hears me.

Adam.

I can't get out.

"Adam!"

I'm half-sitting, half-lying on the fold-out bed in the hospital room. No bugs, no noise except the chirping sounds of Julian's machines. I sit up, still disoriented and afraid. Julian's watching me, the television projecting light across his face.

"You were having a nightmare," he says. "Are you okay?"

I'm not. I'm still scared, and the room's too small. "Yeah. Sorry. Didn't mean to wake you up."

"What were you dreaming about?"

I kick the blanket off, feeling hot even though it's always freezing in here, and I stand up. "Prom. I had three dates, but they didn't know about each other."

Julian laughs softly, recognizing the plot of about five different Nick at Nite episodes we've seen this week.

"They found out about each other, of course, and then they all teamed up to plan some seriously scary revenge scenarios."

He laughs again, looking like a little kid under his mountain of blankets.

I glance at the clock. "It's late. You should go back to sleep."

He nods agreeably, but waits till I'm on the fold-out bed and I've pulled the blanket up to my chin before he closes his eyes.

FIFTY-SIX

ADAM

JULIAN'S WATCHING SOME god-awful show about two twin brothers who run a hotel, and I'm making a halfhearted attempt to finish my Calculus homework, when Charlie peeks his head in the room.

"Can I come in?" he asks.

"Hey, man," I say. I look over at Julian, who nods. "Yeah, come in."

Charlie glances around at the flowers and balloons, looking huge and out of place in this room with all its happy animals. "I didn't bring anything."

"That's okay," I tell him.

He stands there looking totally awkward till I kick a chair in his direction. The three of us watch TV without talking for a few minutes, then a nurse pops in and announces it's time for another test. She transfers Julian to a wheelchair and rolls him away.

Still looking at the TV, Charlie mumbles, "He's pretty beat up."

"You should've seen him last week."

"Yeah." He looks guilty. "I wanted to. I just didn't know if . . . I wasn't sure if—"

"It's fine, Charlie."

Another long stretch of nothing but those annoying, screeching twins till he says, with the tone of someone confessing a mortal sin, "I used to be jealous of him."

"I know."

"I mean really jealous." Guilty eyes study his hands. "I don't know why, but it was like I-wanted-to-punch-him-in-the-face kind of jealous."

"But you didn't. You'd never actually hurt anyone." He's still looking down when the ice-cream truck lullaby plays overhead. "Another baby."

"What?"

"The song. It means a baby's been born."

"That . . ." He smiles weakly. ". . . would be my brother."

A couple hours later, Mom stays with Julian while I leave the hospital room for the first time in days. Stretching my legs feels so amazing that I practically jog out of the colorful pediatrics ward to the colder white of the rest of the hospital.

I find Charlie in a half-lit hallway holding a tiny creature wrapped in yellow. His hands are bigger than the entire length of the baby. He smiles at me—not a smirk, but a real smile. No one else is around, so I guess his dad went home with his nine million other kids.

"Is that Shiv?" I ask.

He shakes his head. "I talked my mom out of it."

"What'd you go with?"

"Elian."

"Elian?"

"Yeah, like those books. I used to love them when we were kids."

"Me too."

Charlie looks down into the tiny face. "He's pretty cute, huh?"

He is. I mean, he looks like a hairless Shar-Pei puppy, but he's a brand-new human with brand-new eyes, and . . . Jesus, it's happening again. The burn in my throat, the pressure in my chest.

"Adam?" Of course, Charlie looks panicked. He probably thinks I'm dying. I wipe at the tears streaming down my face, but since there's an endless supply, more come. I wonder if this is what having a nervous breakdown is.

Charlie stands and places the baby in a little rolling crib, then he raises his arms like Frankenstein's monster, or if he were someone else, like he's about to hug someone. But if Charlie Taylor actually hugged me, it would mean the End of Days. His monster arms get closer.

It's the End of Days.

FIFTY-SEVEN

ADAM

MOM IS WATCHING Julian, while Julian watches TV, when Emerald stops by with a paper sack. "Your assignments," she says with a strained smile. I walk her into the hall, and we stand in front of the under-the-sea party.

"I texted you," she says.

"Yeah, I'm sorry."

"I know it's been stressful around here."

"Yeah." There's tension and a strange disconnect between us, like we're not the same people we were a week ago. "Well, thanks for bringing these."

"Adam?" Her face is pale. Her blue eyes are wide, and I notice her hair is loose and falling around her shoulders. "Never mind," she says, turning away abruptly. "It's nothing."

It's not till later, when Julian's asleep, that my mom asks, "Are you and Emerald okay?"

"Yeah. Why?"

"You're acting strange. Like you're mad at her."

I sigh deeply, because seriously, there are bigger things to worry about. "And why would I be mad at Emerald?"

She doesn't answer, just looks at me, and I wish for once people would say what they're thinking. Or just tell the truth. If I'd just told the truth . . . but I didn't. I listened to Emerald.

Logically, I know it's not her fault, but I have this nagging thought that if I'd taken him to my house, I would have called the police. And if I'd called the police, all the things that followed never would have happened. But that's the kind of horrible thought you can think, but you can never say out loud.

FIFTY-EIGHT

ADAM

"YOU HAVE TO go back to school." It's Sunday night and Delores is telling me off next to a tap-dancing lobster outside Julian's room.

"I can't." She knows how panicked he gets when I'm gone.

"You've missed over a week. How's it going to look to a judge if the woman who wants custody of Julian has a son up next on his docket for truancy?"

It would be worse than truancy. My finals are this week, and if I don't take them, I don't graduate. "Why can't they just let Julian leave already?"

"He'll be released when he starts eating."

"He *is* eating . . . a little."

"Yes, I've heard. Protein shakes, but not *food*. He can't keep going on like that."

I know I should've been pushing him to eat, but I also know from eating the companion lunches that the food here tastes like microwaved shit. If you're already having trouble with your appetite, those won't spark it.

"What'll he do all day? He can't be alone. He has to—"

"He won't be alone. There's a teen-counseling program downstairs. Could be good for him."

"God, he'll hate that."

"But he won't be alone."

Later, after everyone leaves and it's just Julian and me, I say, "You've gotta start eating."

He looks startled and a little defensive. "But I'm not hungry."

"They won't let you leave till you eat."

"Could you . . ."

"What?"

"Just throw it away? Pretend I ate it?"

"No."

His shoulders sag, defeated. "I'm not hungry," he says again, eyeing the waxy chicken, limp green beans, and hard dinner roll.

"At least try the pudding, huh? I got these from the fridge down the hall. We've got chocolate and vanilla." I wave one in each hand. "Which kind do you want?"

He shakes his head, disgusted. "Neither."

"Vanilla it is." I tear away the plastic lid and plunge in the spoon.

He crosses his thin arms over his chest with the same sulky expression he used to pull when we were in elementary school and I'd force him to read. If these weren't such horrible circumstances, I'd laugh.

"You're eating this, Julian."

He tilts his head to the side like a confused puppy and sinks back against his pillow.

He takes a small bite, then shudders, and for a second I think he's going to throw up. Then he takes another.

"Keep eating and you'll get out soon. You wanna leave, right?"

He hesitates, just a little too long. "Right."

FIFTY-NINE

JULIAN

I'M NOT ALLOWED to walk long distances yet, so Adam pushes me in a wheelchair while Delores strides alongside us. The bright, busy hallway is overwhelming, and I'm still nauseous from the breakfast he made me eat.

When Delores arrived this morning, she told me she wanted me to join a *special group of teenagers*. Ones who were originally confined to the psychiatric ward on the sixth floor but have graduated to the outpatient program. Adam didn't look shocked at all that Delores wanted me to spend the day with mental patients.

The two of them talk cheerfully above my head as we take the elevator down to the first floor. Adam pushes me through a maze of hallways, then into a large white room with a long row of windows where the sun hurts my eyes.

At the far end of the room there are about twenty plastic chairs in a circle, and half are filled with older kids. I'm the only person not dressed in real clothes, the only one wearing pajama pants and hospital-issue treaded socks.

A girl with a shaved head immediately zeroes in on me and aims sympathetic eyes at my hospital bracelet and wheelchair. Two boys, one with more piercings than skin, begin to argue, then they stand and yell into each other's faces. The other teens try to calm them down while a woman in a white coat wedges herself between them.

"I don't want to stay here," I whisper.

"You'll be just fine," Delores says.

Adam wheels me across the long room, right into the circle.

"You're new," the bald girl says.

"No," I answer quickly. "I'm not staying." I can't breathe. *"Adam."*

He reverses me so fast I get dizzy, and then I'm flying to the other end of the room. He stops behind a bookcase full of art supplies.

Delores bends down. "Take a deep breath with me," she says, inhaling loud and deep. "Lower. Not from your chest, from your diaphragm."

"I can't. It hurts."

She taps my chest. "These are short, panicked breaths. Try to go lower."

"I don't need to breathe. I need to leave!"

"Julian." Her voice is stern. "Adam has to go to school today, and you're going to stay here."

"I *can't.*" There's not enough air. "It's too dark."

"Delores, come on," Adam says. "I can stay with him one more day." He crouches in front of me and wipes my wet face with his sleeve.

She tugs him up, then leans into his ear. The only full sentence I can hear is, "Let's not drag this out."

He nods solemnly. "This'll be fun!" His voice is suddenly loud and filled with false cheer. He grabs a container of Play-Doh off the shelf, holding it up like it's evidence. "You like art."

"I don't like art."

"But you said—"

"It wasn't true. I don't."

"Well . . . you like writing stories. You've got a roomful of crazy people over there. You're gonna have so many great stories for me later."

"Adam!" I can't tell if Delores is playfully scolding or not. "In all seriousness, Julian, everything here will be confidential."

Confidential. I hate that word.

She gives Adam a brusque nod.

His face is overly bright. "All right, let's do this." He pushes me back into the circle. "I'll be here as soon as school's out," he promises, then he kicks the wheelchair brake into place so I don't roll away.

ADAM

The cafeteria's like it always was—warm and dangerously crowded—but for some reason the noise irritates me. Exhausted, and fueled on hospital coffee that's making me edgy, I squeeze into our table between Jesse and Matt, across from Charlie and Allison. A few people I didn't see this morning hug me and ask about Julian.

"He's fine," I answer, not in the mood to get into it.

I can't stop my foot from tapping, but so far no one's told me to settle down. I'm half-listening to conversations, half-thinking about what about what happened when I got to Dr. Whitlock's last period. She and Principal Pearce were both there, standing shoulder to shoulder. He was holding on to his cane, looking particularly fierce, as Dr. Whitlock asked:

Did you know?

Did I know what was happening? Did I know and not tell her? I looked back and forth between them, then admitted, *Yes. I knew.* Her eyes went a scary sort of livid. *You should have told me.* *I'm sorry,* I said, throat convulsing and eyes suddenly blurry. She turned away and shut her office door.

"You're not eating," Matt says. It takes me a minute to realize he's talking to me.

"I guess that means I'm not hungry." His eyes widen in surprise, because I did kind of snap at him, but I'm too annoyed to apologize.

"HOLY SHIT!" Jesse's loud voice grabs the attention of the entire table. "Somebody write this down. May twenty-sixth. Adam Blake is in a bad mood."

Charlie shakes his head, shooting secretive glances from Jesse to Emerald to me. Looking abashed now, Jesse aims apologetic eyes back at them. It's like they've all developed some kind of Morse code out of blinks and head shakes.

I look up and realize *everyone* is staring at me like I'm a mental patient around whom they need to lightly tread. My arms and legs start to itch like crazy. It's gotta be the caffeine, but I can't just sit here anymore. I don't bother saying anything. I just go.

All day is like this: a pointless biding of time until each class ends. I feel this growing buzzing tension, too many thoughts crowding my head, and I wonder if this is how Julian feels all the time. And if he does, how does he even freakin function? How does he walk down the hall without it leeching out? It seems like there should be an obvious wound branded across your forehead when you feel like this.

I'm heading to seventh period when I stumble over some invisible obstacle, right into a guy I sort of recognize. He's not in my grade—a junior, maybe—but he's taller and wider than me and he's got a sharp jaw and mouth that make him look part-velociraptor.

"Watch it, asshole." He sneers like I intentionally tripped and fell into him.

"It was an accident, *asshole*."

Super fast, his hands are fisted in my shirt, and he propels me toward the wall. My hips smack against a water fountain—turning it on—but my back hits air so I end up awkwardly flailing. This immediately grabs the interest of the entire hallway. Bloodthirsty kids encircle us. Their excitement depresses me.

The guy is really glaring now, over-the-top-WWE-style. He keeps me pinned to the fountain, every sharp tooth showing, but not saying anything.

"So are you gonna hit me, or can I go?"

My question seems to catch him off guard, and he unfolds his fingers from my collar.

I straighten. The back of my hoodie is wet, soaked through to my skin. I can feel the disappointment of the crowd when he steps back just enough to let me pass.

You got in a fight??

Sometimes it's difficult to interpret tone from a text message, but with Charlie you can always assume he's yelling.

It wasn't a fight, I text back while walking down the colorful pediatrics hall.

WTF happened??

He's either worried or he's impressed. I don't care which at the moment, so I stuff my phone back into my pocket.

I find Julian sitting in the chair in front of the window in his room, writing in a spiral notebook. Delores sits next to him, wearing a bright yellow dress and an orange hat like an advertisement for springtime. She says hello to me, then pats Julian's back and tells him she has to run.

"So how was it?" I ask, dropping into a metal chair.

"Do I have to go back?"

"Was it that bad?"

"Yes."

"Why?"

"They make us say things."

"Like what?"

"Like things about ourselves. All the good things we can name about ourselves. We had to write them down, then read it out loud."

That does sound like Julian's own personal brand of hell. "So what'd you write?" I reach for his spiral, but he pulls it away.

"It's confidential," he says, and I think he's actually being a smart-ass. Funny.

"Just a couple more days. Then you can get out of here."

"Does Russell . . ."

My smile wobbles. "Does Russell what?"

"Do you think he still wants me to live with him?"

"It wouldn't matter if he did. You're not going back there." Instead of relieved, he looks like he's going to throw up. "Do you *want* to live with Russell?"

He shakes his head.

"Then what?" I'm constantly confused these days, like an English speaker air-dropped into Russia.

"I don't have anywhere else to go."

Julian's smart, but in some ways he's so staggeringly clueless.

"You're coming home with me." I thought that was obvious. "My mom's been working on getting permission to be your guardian since you got here."

"She is? But . . ."

"What?"

"Well, before . . ."

"Before what?"

He shakes his head, leaving me frustrated and baffled. "Last time."

"Last time *what*?"

"I . . . I know I caused problems. And you and Catherine couldn't handle it anymore. I know."

"Who said you caused problems?"

He doesn't answer.

"Russell?"

He shrugs, then nods.

"Jesus, Julian. He was *lying*. It wasn't our choice for you to go. That was him. Do you know how freakin devastated my mom was when he wouldn't let us see you?"

Julian looks doubtful, and it pisses me off.

"Hey!" I say sharply, and he flinches. "I don't lie to you." Julian's eyes are like saucers, shocked and a little wary. I'm still frustrated, but it's dwindling, or maybe it's splitting. Locking onto Russell. Onto Emerald. Onto me. "I don't lie."

SIXTY

JULIAN

SITTING IN A circle in the room with too many windows, I wait for the day to begin. As I watch the other kids talking and hugging, it reminds me of the concert I went to with Adam last fall, when I saw the intimacy of his friends. All these kids were once confined together, and they all love and hate each other like family.

Annie, the girl with round red cheeks and no hair, takes the empty seat next to me and asks without warning, "Who put you in the wheelchair?"

Over the past couple of days, she's the only person who's tried to talk to me other than the staff. While the other kids have a hard, almost-scary toughness about them, she's soft and sweet. Like Shirley Temple, if Shirley was a teenager who fell on hard times.

"N-no one," I say. "I'm just . . . weak. Because I haven't been eating." I can tell she doesn't believe me, and I know what I must look like with all the cuts, bruises, and broken fingers. It's humiliating.

When the counselor, a woman with short spiky brown hair and a white coat, takes her seat, we start as usual by setting goals, then *checking in.* I hate it. It's worse than school, where the teachers actually prefer it if you never speak.

After an hour of this we're allowed to write in our journals. I use my hands to spin the wheels of my chair, propelling myself into a corner of the room.

At lunchtime, trays of food are delivered from the kitchen. Mine is the only one with a name taped to the lid, since I have a special diet of bland foods. I study the baked chicken, brown rice, sliced carrots, and yogurt. I can't imagine eating anything, but I know Adam will ask, and I don't think I'll be able to lie.

I open the container of plain yogurt, taking a cautious bite. It has a strange texture, not quite solid, not quite liquid. It's like . . . tooth-paste. I gag and spit into my napkin.

Back inside the circle, I fiddle with the hem of my T-shirt. My pajama pants are long, but when I cross my legs I can see dark hair sprouting on my shins. It looks strange. I'm wearing hospital socks and I want to wear shoes like everyone else, but my sneakers are still somewhere inside Russell's house.

The woman who's running group pulls a question from a plastic box. *What would you like to change about your lives?* No one wants to answer first, so we go in order around the circle.

The group leader pulls out another question. *If you could confront someone who has harmed you, what would you say?* Around the circle again.

When she stops at me, I shake my head. She looks unsatisfied, but turns to the boy with all the piercings. He tells us again why he hates his mother and why he still thinks she deserves to die.

Annie is next, and she says in her soft, small voice that she'd confront her stepbrother Chris. She tells us that she and Chris always fought, and sometimes it got physical. One day, she was so frightened she ran and hid beneath the car in their neighbor's driveway. Chris found her and took hold of her ankles to drag her out. She reached up to stop him, not realizing that beneath the car, the engine was still hot.

Annie lifts her arm to show us the long shiny burn. She tells us about the pain, how much it shocked her, how she cried and told Chris that she was hurt, but he didn't care. He crouched down, reached under the car, and dragged her out by her hair.

Annie looks away from us, ashamed. I imagine her stepbrother, someone bigger, stronger. Then I imagine her, burned and afraid. "The things that went on in our house," Annie says, "you wouldn't believe. I feel sorry for him really. I was the stupid one who . . ." She goes on, insulting herself, pitying him, explaining away everything he did as if it's okay for him to hurt her.

It's not.

SIXTY-ONE

ADAM

IT'S OFFICIAL—MY MOM'S been granted temporary custody of Julian. Delores comes into the room to say her good-byes, and then I follow her out into the hall. She gives me a strong hug. "I'm going to miss you, Adam, you know that?"

"I'll miss you too."

"I know as soon as you all get out of here, you won't want to think back on any of this, but if you ever do, you come see me."

"I will." I hug her again. "Delores, before you go—has there been any word on Russell?"

"No." She sighs. "The police did their interviews. They know he was fired last year after some incident with a woman at work, but no one there seems to know anything about him."

"It's so weird that he wasn't working. Julian said he was always gone on business."

"The last job he had that required any sort of travel was four years ago. He was fired from that one too."

"How was he paying for everything?"

"Julian was paying."

"What do you mean?"

"Julian's parents both had life insurance policies that went to him. The money was supposed to be used to take care of him."

I think of Julian's ragged clothes and shoes and no cell phone, then Russell's suits and flashy car. "Bastard."

"Agreed," she says seriously. "Listen, Adam. It's best you hear this now. Russell's got a warrant out on him, but so far it's for a child abuse charge and nothing more. Do you get what I'm saying?"

"B-but," I sputter, "how is that possible? He tried to *kill* him." Delores nods slowly. "You think Russell's going to get away with it, don't you?"

"I don't know. You never can tell. Running off like that makes him look a lot guiltier, but the thing is, no one's really chasing him. Fortunately for Julian, Russell doesn't seem to know that."

SIXTY-TWO

JULIAN

WHAT KEEPS YOU trapped?

Group starts out like it always does, the other kids resisting and rolling their eyes as if it's an idiotic question.

I'm out of the wheelchair and sitting in an actual chair in the circle, wearing the brand-new sneakers Adam brought me today. They're bright red, and I can imagine myself running in them.

No one speaks, but there's a nervous strain in the air as if a live wire is snapping through the room. Kids are looking at the floor, at the ceiling, out the windows, at their hands. I squeeze my eyes shut, and I can feel it—pain—pouring out of everyone in the circle like smoke.

The counselor asks again: *What keeps you trapped? When you're done with this program and you go back to your lives, what can stop you? What keeps you from living the life you want? What keeps you from being free?*

And I see it all at once—all the things that have kept me trapped. Not just Russell, but me—my fears.

Afraid of talking.

Afraid of trying.

Afraid of wanting.

Afraid of dreaming.

Thinking about the people I've lost—and afraid of losing more.

The counselor pushes until a few kids mutter answers. They pretend not to care, but they do, and like me they already know the answer to her questions. Soon their responses are rapid-fire. Drugs pills parents teachers him her fear friends me me *me*.

The things I know stay in my head as I stand on my own two feet at the end of the day, and I walk back to my room with my journal to write my list of cages.

SIXTY-THREE

ADAM

"I NEED TO go back," Julian says. "Back to Russell's house."

We've been home from the hospital for less than an hour. His bruises have faded, but you can still make them out like smudges around his eye and mouth. His fingers are still bandaged and broken, and there are scars on his back that'll probably never disappear.

"Why?" I ask.

"There are some things I need."

"Did you look through everything?" Delores and the police went to the house a couple of days ago to box up the contents of his room.

"Not everything is there."

"If you need clothes, we can get clothes."

"It's not that. It's . . . everything that was in the trunk." Neither of us says anything for a minute, like we both need to recover from hearing that word.

As much as I don't like that douche bag Clark, I say, "Okay, but we need to call the police, get an escort or something." I'm not halfway through the sentence before he starts shaking his head.

"I can go by myself."

"That's not going to happen."

He takes a seat on the sofa, looking exhausted. I feel bad for him, because he's finally using his freakin words, but it seems like every time he does, the answer's no.

"Fine," I say. "No police, but we bring people with us." I interrupt his protest before he can start. "That's the only way. They can wait outside, okay? It'll just be safer."

"In case Russell comes?"

"Yeah."

"But you said it doesn't matter what he wants. That I'm not living with him either way."

"I know."

"So why?"

Because he tried to kill you! I want to shout. But sometimes it's like talking to a five-year-old, and there are certain things you can't tell a five-year-old.

"Can you just trust me on this?"

"I do trust you."

Julian stands on the front porch with his key, but he's making no move to actually insert it into the lock. Sometimes with Julian you have to push, but sometimes you have to wait.

I glance over my shoulder at Charlie, Jesse, and Matt. We've just finished our last day of high school—ever—and they should be out celebrating, so it says something that they're all here, leaning against my van like a row of bodyguards.

Julian takes a shaky breath, unlocks the door, and we walk inside.

I expected signs of an investigation, drawers yanked open, tables over-turned, but the house is just as insanely neat as I remember it. He tiptoes carefully down the hall like he's watching for land mines, then stops outside his bedroom door.

"Nothing's in there," I say, stepping in front of him. "It's already been cleaned out." I don't know if the trunk is still in the room or not, but I don't see what good it would do to look at that.

Julian nods, then turns around. On the opposite end of the house, he opens a door to the neatest garage I've ever seen. Everything's boxed in plastic containers and marked with typed labels. We search through the orderly rows but come up with nothing that looks like it belongs to Julian.

Julian starts shivering and breathing hard.

"You need to sit down?"

He shakes his head.

We go back inside, and again Julian pauses anxiously outside a door. This time when he opens it, it's obviously Russell's room. There's an antique four-poster bed in the center, so enormous I'm not sure how it fit through the door, and a matching dresser and chest of drawers.

There's something strange about the room I can't quite put my finger on. Then it hits me. It's *just* furniture. Like he moved in yester-day. Nice enough, but there's no indication that someone actually lives here. I pretend I'm not creeped out, but I am. No one knows where Russell is. What if . . . what if he's hiding *inside the house*?

"Jesus!" I jump at the sound of my cell. "It's okay," I tell a startled Julian. "Just Charlie." Then I say into my phone, "We're fine. Just a lot to look through."

"Sure you don't want us to come in?" Charlie asks.

"No, we're cool."

I end the call, then start yanking open drawers. Inside the dresser are neatly folded clothes. Julian hesitantly opens the closet while I peek under the bed. It's totally empty and dust-free, like maybe Russell actually crawls under here to clean.

I stand up and find Julian getting bolder and more panicky, digging through the closet. "It's not here!"

"Let's keep looking. We've got a whole other floor."

The guest room upstairs looks a lot like Russell's bedroom—nothing but furniture. I open the drawers, which are totally empty, and it makes me think of this *Twilight Zone* episode where a married couple gets stuck in a strange, empty town and it turns out everything—the trees, the houses, the animals—are just props in an alien child's train set.

When I hop up, I take one look at a too-pale Julian and tell him to sit down. He shakes his head. "Seriously," I say. "Do it before you pass out."

He sits on the bed while I pretend to look around, even though it's obvious there's nothing here. "I think he threw it away," Julian says bleakly.

I'm starting to believe the same thing. "Where else can we look?"

"His office."

"Think you can get up?"

"I never said I needed to sit down."

I jump when my phone rings again. I open it and snap, "Jesus, Charlie. We're fine."

"Making sure," he says.

Julian gets up, still too pale, but we head down the hall to Russell's office. I open the door, Julian right behind me, and stop short. "Holy shit."

SIXTY-FOUR

ADAM

I CATCH JULIAN'S expression—just as shocked as mine—then look back to the room. It's the office of a diagnosed hoarder, crammed so full it's hard to even walk inside.

I take a giant step over a crooked stack of boxes and look around. There are rows of glass-doored cabinets like the one downstairs, but instead of the contents artfully arranged like a store window, if you opened one, everything would probably fall out on top of you like in a cartoon. What's really weird is that none of the cabinets are against the wall. Instead they're staggered haphazardly around the room.

I dodge a teetering stack of books to get a closer look. One of the cabinets is full of ancient calculators—or maybe they're cash registers. Another's full of stick-figure sculptures twisted into weird metal poses. The walls are covered with more stuff—masks, coins, a huge white canvas with a thousand impaled butterflies. It makes me think of Emerald, all those butterflies she collects. But this man collects *everything*. Looking through all this could seriously take hours.

"I guess we should get started," I say.

Julian nods uncertainly and kneels to open a cardboard box.

The room's so crazy full that it takes me a while to even notice the desk against the wall. I yank open the top middle drawer—pretty typical office stuff except everything's in multiples, like five staplers and eight pairs of scissors. The next few drawers are filled with the same kind of junk.

I tug the bottom drawer on the left. Locked. I grab a letter opener—he has a collection of those too—and stab it while Julian prowls the room, pushing aside papers and boxes. The drawer slides open just as he gasps, "It's here!"

I look up to find Julian hugging a green spiral notebook to his chest, and I smile. I'm about to stand when I spot a folded red T-shirt with a picture of a cartoon dog on it—obviously a kid's shirt—in the open drawer.

"Is this yours too?" I ask. When I grab it, a sleek black object clatters to the floor—an external hard drive.

Julian squints at the little red shirt in my hand. "Yes. I remember that shirt. I haven't seen it in years, though."

Why would Russell have Julian's shirt locked in a drawer? And why would it be carefully folded around a hard drive? When Julian goes back to digging through his box, I stuff the drive into my pocket.

"Let's go."

I wait till we're back home to show Julian. I wasn't planning to show him at all, but without really thinking, I've asked, "Is this yours?"

"No."

"It was in Russell's office."

"You took it?"

"It was in your shirt." He looks puzzled, but not exactly concerned. "Do you care if I see what's on it?"

"It's not mine." Taking this as permission, I plug it into the desktop computer in the living room. A window full of files opens on the big screen—all of them videos. I click the cursor down and open the oldest one.

The screen fills with a small shaking boy standing with his back to the camera in Russell's living room. Russell enters the shot. Next to the boy, he's a giant. He's holding a long thin stick in his hand.

My stomach fills with acid.

Take off your shirt, Russell says.

The boy takes off his shirt, then grips his bare upper arm with one hand.

Turn around.

JULIAN

It's me. I'm smaller and younger, probably only nine or ten years old, but it's me. I see my face, twitching in fear before the switch falls. I see my eyes, filling with pain before they squeeze shut. I see what I look like when I cry. And for the first time I see what Russell looks like too, an expression I never saw when my back was turned.

"He *taped* them?" I whisper. "Why did he tape them?"

"Julian." Adam says my name, then says nothing more.

The boy starts to scream.

"So he could see it again?"

I feel Adam watching me as I watch myself.

"Is that why?"

The boy's screams get louder.

"Jesus." Adam's hands fumble to close out the screen. We're left with silence, and a white square containing a list of so many more files.

"Delete them."

"I can't," Adam says. "This is evidence. I can't just—"

"Please."

"We have to show this to the police." He ejects the hard drive.

"Give it to me."

"No." The firmness in his tone and the fact that he's holding something that holds all my secrets have my eyes watering.

"You can't show that to anyone." I imagine police, detectives, judges, everyone, seeing me cry, seeing me . . . I don't want them or anyone to look at me. "Some of the other videos will be worse."

"Worse how?"

"In some . . . I'm . . . I'm not wearing clothes."

"What do you mean you're not wearing clothes? What the fuck did he do to you?"

The humiliation is unbearable, as if he can see me from the inside out.

"Julian. What did he do?"

I shake my head. Push my fingers against my eyes. "The same," I finally answer. "The same as that . . . without my clothes. Please just delete them."

"I *can't*." Adam's voice breaks. "I won't show them to anyone, but I can't delete them. Not yet."

The screen is blank now, but I still see Russell's face and the way he looked when my back was turned. You don't really know people when your back is turned. "You want to look at them."

"Jesus, *no*." Adam grimaces like he's going to be sick. "I just want to do one thing that isn't stupid. Throwing it away would be stupid. I'm holding on to it, just in case."

"In case what?"

"In case he comes back."

SIXTY—FIVE

ADAM

"WHAT COLOR WOULD you like to paint your room?" Mom asks Julian. She's got that weird, overbright face on—the one that means she's pretending to be happy but she's really worried.

The guest room—now Julian's room—is insanely girly. White wicker furniture, pink and yellow daisies stenciled all over the place, and white straw hats nailed to the wall, as if that's any kind of decoration. To top it off, there are framed photos of Mittens, the Persian cat she used to have, *everywhere*.

Julian looks around the room. "I don't need to change the walls."

"Are you sure?" Mom asks.

"It's fine. I mean, nice. Thank you, Catherine."

"This is definitely not fine," I argue. "How are you gonna sneak a girl into your room if it looks like this?"

"Oh, Adam," Mom says, amused and scolding.

Julian just looks puzzled. "I won't sneak a girl into this room."

"Hopeless," I say. "We're painting."

☆ ☆ ☆

Around ten o'clock, Mom sits on the edge of the white wicker bed, actually tucking Julian in like he's five, but either it doesn't embarrass him, or he's too polite to protest. Even though it's not that late, I'm tired enough to go to bed myself. I shut my eyes, but I can't shut out the sounds in my head, the screams I heard earlier today, and I can't stop thinking about all the obvious and weird things I should've noticed before.

Like Julian being out sick all the time. And the fact that his uncle made him shave his legs. I figured the guy was some kind of germophobe, but now . . . was he trying to make Julian look more like a girl? Or a child? Both answers do weird things to my stomach.

God, I can't freakin sleep. What did I used to do when I couldn't sleep?

Think good thoughts.

I try, I really try.

SIXTY-SIX

ADAM

I WAS PROBABLY naïve to assume everything would be perfect once Julian got home from the hospital. That first night I almost stepped on him when I got out of bed—he'd used all his blankets and pillows to make a pallet on my floor—and he's done this every night since.

Days aren't any better. He follows me from room to room, trailing after me even if I'm just going to the kitchen or to use the toilet. It'd be okay that he has to be glued to my side, except he refuses to leave the house, like, at all. Which means I can't leave either. Maybe the house isn't as cramped as the hospital room, but by the end of a week, I can't take it. I need to go out. I need fresh air. I need five to seven minutes in the bathroom without someone standing right outside.

When Charlie shows up unannounced in the middle of the afternoon, I'm ready to hug him. "You want to go get something to eat?" he asks. "You too, Julian."

Looking wary, Julian doesn't answer.

"No, I think we're good here," I finally say.

Charlie shrugs, then holds up a couple of video games. Soon we're sitting on the floor in front of the TV, while Julian watches from the couch. When I ask him if he wants a turn, he answers, "We never had video games." Because if it didn't happen while they were alive, it never would.

For about a week, this is our ritual: Charlie coming over after work with games. Us playing. Julian watching. Till the day Charlie tells me my hyper-cricket-legs are driving him fucking crazy.

"Go for a run or something," he orders.

Julian sits up straight, obviously concerned. Charlie continues to obliviously click his controller.

"It's cool," I say. "I'm fine."

"You're not fine. You're annoying. When's the last time you left the house?" Charlie leans his whole body as he tries to get his car on course again, clicking furiously, but it falls over the edge of the cliff. "Fuck!" He starts to pass the controller to me, then yanks it back. "I'm playing again. Go. Get out. I'll babysit."

I glance over at Julian, who looks more worried than offended.

"We'll be fine. Right, Julian?" Charlie says.

Julian gives me a totally unconvincing nod, but leaving the house is so tempting that I pretend he means it. I pull on sweats and sneakers, tell them I won't be long, and then I'm out.

The sun feels amazing. God, I forgot how much I used to love running. I went for runs all the time before I got the van. I really need to force Julian to leave the house. It's not healthy staying inside all the time—you need the vitamin D. But without literally dragging him, it's probably not going to happen. For such a quiet kid, he can be seriously stubborn.

I turn a corner, running faster. My whole body feels lighter, my mind clearing enough to realize that no matter how much things suck right now, it's all temporary. I can see the big picture, the aerial view. Things will be like they were—better, even. I know it.

I run another few blocks, starting to sweat a little. I've been gone for at least an hour. Julian's probably freaking out.

I turn around and jog home.

When I arrive, out of breath and sweaty, I find Julian sitting on the floor beside Charlie, holding a controller in two hands while Charlie cheers him on.

SIXTY–SEVEN

ADAM

AT MIDNIGHT I find Mom in the living room watching *Family Feud* without much enthusiasm, not even bothering to yell at the contestants for being so stupid. When I fall onto the yellow couch beside her, she says bluntly, "I'm worried about you."

"Why?" I ask, surprised.

"You're too together."

I laugh. "Would you be happier if I had a mental breakdown?"

"You still aren't talking to Emerald, you aren't going out, but you're bouncing around the house like you're happy."

"Wait, so are you worried that I'm together or that I'm pretending to be together?"

"I don't know."

"I'm *fine*."

Julian's been with us for almost a month now, and yes, there were some adjustments, and yes, he still sleeps on my floor and refuses to leave the house, but things are better. I can see things getting better every day.

"I'm serious, Adam."

"Please feed whatever this is with Julian." I've lost my playful tone, and she catches it.

"What does that mean?"

"You're the one who has to break up fights and find drama everywhere you go."

She winces. "Is that what you really think?"

"You don't need to worry about *me*. Julian's the one this happened to."

"I *am* worried about him. Of course I am. But that doesn't mean I'm not worried about you too. You're leaving soon, and I just want—"

"I'm not leaving."

"What?"

"I'm not going."

"You're not going to college," she says flatly.

"Of course I'm going to college. I'm just not moving. I'm going to commute."

"This is crazy. You can't just—"

"I thought you'd be happy. All you ever talk about is how much you're going to miss me."

"I will miss you." She sighs. "Very much. But that doesn't mean I don't want you to go."

"Well, I'm not."

"Julian will be fine, Adam. I did a good job raising you, didn't I?"

"Adequate."

She laughs and mutters, "Punky Brewster." Then she gets serious again, but I wish she wouldn't. I've had enough serious to last a lifetime. "I know you want to take care of him. Everyone you're close to . . . they all need you so much."

For a minute, we don't talk, just half-watch the final round till she says, "Someone like you has to be around people. You can't be alone so much."

"I'm not alone."

She frowns at me like I'm deliberately trying to be difficult. "If you won't go out, then have people over. You were planning that graduation party. You could still have it."

"It's a little late for that now."

"Have one anyway." She sounds way too insistent about something that doesn't even really matter.

"I don't know."

"Just something small. It would be good for you. For *both* of you."

"Yeah . . . maybe just a few people."

"Like Emerald?"

"Maybe."

SIXTY-EIGHT

JULIAN

IT'S A SMALL party compared to the one Emerald had back in December, only fifteen or twenty people, but the noise and chaos are still too much. I open the back door, and cross the yard to sit on the grass beneath a giant tree. Its branches dip low and wide, hanging around me like a curtain.

The last time I was outside was when we went to Russell's house. Once we got home, Adam parked in the garage.

He keeps telling me I need fresh air, that sitting in front of the window like a cat isn't the same. Part of me misses the sun and the way it felt to ride my bike as fast I could. But whenever I would imagine leaving, I'd see the blue sky like the ocean—no walls or shore or end in sight. And I'd see myself disappear.

Tonight, when all Adam's friends arrived, I could tell how much they missed him. Most of them told him openly, and the others just kept watching him like they couldn't get their fill of his face. They were nice to me too, almost but never quite hugging me, as if they were afraid touching would hurt me.

I breathe in deep. My lungs expand and it only hurts a little.

The air smells sweet, warm, real. Maybe Adam was right about going outside. It's nice. I dig my fingers into the grass. Press deeper, into the soil, and I picture my mother standing on our old back porch, shielding her eyes from the sun.

I can still hear the music from inside, but I'm far enough away that it's just a pulse without words. I close my eyes.

"Julian?" It's the voice I've heard in my head like a rusty echo a million times.

My eyes fly open. Russell's silhouette is near the open gate, just a few feet away. He begins walking toward me. I want to run or yell, but I can't. I have absolutely no control over my body.

As Russell passes the back porch, the motion sensor light turns on, and I can see him clearly. Unshaved, unwashed, unhappy. He's looking at me, and I realize that I have no control over my body because it's not my body to control.

My eyes flick to the back door. He seems to know what I'm thinking. Quickly, he crouches down—then he springs all of his weight toward me. *On* me. One of his arms winds around my stomach, pulling my back into his chest, while his other arm encircles my neck. I can feel his heart against my shoulder blades, his chin on top of my head. I can smell him, bitter soil and sweat. He tightens his hold, both arms wrapped around me. It's the closest to a hug we've ever shared.

"Why did you leave?" he asks. "You told me you wanted a chance, and you left."

"I had to. Adam—"

His forearm tightens across my throat. "*I'm* the one who took you in. Me. But no matter what I do for you, you still *hate* me."

I grab at his arm, twisting in his grasp. I can't breathe.

Abruptly, he lets me go. I suck in a pained breath before turning around to face him.

"I . . . I don't hate you," I say, and I mean it. "I know you're just unhappy."

His eyes flicker in hopeful confusion. "Then you want to come with me?"

I remember the video. The expression on his face when he was hitting me. All the times he found a reason to punish me. Not to make me better, but because he enjoyed it.

"No. You hurt me. It's not okay to hurt people. Even if you're unhappy."

His face turns to ice, and then it cracks. "I never touched you," he growls. "In all these years, I never put my hands on you." He leans in close, his eyes on fire. "Did I?"

I shake my head.

"I could have, but I didn't. You don't even think about that. About what I had to do."

The porch light dies, plunging us into darkness, but it doesn't really matter. I was never good at reading him anyway.

I feel one hand wrap around my throat, and there's just a hint of pain. I should be afraid, but I feel empty. I remember my father's hands. My mother's hands. What hands are meant to do.

His fingers tighten, lifting me like a puppet until I'm on my feet. When he starts dragging me toward the open gate, the numbness flies away. My mouth goes wide. His hand slaps across my lips. As I kick and claw at his arm, I feel something wet against my neck, then the sharp sting of teeth.

Russell pulls an object from his waist, one I recognize from the same cabinet that holds the switch. "This is my father's gun," he says.

"I—I'm sorry about your father. I miss my father too."

He starts to laugh, and turns his head just enough for the moon to shine against his face. It's the clown mouth, a smile around a sneer. "You think I miss my father? I *hated* him."

"I—I—"

Russell laughs again and holds the gun out in his palm in front of me like an offering. "He used to talk so much about what it meant to be a man, but I always thought there was something small about using one of these. A man should rely on his own power, not tiny pieces of metal you can't even see coming." He pulls the gun back in his tight grip. "But they're quick, and sometimes you need things done quick. Isn't that true?"

I try to nod.

"Adam is something that could be done quick."

I try to speak, but Russell squeezes my face so hard with one hand that my teeth catch against the inside of my cheek and I taste blood.

"You know how quickly it can happen. One minute you have them. Then, in an instant . . ." He releases my face and snaps his long fingers. ". . . they're gone." I go cold and sweaty at the same time. "All of them. Gone."

This time when he drags me, I go limp. I don't walk, but I don't fight, letting him pull me farther from the house to the gate, where he could take me anywhere.

ADAM

Lately I've been wondering if anytime I get nervous or worried or whatever, I'll think it's a bad feeling. Because this could just be stress, or it could be an actual premonition when Julian's not in his room or in the kitchen or anywhere else in the house.

I open the back door, and the porch light illuminates two figures: Julian—and Russell. His giant arm is wrapped around Julian's neck. He's pulling him toward the gate.

I break into a run, shouting, "Stop!"

They freeze, and there's this expression on Russell's face, a terrifying kind of hatred that's never been directed at me before. Slowly he raises his arm, and the expression becomes one of immense satisfaction.

I've always thought if a gun was pointed at me, I'd know what to do. If you've seen a million superhero movies like I have, you think you'd throw out a smart-ass comment, then maybe spin-kick it from the bad guy's hands.

Instead it's just white and so much fear I can't think, and I'm stammering and doing what stupid people do in movies—trying to reason with the crazy person holding the gun and you can't do that. You can't.

"It's okay, Russell," Julian's saying. "I'll go. I want to go with you."

I hear the door open behind me. "Adam, are you—?" Emerald. She screams, then there's a smattering of terrified voices.

My mother pleading.

Someone crying.

Someone running.

These are all the wrong things to do. They're going to make him panic.

Russell's arm—choking.

Julian's face—crying.

The gun—closer, closer, till it's resting cold against my forehead.

I can't see anything now. I know to stop him I need to be able to see, but everything's blurry because my eyes are full of tears. I squeeze them shut, feel the tears spill over.

A sudden sound and smell that reminds me of fireworks.

SIXTY-NINE

ADAM

CHARLIE AND RUSSELL are rolling across the grass. Charlie's taller, but Russell's bigger and looks a hell of a lot stronger. Somehow, in the seconds my eyes were closed, Charlie must've tackled him. The gun must've fallen, must've gone off.

Where is it?

Julian's on the ground, scrambling backward while they twist and grapple.

I don't see the gun.

I don't know how, but Charlie's gotten the better of Russell. Digging his knees into the bigger man's chest, he brings his fist high into the air, and smashes it right into Russell's face. I see the exact moment when he breaks Russell's nose, a wet crunching sound and flood of blood.

Russell roars, links his huge hands together, then slams them like a battering ram into the side of Charlie's head. Charlie topples over onto the grass with a heavy thud beside a still-stunned Julian.

I see the gun.

Charlie and Russell and I all move at the same time—but Russell's faster. Charlie tackles him like a linebacker and there's another firecracker blast. It's still echoing in my ears when Charlie and Russell fall. Now both of them lie still, the front of their shirts blooming blood.

Arms tighten around me. I try to get away.

"It's okay, baby. It's okay, you're okay," my mom is saying over and over. I half-hear, half-see the yard full of friends, most of them crying, some of them placing panicked phone calls.

I pull away from my mom and drop to the grass. "Charlie?"

He doesn't move.

Julian's sitting completely still, like a photograph of a painting. Julian, twice removed.

"Charlie!" I yell.

He grunts and sits up.

"Jesus!" I take in a huge breath. "Are you okay?"

He looks down, touching his blood-soaked chest, confused and scared. "I'm not hurt," he says. "Unless it's shock. Am I in shock?"

I laugh, a crazy, hysterical noise. "No. I think it's his." I nod to Russell, who's watching me with malevolent and not-quite-dead eyes.

I half-hear my mom organizing, sounding counselor-composed while she gathers crying kids and tells them to come inside. Emerald takes Julian by the hand and leads him away like a child.

"I didn't—it was an accident," Charlie stammers. "I was just try-ing to—" He scrambles away, rubs his shaking, bloody hands in the grass, and falls back against the fence. "He was gonna take Julian. He was gonna kill you."

"I know."

"I stopped him."

"I know."

SEVENTY

ADAM

I'M NOT SURE how Emerald found me way the hell out here. I didn't tell anyone where I was going. Just took off and didn't stop till I reached the lake and couldn't walk any farther. She takes a seat on the wet grass beside me, and for a few minutes we watch the blue-green water without talking.

She breaks the silence. "I remember coming here when we were kids. Wasn't there a rope tied around that branch?" She points over my head to a tree with limbs that extend over the lake.

"A hose," I answer. "They took it down after someone drowned." I made that up—I actually have no idea why the Tarzan-swing garden hose is gone. Now she's looking bleakly out at the water like she can see someone's ghost. That feels appropriate.

"Are you okay?" It's only been a week since I sat in the back-yard with Charlie and watched Russell die. I looked him in the eye, while Charlie looked at the sky, then something happened that I knew I wouldn't be able to explain later if I tried. Russell's eyes were so full of hate. So full, then just empty, just glass, just nothing.

After everything that'd happened, I expected Julian to get even worse. Instead, he seems stronger, actually speaking at a normal volume now. It's almost like he was afraid to talk before, afraid Russell could hear him no matter where he was.

I remember when Julian was a little kid, he was so stubborn, but maybe that's a good thing to be—a force of will that doesn't die no matter how many horrible things happen to you. But me, I just have this one thing, this one bad night, and I'm—"I'm fine."

"What did I do?" Emerald shouts, startling me and the ducks swimming just a few feet away.

"You didn't do anything."

"Then why won't you talk to me?"

Because I'm an idiot—like as stupid as Brett was, if he'd actually existed. Because I blamed her for what happened to Julian even though it's really on me.

"Do you know how scared I was?" She's crying, her face all blotched like she rolled around in poison ivy. "I thought he was going to kill you. And when you were okay, I never felt so grateful in my life. I didn't want to take anything for granted anymore. I thought you'd feel the same way, but you didn't. I love you, and you won't even talk to me. I told you." She sobs. "I told you I would *break*."

It's like we're back inside the center of the labyrinth and I'm struck with so much regret and so much love, it's worse than a heart attack. "I'm sorry, Emerald. I can't. I'm not helping anyone right now."

"You *do* help." She wipes the tears off her red cheeks. "You helped him. You were so brave—"

"*Brave?* I'm not brave. As soon as I saw that man I should have been, I don't know, so fueled with homicidal rage that I *did* something.

But I just stood there, crying. It was Charlie who actually did something, and I'm not even sure he *likes* Julian."

We go back to silence, until again, Emerald breaks it. "Everyone watches you, and you don't even know it. You just . . . It's like you come into a room and you're glowing or something."

I laugh, but it's not a happy sound. "Yeah, glowing is my superpower."

"And when you smile . . . my grandmother calls them big-soul smiles. She says some people have souls so big that they spread out, touching everyone they pass." Emerald wipes her wet face again. "There are different ways to help people, Adam. There are different ways to do good."

I don't know if it's the fear or the sadness or all the pure emotion from the last month, but I'm embarrassingly close to crying, so I respond the way I normally would. "Are you going to start singing that what makes me beautiful is that I don't know I'm beautiful? Because I don't think I can take that."

"You are." Her voice is more tender than I've ever heard it, and I can only stare at her, no longer in the mood to joke. "Beautiful." And her fingers touch my face, carefully, like I'm something that might break.

SEVENTY-ONE

ADAM

JULIAN'S TYPING AWAY on the desktop computer in the living room while I'm watching TV and texting Emerald. All of a sudden he leaps up and stares at the television—some show on the Travel Channel.

"Can I borrow your laptop?" he asks, which is weird, since he's already using a computer.

"Uh, yeah, I guess." He grabs it off the coffee table and bolts from the room. A few minutes later I hear the sound of breaking glass.

I head into Julian's room to find one of the framed photos of Mittens smashed against the wall. I step over the pieces and try for a joke. "I told you we could redecorate."

Julian's either ignoring me or doesn't hear me. Sitting in the center of his bed, body thrumming with tension and face furrowed with intense concentration, he leans over an open spiral notebook. His fingers run along the page, tracing the words like they're Braille.

"Julian?"

Getting more agitated, he thrusts his finger into the paper.

"Julian."

He keeps stabbing the page, starts whispering something to himself. I cross the room and grab his wrist. He goes still and looks up at me with eyes that are too huge for his face. I let him go, then sit on the end of the bed.

"Why didn't she write titles?" he asks, looking back down at the notebook.

"What?"

"Titles. None of them have titles. I was always sure they meant something."

I give a closer look to the neat round letters on the page.

1. ALMA, COLORADO

2. BRIAN HEAD, UTAH

3. VILLAGE OF TAOS SKI VALLEY, NEW MEXICO

"Who wrote this?"

"My mom. This whole notebook is full of lists. I always knew these cities, these lists, had to be important. She wouldn't write them unless they were important. But you just have to guess at what they mean, you know?"

I nod, but I don't know. I don't know at all the pain of trying to know and understand someone after they've gone.

"I finally get what this one means." He points to my laptop on the nightstand. A webpage is opened to a list of U.S. cities with highest elevation. "It looks like they're all probably explainable. The movies are just Best Picture winners. The songs are number-one songs from different years."

"So . . . that's good, that you figured it out?"

"Good?" Such a venomous expression on Julian's face is unnerving.

"They're just facts she recorded. They don't tell me anything about her. She wrote all these lists, but they don't *mean* anything!"

Suddenly and violently, he starts ripping the pages out of the notebook.

"Nothing means anything! People just go. They don't finish." He grabs the loose sheets, wildly tearing them into shreds. "We don't die after we complete some mission, we just *die*." He yanks the green cardboard away from the silver spiral till that's all that's left. "Do you know how I know?"

I shake my head.

"Because if they could have chosen, they wouldn't have left me. I know them. They weren't finished with me!"

He folds in on himself like a closing shutter. Surrounded by torn bits of paper, he begins to sob. It's horrible to watch when you can't do anything to fix it.

He goes abruptly silent, like someone turned off his voice, and he picks up one of the torn pieces with two fingers. "Oh no."

He starts to cry again, bending till his face is pressed into the mattress.

He shoots back up and kneels, wrapping his arms around his stomach.

Then he collapses again.

It's the kind of desperate thing I did when I was on the meds that made me so sick. Miserable and nauseated, I was in so much agony I didn't know what to do with myself. Should I lie in bed? On my side? On my back? There was nowhere to go that me and the pain didn't follow. I remember my mom watching, looking totally helpless because she couldn't fix it.

"Stop, Julian. You're going to give yourself a headache."

He freezes, looking stunned. His crying becomes less hysterical, but deeper. My mom couldn't fix me, but I remember she'd pet my back, and I know Julian's father used to rub his head.

There are different ways to help people, Adam.

I extend my fingers like I'm playing the piano across his face.

Gradually, he goes quiet and turns to stare vacantly at the wall. "I know." He sounds so tired. "I know if there was any choice at all, they wouldn't have left me alone. They would have made sure I was taken care of."

In a heartbeat, a thousand memories at once. All the times I knew things I couldn't have known. All the times he was assigned to me.

"Julian," I say, "maybe they did."

SEVENTY-TWO

JULIAN

EMERALD'S BACKYARD IS strung with paper lanterns and golden lights. There are tables covered with food, streamers, balloons, party hats, stacks of wrapped gifts, and an enormous cake.

The last birthday cake I had was the summer I turned nine, the summer my parents bought me the trunk and told me I was brave. It was always just the three of us on my birthday, never a party with other kids, since school was out. That year we wore hats and I opened gifts, then we walked along the rocky beach where I found the conch.

Emerald's yard fills with people, too many to fit at the picnic table where I sit at the head. Everyone sings "Happy Birthday" and watches me open presents. Adam gives me a novel, and Emerald gives me a journal, and it's overwhelming to have so much attention, but it's not embarrassing, not really.

Later I say to Adam, "Fifteen seems a lot older than fourteen, doesn't it?"

Tilting his head, he laughs. "Yeah, I guess it does."

We listen to music and eat cake while the sun shines on everyone, making them glow like angels. Adam's and Emerald's faces are close together, whispering things I can't hear. Jesse pulls out his guitar and asks me if I want to sing. I shake my head. Today I just want to listen. Charlie passes out popsicles. Everyone's lips change color. The last day of July slowly fades, but everyone keeps talking and laughing like they could stay here forever.

It's dark when I stretch out on my back on the trampoline. Listening to the voices of all the people I love, I gaze up at a perfect night sky. It's as if the lights strung through the trees have moved to float above us. Beautiful and too many to see all at once.

Ten million stars.

Acknowledgments

Not long ago, I told my son I love him so much that sometimes my chest fills up like it's going to burst, and I have to take a deep breath. He responded, "That sounds like a medical condition." Did I mention he's a bit of a smart aleck?

Well, that's what I'm feeling now—an I-can't-breathe kind of love and gratitude for the people in my life. So much that even though my editor's given me a year of extensions, I *still* don't know how to put it into words.

But here goes.

I would like to say thank you to:

★ Peter Steinberg. When I pictured my dream agent, he was smart, dedicated, and above all else, kind. I got my dream agent. I'm also very grateful for my foreign-rights agents (Jess Regel, Kirsten Neuhaus, Heidi Gall) and Foundry Literary + Media.

★ Stephanie Lurie—my warm, wise, endlessly encouraging editor, who showed such sensitivity and patience with a first-time novelist—and everyone at Hyperion. They all made this journey such a joy.

★ Kate Hawkes—the kind of friend who'll hop on a plane when you need her, never judges, and has so much love to give—and the entire Hawkes family, who I'm claiming as my family too.

★ Sandra Francis, the embodiment of unconditional love. And all my friends in Dallas (Tracy, Jody, Dina, Daphney, Petra, and the list goes on). Life is better than I ever could have imagined because of them.

★ Joshua, who came into our lives singing and made us a family.

★ Michael—my hyper-friendly-wild-running-resilient-brown-eyed boy.

★ And Joe. For several years I had a debilitating illness. There were times I couldn't walk. There were times I couldn't see. And through all of this, Joe was there—kind and funny and nurturing and giving, with a maturity so far beyond his years. He told me I would get better, every single day, until I did.